A DREAM

Of course, she thought, relieved; that's all it had been, just a dream.

Sliding out of bed, she pulled on her robe and went downstairs. She told herself she was going into the kitchen for a glass of grapefruit juice, but some invisible power drew her toward the living room, and the painting.

After switching on a light, she walked toward the hearth.

The man was in the castle, looking out of a tower window. He seemed to be staring at her, his deep blue eyes filled with a silent plea for help.

Kari wrapped her arms around her waist as she looked at the painting, unable to draw her gaze away from the figure in the window.

Help me.

Other titles available by Amanda Ashley

A WHISPER OF ETERNITY

AFTER SUNDOWN

DEAD PERFECT

DEAD SEXY

DESIRE AFTER DARK

NIGHT'S KISS

NIGHT'S MASTER

NIGHT'S PLEASURE

NIGHT'S TOUCH

Published by Kensington Publishing Corporation

Immortal Sins

Amanda Ashley

ZEBRA BOOKS
Kensington Publishing Corp.
http://www.kensingtonbooks.com

ZEBRA BOOKS are published by

Kensington Publishing Corp.
119 West 40th Street
New York, NY 10018

All Kensington titles, imprints, and distributed lines are available at special quantity discounts for bulk purchases for sales promotion, premiums, fund-raising, educational, or institutional use.

Special book excerpts or customized printings can also be created to fit specific needs. For details, write or phone the office of the Kensington Special Sales Manager: Attn. Special Sales Department. Kensington Publishing Corp., 119 West 40th Street, New York, NY 10018. Phone: 1-800-221-2647.

ISBN-13: 978-0-8217-8064-0
ISBN-10: 0-8217-8064-6

First Printing: October 2009
10 9 8 7 6 5 4 3 2 1

Printed in the United States of America

*To Wendi Gabbidon
and Jackie Robinson
for adding to my* Star Wars *collection.*

*To Sue-Ellen Welfonder, once a fan, now an author
(and hopefully still a fan)
for sharing her knowledge with me.*

*And especially to Bronwyn Wolfe,
who gave me the idea in the first place.
I couldn't have done it without you!*

Chapter 1

There was nothing the least bit remarkable about the old Underwood Art Gallery located on the corner of Third Street and Pine. And nothing particularly remarkable about the paintings displayed inside. For the most part, the works of art were uninspired scenes of landscapes and seascapes and an occasional still life, except for one rather large painting in the back of the gallery. It depicted a tall, fair-haired man wandering in the moonlight through a heavily wooded forest that bordered a calm blue lake.

The painting was by an artist named Josef Vilnius and was aptly titled *Man Walking in the Moonlight*. Karinna Adams had never heard of Vilnius, but it was an interesting piece in that the colors seemed to change depending on the time of day: the blues and greens and golds bright and cheerful when she observed the painting during the afternoon, the hues more somber and subdued when she arrived at the gallery in the evening. The changes in hue were especially puzzling since they had nothing to do with the gallery's interior lighting and seemed to be some anomaly inherent in the painting itself. It was most peculiar, and it had drawn Kari back to Underwood's time and time again.

Tonight was no different. Kari stood in front of the mysterious painting, her gaze moving from the old rowboat tied up alongside the narrow wooden dock to the gray stone castle perched high atop a grassy hill. A shaggy black and white dog slept in the shade on the north side of the castle, and a gray kitten frolicked in a bed of flowers. A lamp burned in an upstairs window. Swirls of blue-gray smoke curled up from one of the castle's many chimneys. A white horse grazed in a large grassy field, its coat shining like silver in the moonlight. The horse looked so real, she wouldn't have been surprised to see it galloping across the greensward.

Kari had visited the Underwood gallery every night after work for the last two weeks. And every night, the man in the painting had been either in a different pose or in a different location, first walking in the moon-shadowed woods, next fishing from the boat under a starry sky, next looking out at the night from one of the castle's second-story windows, next resting on a large rock near the water, next sitting on the edge of the dock.

Tonight, he was astride the horse, his head turned to look back at the castle on the hill. Moonlight shimmered in his hair, which fell past his shoulders. He wore a loose-fitting white shirt, snug buff-colored breeches, brown boots, and a long black cloak that fell in graceful folds over the horse's hindquarters.

His hair was dark blond, as were his brows, above crystalline blue eyes that were so vibrant and alive, it was hard to believe they were just paint and canvas. He had a sharp nose, a sensual mouth, a strong, square jawline. He was a remarkably handsome creature, and she often wondered if the artist had used a live model, or if the figure had been drawn from the artist's imagination.

Kari moved closer to the painting, trying to determine how the figure of the man moved from place to place. So far, she hadn't been able to determine how the artist had managed such a remarkable feat. At first, she had thought the man might not be a part of the painting itself, but perhaps a cutout figure that could be moved and posed at will. But she had quickly dismissed that idea. He had to be part of the painting, just like the boat, the dog, the kitten, the horse, and the castle. She wondered if the artist had painted several versions of the same scene and the gallery owner changed them from time to time, just to mystify the public, but that hardly seemed likely. Perhaps Vilnius had just used the same technique that made it seem as if the eyes of a painting were following you, like the ones in Disneyland's Haunted Mansion.

With a shake of her head, Kari glanced at her watch. The gallery would be closing in a few minutes. She could scarcely believe she had been standing in front of the painting for almost an hour!

When she looked back at the canvas, the man was staring at her.

Startled, Kari took a step backward, then leaned

forward, her eyes narrowing as she studied the figure. His lips seemed to be moving, forming the words *help me.*

That did it, she thought. She was losing her mind; that was the only answer. Painted figures did not move, nor did they speak. Filled with a sudden cold fear, Kari turned and ran out of the gallery.

She was breathless by the time she reached her car. Sliding behind the wheel, she locked the door, then drove home as if pursued by demons. It wasn't until she was safely inside her own house, with the front door securely locked behind her, that sanity returned. She was behaving irrationally, letting her imagination get the best of her. People in paintings didn't move. They certainly didn't speak. Tomorrow, she would go back to the gallery and the man would be walking in the moonlit woods, where he belonged. He wouldn't move, he wouldn't look at her, and he definitely wouldn't speak!

Blowing out a sigh, she went into the bathroom. After turning on the water in the tub, she added a capful of bubble bath, then lit a blue candle. Blue for serenity and harmony and to soothe a troubled mind. And her mind was more than troubled. It just wasn't normal to be so obsessed with a painting. And, as if it wasn't bad enough that the man in the painting dominated her thoughts during the day, he had started haunting her dreams at night.

With the candle glowing softly and the bathtub filled almost to overflowing with fragrant bubbles, Kari stepped into the water for a long, leisurely soak. She had been working too hard. That's all it was, just job-induced stress combined with a vivid, overactive imagination.

She closed her eyes. It was just stress. Nothing to worry about. Lots of people suffered from it these days and it was perfectly understandable, what with the state of the economy, the high price of gas, ever-growing tensions in the Middle East, and the ongoing investigations into the questionable benefits and possible risks of several high-profile, over-the-counter drugs. Add to that the ever-increasing number of floods, earthquakes, and tornadoes that were pummeling distant parts of the earth and it was a wonder the whole world wasn't going quietly insane.

Kari blew out a sigh of relief. Stress, she thought again. Of course, that's all it was. She wasn't going crazy after all.

Chapter 2

The gallery had closed for the night. Now that he was free to move about with no one watching, Jason Rourke roamed through the painting's lush landscape, searching, as always, for a way out, even though he knew there were only two avenues of escape, and both were beyond his power to control. He had been trapped inside this painted hell for three hundred years, cursed to remain imprisoned behind a wall of glass until the wizard who had cursed him died, or until a mortal woman called him forth of her own free will.

Sunk in the depths of a cold and bitter despair, he walked down to the lake and sat on the rock at the water's edge. It was a unique prison, appearing flat to those who viewed it from the outside, yet three-dimensional on his side of the glass. The water, the rocks, the grass, the animals—all were real, giving him an illusion of life and freedom.

He swore softly, plagued by his unnatural hunger, the same unrelenting hunger that had been his downfall. Damn! How was he to have known that the pretty young woman whose maidenhead and blood he had taken had been the only daughter of a powerful wizard? Drunk with wrath, Vilnius had called down a horrible curse upon them both, on Rourke for defiling his daughter, and on his daughter for lying with a man who was not a man at all, though she'd had no idea, before or after, what manner of creature she had taken to her bed. Rourke had pleaded with Vilnius to relent. Ana Luisa had begged for mercy, but to no avail. Rourke had listened in horror as Vilnius had said the words that imprisoned him, watched helplessly as the wizard had pronounced the same horrible curse on his own daughter.

And now he was here, condemned to this hellish existence, denied the pleasures of the flesh, with no way to ease the awful hunger that burned through him with every waking moment. Three hundred years of torment for thirty minutes of pleasure! He slammed his hand on the rock. Dammit, where was the justice in that?

He cursed again, frustrated by his helplessness. He had been trapped in this nightmare for three centuries and only in the last few weeks had he regained strength enough to be able to move around within his pictorial prison.

Much had changed in the last three centuries. Though his view of the world was limited to what he could see from the inside of the art galleries or private homes where the painting had resided, he was well aware that life as he had once known it no longer existed. Automobiles had replaced the horse as a means of transportation. Electricity now provided power and lights, although candles were still used on various occasions. Men and women wore strange clothing, and far less of it! People worried about things that had been unheard of in his time, like the rising price of gasoline and global warming, swine flu, terrorists, and weapons of mass destruction. He had watched scenes of warfare in far-off lands, noting that mankind had learned to kill far more efficiently. In his time, a strong man armed with a good sword might kill half a dozen of his enemies in battle. Today, one terrorist with a car bomb could destroy a building along with every man, woman, and child in the vicinity.

Rourke placed his hands on the thick glass that enclosed his prison and stared into the darkness visible beyond the front window of the art gallery. The silent beauty of the night called to him, teasing him, tempting him. The hunger burned hot and deep in his belly, an insatiable hunger that had not been fed for three hundred years. Had he still possessed a soul, he would gladly have traded it for one drop of rich red blood, for one moment of relief from the constant pain. He curled his hands into tight fists as he wondered how much longer he could endure this existence before he went completely mad.

Pressing his forehead against the cool glass, he closed his eyes. And the image of the woman appeared in his mind. Tall and slender, she was, with hair like fine black silk, and the bluest eyes he had ever seen. She had come to the gallery every night since his painting arrived. And every night she stood in front of it, a bemused expression on her lovely heart-shaped face. He knew, of course, what it was that troubled her. Paintings were supposed to be immutable, unchanging, inert. It bothered her that he was rarely in the same place twice. He might have found her confusion amusing if not for the hunger that tormented him, the anger that plagued him, the never-ending desire for freedom that haunted his every waking moment.

Freedom! He craved it with every fiber of his being even as he yearned to taste the warm, crimson nectar of life on his tongue. He longed to draw a breath of free air again. To feel the wind on his face, to know the pleasure that came from a woman's touch, to feel a woman's body writhing in ecstasy beneath his own. He yearned to feel the earth beneath his feet, to run through the shifting shadows of the night in search of prey, to listen to the sweet symphony of a thousand beating hearts.

To be whole again, to have substance, to have depth and breadth, to indulge his senses, all of them. He was weary, so indescribably weary of his current state of being. He might have taken his own life had it been possible. He would certainly claim the life of the wizard who had cursed him should he ever have the chance!

Revenge. The thought of it was the only pleasure left to him in the unchanging hell of his existence.

Chapter 3

Friday night after work, Kari hurried down Third Street, her shoulders hunched against the rising wind. People rushed past her, eager to reach the shelter of their homes before the storm broke. Kari was eager to get home, too, but first she had to prove to herself once and for all that she hadn't seen what she thought she had seen. Otherwise, she was going to spend the rest of the weekend wondering if she really was losing her mind.

When she saw the painting again, she would prove to herself once and for all that she wasn't crazy. She would see that the figure of the man was walking in the moonlit woods, just as he had been the first time she had seen the painting, and then she would leave the gallery and never, ever return.

Opening the door, she stepped inside, grateful to be out of the cold and the wind. She nodded at the owner's brother, Felix Underwood, who smiled and nodded in return. Felix was looking after the shop while his sister, Janice, was on vacation. Every time

Kari saw Felix, she was reminded of Walter Matthau. The two looked enough alike to be twins.

"I knew you would come again tonight," Felix Underwood said cheerfully. "You should buy the Vilnius. I'll make you a good deal."

"About that painting," Kari said, "have you ever noticed anything strange about it?"

"Strange?" Mr. Underwood looked up at the ceiling, as if he might find the answer to her question lurking there.

"Mr. Underwood?"

He shook his head. "Nothing strange comes to mind, but then, I don't really know anything about fine art," he admitted with an affable grin. "I'm a plumber by trade."

"Do you know where the painting came from?"

"I believe Janice bought it at an estate sale a few weeks ago. I seem to recall her telling me that the former owner, Mrs. Amelia Van Der Hyde, had kept it in the attic."

"In the attic? Do you know why she kept it there?"

Felix Underwood shrugged. "Perhaps she grew tired of it."

Or perhaps it had spooked Mrs. Van Der Hyde, too, Kari thought, though she didn't say so aloud.

"Shall I ring it up for you?"

"No, thank you." Kari glanced only briefly at the other works of art as she made her way toward the back corner of the gallery where the Vilnius sat on a large easel.

Taking a deep breath, she stopped in front of the painting, her gaze seeking the painted figure of the man who plagued her thoughts by day and haunted her dreams at night.

Her stomach clenched when she located him. She had convinced herself that he would again be walking in the woods, where he belonged, but he wasn't.

Tonight he was standing at the edge of the moonlit forest, one hand resting on the neck of the white horse.

A cold chill slithered down Kari's spine. It was true, she thought, she was going out of her mind.

"Why don't you take it home with you," Mr. Underwood suggested, coming up behind her. "Live with it for a few days. If you don't like it, you can bring it back. But don't tell anyone, especially my sister! All sales are supposed to be final."

"It's a deal." Kari clapped her hand over her mouth, wondering what had possessed her to say such a thing. She couldn't afford to buy a painting, not even one by an unknown artist. Heck, until she paid off her car, she couldn't even afford to buy a cheap print! But Mr. Underwood was already lifting the painting from the easel and carrying it to the front of the store. Besides, if she changed her mind, she could return it.

Ten minutes later, she was the owner, however temporary, of a genuine work of art.

Mr. Underwood carried the Vilnius out to her car, but it was too big to fit in the backseat, and too wide to fit in the trunk. Assuring her that it was no trouble, he put the painting in the back of his pickup truck. Returning to the gallery, he hung the "closed" sign in the front window and locked the door, then followed her home where he obligingly carried the painting into the house.

Kari thanked him profusely, then bid him good night.

After turning on the lights and the heater, she propped the painting against the living room wall. Standing in the middle of the floor, she did a slow turn, wondering where best to hang the picture. Over the sofa? No, she would have to keep looking over her shoulder to see it. Over the mantel? Maybe. Between the front windows? Another maybe. In the bedroom? No!

Over the fireplace seemed the most likely spot. She found a hammer and a couple of large nails, then dragged a chair over to the hearth. After doing some measuring and a little cussing, she figured out where to drive the nails; then, praying that she wouldn't drop the darn thing, she wrestled the painting into place. After making sure it was straight, she hopped down off the chair, then stood in the doorway to observe her handiwork.

She had to admit, the Vilnius looked great. The painting was just the right size, the colors perfectly complemented her décor, and it added the finishing touch to the room.

Standing there with her arms crossed under her breasts, she searched for the man in the painting. Where was he?

Moving closer, she looked in all the usual places but he wasn't walking in the woods or looking out the window of the castle. He wasn't riding the horse or sitting on the rock near the edge of the water or reclining on the grass. Had she imagined him? Maybe she was crazier than she thought.

Standing on the chair again, she perused the painting through narrowed eyes. How could he not be there? Thirty minutes ago he had been petting the horse . . . but now the horse was gone, too.

She really was losing it, of that there could be no doubt. Maybe she had imagined the whole thing. Maybe there had never been a man in the landscape at all. Heck, maybe the canvas was blank . . . but no, what was that? Leaning closer, she stared at a dark speck on the right side of the castle. Was that him?

After jumping off the chair, Kari rummaged in her desk for her magnifying glass, then climbed back up on the chair, and looked again. A horse and rider were barely visible in the shadows alongside the castle.

Her relief at finding him warred with the renewed fear that she was losing her mind.

Paintings simply didn't change from day to day. Painted figures of people and animals didn't move.

Feeling horribly confused and afraid, she put on her nightgown and went to bed, only to lie there imagining a history for the man in the painting. He was a nobleman who lived alone in the castle, with only a horse, a dog, and a kitten for company. She frowned, unable to decide why he was so sad. Maybe he was nursing a broken heart, or perhaps he was grieving for a lost loved one. Or maybe he just liked living alone.

With a faint smile, she closed her eyes. Maybe the answer would come to her in her dreams.

It seemed she had been asleep for only a few moments when she woke with a start. She stared at the ceiling blankly, and then frowned. Her ceiling was sky blue, not gray. She turned her head to the left, but instead of a window, she saw a blank wall.

A shiver ran down Kari's spine. All the walls were blank. And they were made of uneven dark gray stone.

She sat up, the sound of her heartbeat pounding in her ears. Where was she? And how had she gotten here?

Slipping out of bed, she left the room and tiptoed down a narrow circular stairway. The stone floor was icy cold beneath her bare feet. She paused at the bottom of the stairs, her gaze darting nervously from side to side. There wasn't much to see save for a large, rough-hewn chair in front of an enormous fireplace. A painting of a sword hung above the mantel. She paused a moment to study the weapon. She didn't know anything about such things, but this one was beautiful, from the long, slender blade to the intricately wrought hilt. It reminded her of Inigo Montoya's sword in one of her favorite old movies, *The Princess Bride.*

Moving on, she passed several other rooms. All were empty. All had high ceilings, gray stone walls, enormous fireplaces, and tall, narrow windows.

She was in some kind of a castle, she thought, her trepidation growing with each moment that passed.

In the scullery, she glanced out a small, square

window, felt her eyes grow wide as she found herself looking out at her living room at home.

It hit her then. She was inside the castle in the painting!

Panic rose hot and quick within her. Was this how the man had gotten into the painting? Had he bought it and then become its prisoner? Had she now taken his place?

She whirled around, her gaze flitting around the room. Where was he? And how was she going to get out?

She searched the downstairs, went back up to the second floor and then up to the third. There was no sign of him. Returning to the main floor, she opened the heavy wooden door and went outside, but he wasn't there, either. Maybe she really had imagined him!

She hadn't imagined the horse, though. Even now it was trotting toward her, its dainty, foxlike ears flicking back and forth, its nostrils flaring.

"Hello, you pretty thing," she murmured.

Hesitantly, she held out her hand. The horse sniffed her palm, then whinnied softly, its breath warm against her skin. Captivated, she stroked the horse's neck, then ran her fingers through its long, silky mane. It didn't feel like a painting of a horse; it felt like a living, breathing creature, but how was that possible?

Kari shook her head. She was dreaming, she thought. In a dream, even the impossible was possible.

"So, where's the man?" she wondered aloud.

If the horse knew, it wasn't saying.

After giving the animal a last pat, Kari returned to the castle. With a sigh, she went into the scullery and sat at the table. For a kitchen, it was surprisingly unkitchenlike. There were no cupboards, no oven or stove, no sink, no food that she could see. So what was the table for?

She had to be dreaming, she thought again. That was the only plausible explanation. She would just sit here until she woke up and . . . was that a door?

Rising, she hurried across the room. It was, indeed, a door, a very small door. Maybe it was a way out, she thought, a way back to reality! Feeling suddenly like Alice lost in Wonderland, she reached for the brass knob. It was hard and cold beneath her hand. The portal opened with a creak and she peered down a flight of uneven stone steps. Certain she was doing the wrong thing, she nevertheless found herself carefully descending the narrow stairway.

She shivered when she reached the bottom. It was colder down here, though she saw no reason why it should be any colder than the rest of the castle. She was about to hurry back up the stairs when she felt the hair rise along her nape. Slowly, so slowly, she turned around.

At first, she didn't see anything, and then she saw a tall shape rise up out of a dark corner. A pair of unblinking red eyes stared at her, growing larger, coming closer. Spooked as never before, Kari opened her mouth and screamed bloody murder.

She woke with the sound of her own cries ringing

in her ears. A dream. Of course, she thought, relieved; that's all it had been, just a dream.

Sliding out of bed, she pulled on her robe and went downstairs. She told herself she was going into the kitchen for a glass of grapefruit juice, but some invisible power drew her toward the living room, and the painting.

After switching on a light, she walked toward the hearth.

The man was in the castle, looking out of a tower window. He seemed to be staring at her, his deep blue eyes filled with a silent plea for help.

Kari wrapped her arms around her waist as she looked at the painting, unable to draw her gaze away from the figure in the window.

Help me.

She heard the voice inside her head, deep and decidedly male. *His* voice.

Startled, she backed away from the hearth, a cry escaping her lips when she hit a corner of the coffee table and almost fell.

Great! Now she wasn't just seeing things, she was hearing things as well.

Tomorrow she would call Tricia and ask her to come over, take a look at the painting, and tell her what she saw.

Tricia McPhee was Kari's best friend. Tricia was cool, calm, and level-headed. She had the imagination of a tomato yet she attracted the strangest people; people like Mel Staffanson, who kept a hearse, complete with a full-sized coffin, in his garage. Mel drove the hearse around town on Hal-

loween and rented it out for parties. Then there was
Sheri Hunt, who only wore green and had dyed her
hair to match. Sheri raised silkworms. Angie Delgado
was another of Tricia's eccentric friends. Angie had
been married and divorced six times and now lived
with four Pomeranians and five Siamese cats, declaring they were easier to get along with than men.

It always amazed Kari that she and Tricia were
friends, because they were so different. Tricia was
an only child. She had been spoiled and pampered
from day one. She had gone to the best schools,
graduated at the top of her class, married a sur-
geon, had two adorable children and lived in a big
house. Kari had been poor her whole life. She had
been an average student with a vivid imagination
and had managed to get into college only because
she won a scholarship.

Yes, Tricia was the answer.

Tricia arrived the following evening. She spent
several minutes studying the painting and then she
looked at Kari.

"All right," Tricia said, her hands fisted on her
slim hips. "I give up. What am I supposed to see?"

"The man in the painting."

"I see him. He's right there, in the woods," Tricia
said, pointing with a long, well-manicured finger.
"So, what's the big deal?"

Kari let out a sigh of resignation as Tricia confirmed her worst fears. She was losing her mind.
This morning and this afternoon, there had been

no sign of the man. She had searched the painting a dozen times during the day and he had been nowhere to be found. The horse had been grazing in the field, the dog had been asleep in the shade, the kitten had been playing in the flowers, but the man had been gone, as if he had never existed.

She had checked the painting just before Tricia arrived and the man had been in the castle, staring out the tower window. In the time it had taken Kari to open the front door and return to the living room with Tricia in tow, he had moved back to the woods, where he belonged.

Tricia tapped on a corner of the frame. "Did it come this way?"

"What way?" Kari asked, frowning.

"Framed like this. Oil paintings aren't usually framed under glass."

Kari shrugged, surprised she hadn't wondered about that before. But then, she wasn't an expert in such matters. Besides, she'd had other things on her mind, like a one-dimensional painted figure that refused to stay in one place.

Tricia stepped up on the raised hearth, her eyes narrowing as she studied the painting. "This is a Vilnius!" she exclaimed, gesturing at the signature scrawled in the lower right-hand corner. "Good grief, Kari, this looks like an original. Did you rob a bank, or come into an inheritance or something?"

"Of course not. What makes you think that?"

"Karinna, this painting is at least three hundred years old, and it's worth a small fortune. Maybe even a big one."

"How do you know that?"

"Hello? I majored in art, remember? Anyway, I remember seeing a picture of it in a book about little-known artists of the Old World. As far as anyone knows, Josef Vilnius painted only a handful of canvases. Three of them were supposed to have been lost or destroyed in a fire or a flood or something. One of them, *The Wizard's Daughter*, is located somewhere in Romania. Bucharest, if I recall correctly. This is the only one that's unaccounted for. Most experts assume it was destroyed, too."

"You must be mistaken," Kari said. "If it was valuable, it would have sold for a lot more than I paid for it."

Tricia shrugged. "Maybe the art dealer wasn't aware of its value. After all, Vilnius never made it really big, what with only five or six paintings to his credit. Or maybe the dealer thought it was a fake, since its whereabouts have been unknown for so long."

Kari looked up at the painting, imagining the nice profit she could make if the canvas was a genuine Vilnius and as rare as Tricia seemed to think.

"It was rumored that Vilnius was a witch or a warlock or something." Tricia waved her hand in a dismissive gesture. "Of course, that was a lot of nonsense. Whoever started the rumor probably thought it would jack up the price, you know?" She shook her head. "Girlfriend, you are so lucky."

Kari forced a smile. She didn't feel lucky. She felt like she was slowly going insane, but then, maybe she wasn't. After all, crazy people never thought they were crazy. But maybe that was only after they lost their minds.

"Listen, I'd love to stay and chat," Tricia said, "but I've got to go pick Brent up from work. His Hummer's in the shop." She gave Kari a hug. "Let's do lunch one day next week. My treat."

Later, after Tricia had gone home, Kari busied herself with housework. She washed the lunch dishes, mopped the floors in the bathroom and the kitchen, vacuumed the rugs and dusted the furniture in every room but the living room. Time and again she was tempted to go in and look at the painting to see if the man was still in the woods, but for her peace of mind, she refused to do so.

She told herself that the pretty white horse was grazing in the field, the shaggy black and white dog was asleep in the shade, the cute little gray kitten was curled up in the flower bed, and the man was in the woods, where he belonged. She had seen him there earlier and that's where he was now, because painted figures didn't move and certainly didn't speak. She wouldn't look at the Vilnius again. Monday morning she would take the accursed thing back to the Underwood Gallery and put it, and the man, out of her mind once and for all.

When she finished cleaning the house, Kari changed her clothes, grabbed her handbag and her keys, and left by the back door.

Getting into her car, she drove to the grocery store to pick up a quart of milk, a dozen eggs, a loaf of bread, and some fresh fruit and vegetables. On the way home, she stopped at Mama Wong's for some

Chinese takeout, then stopped at Polly's and picked up a lemon meringue pie because, well, just because.

At home again, she put the groceries away, poured herself a glass of milk, then sat down at the kitchen table and ate dinner, even though she usually ate in the living room in front of the TV.

With dinner over, she rinsed her dishes and put them in the dishwasher, then looked out the kitchen window, her fingers drumming on the countertop. What was she going to do now? It was too early to go to bed.

Keeping her head turned away from the painting, she went through the living room and up the stairs, grabbed the book on her bedside table, then went into the bathroom to take a bath. She added a generous amount of lavender bubble bath to the running water, lit a candle, and stepped into the tub. She sat there a moment, thinking there was nothing more relaxing than sitting in a nice warm bubble bath. She read until the water was cool and her skin was pruney, and then, reluctantly, she got out of the tub.

Drying off, she blew out the candle, then slipped on her nightgown and robe. Now what, she thought? She was tired of reading. It was still too early for bed. Her computer and the big-screen TV were both in the living room. . . .

"Oh, for heaven's sake, Kari, you can't stay out of the living room for the rest of the weekend!" she muttered, even though it seemed like a good idea.

Squaring her shoulders, she walked briskly down the stairs and into the living room. Sitting on the sofa, she picked up the remote. Keeping her gaze fixed squarely on the screen, she turned on the TV.

It took all her concentration to keep from glancing up at the Vilnius. Was it her imagination, or could she feel the man gazing down at her, willing her to look up?

"Not real," she murmured. "He's not real." Perspiration beaded on her brow. She looked at the fireplace, her gaze slowly moving up, up, until she was staring at the painting from hell.

And he was there, looking at her through the glass, his gaze intent upon her face. His eyes . . . what was there about his eyes that made her want to go to him, to take him in her arms and soothe the ache she saw in his gaze?

She leaned forward, felt her heart plummet to her toes when, with a smile, his lips formed her name.

Karinna.

It was too much. With a cry, she leaped from the sofa and ran out of the room.

Chapter 4

Rourke swore softly as the woman fled the room. Of course, he couldn't blame her for being startled. After all, how often did a figure in a painting move, much less speak? He supposed he should be grateful she hadn't fainted dead away. But, dammit, how was he going to establish contact with her without scaring her half to death? One way or another, he had to communicate with her. She owned him now. His fate, his future, the end to his relentless hunger all rested in her hands.

When she was in the room, he could hear the steady beat of her heart, smell the warm red river of life flowing through her veins.

Three hundred years since last he had fed, and with every passing year, the ache had grown stronger, until what had at first been mere discomfort turned to pain; the pain into never-ending agony. These days, the need clawed at him relentlessly, the pain unceasing. Excruciating. Sometimes, when it became more than he could bear, he fed off the horse. The animal's blood took the edge off his thirst but did nothing to satisfy either his hunger or his endless craving.

He slammed his fist against the glass. Relief was so near. So near. He closed his eyes, remembering the last time he had fed, the rich salty taste, the warmth that had flooded his being as the elixir of life flowed down his throat. It had been but a momentary pleasure, though, as, unexpectedly, the sweetness of her life's blood had turned sour and scorched his tongue. Only then had he realized the seductive young woman in his arms wasn't an ordinary mortal.

He pounded his fist against the glass again, but yet again, to no avail. His preternatural powers had been neutralized by his imprisonment, leaving him with little strength, supernatural or otherwise.

Frustrated and angry, he paced the length of his prison until the worst of his anger dissipated. Someday, he vowed, someday he would reclaim not only his freedom but the sword that Vilnius had stolen from him. Rourke clenched his hands into tight fists. The sword had belonged to his father, Thomas, who had fought with Prince Edward in the Eighth Crusade in 1272. Since becoming a vampire, his father's sword had been the only tangible thing Rourke had owned that held any meaning for him, the only memento he had left of the life he had once known. Thanks to the wizard's twisted sense of humor, a picture of that sword hung over the mantel inside the castle, a constant reminder of all Rourke had lost.

With a sigh, he dropped to the ground, his gaze

moving toward the box with the moving pictures. It was a wondrous creation called television. He marveled at the witchcraft that had conjured such a miracle. Much of what he knew of the modern world he had learned from watching the people trapped inside the mysterious machine. It had taken him quite some time to realize that some of what he saw took place in the present and some in the past, that some elements were fact and some were fiction, though he couldn't always tell which was which. But whether fact or fiction, he found it entertaining most of the time.

He glanced at the doorway, wondering if the woman would return. When she didn't, he spent a few moments perusing the woman's domain. The room he could see was small. The walls were a pale blue, the curtains at the window were white, the carpets a shade darker than the walls. The sofa was covered in a flowered print. A slender vase filled with fresh flowers could be seen on a side table. A three-tiered shelf held a number of small, framed photographs, a collection of blown-glass animals, a large seashell, and a blue marble egg. Another shelf held a trio of candles. Magazines were scattered over the top of the table in front of the sofa. It was a very feminine room. He wondered if she ever had male visitors.

Troubled by the thought of the woman being with another man, he turned and went into the castle on the hill.

* * *

Kari stood at her bedroom window, staring out into the night. It was almost midnight, time to stop acting like a frightened child, go downstairs, turn off the lights and the TV, and go to bed.

Taking a deep breath, she marched resolutely down the stairs. She switched off the TV, careful not to look up at the Vilnius. She was about to turn off the lights when her gaze was drawn toward the painting. What on earth was that?

Curious, she moved toward the hearth. She had never noticed that little white square on the lower left-hand corner of the glass before. Had it always been there? Or was it just another manifestation of her decaying mental state?

She stood on the raised hearth and peered at the small white piece of paper. And there, written in bold script, she read the word *help* written in what looked like blood.

Kari stared at the word as if she had never seen it before while her mind tried to come up with some logical explanation, but, of course, there was only one explanation, illogical and impossible as it seemed. The man in the painting was trying to communicate with her.

With a shrug, she turned away from the fireplace. After all, if he could move from place to place, why couldn't he write a message?

Humming softly, she turned out the lights and went upstairs to bed. There was a simple explanation for everything, she thought as she snuggled under the covers.

She was out of her mind.

* * *

Kari rose early the next morning, ate a quick breakfast, and left the house. She spent several hours at the mall, had lunch at her favorite restaurant, took in an early movie, and then stopped in to visit Tricia, who invited her to stay for dinner and watch a DVD.

"So," Tricia remarked when she switched off the DVD player. "Don't you think it's time you stopped pretending to be a hermit? There's a new guy in Brent's office. . . ."

Kari held up her hand. "Stop right there."

"Kari, I'm not asking you to marry the guy. Just go out with him. Have a little fun for a change."

"I'm not ready to date anyone yet."

"Kari, this is me, Trish. I know Ben hurt your feelings, but it's not like he broke your heart or anything. What's the problem?"

Kari blew out a sigh. She wished she could tell Tricia the truth, that she was falling in love with a man in a painting, but there were some things even your best friend wouldn't understand, or believe.

It was almost midnight when Kari returned home. She went straight to her room, undressed, took a shower, and went to bed.

Surprisingly, sleep came quickly.

She dreamed she was in the castle again. This time, he was waiting for her in the great room. She frowned, thinking that it looked different than it had the last time. There were fresh rushes on the floor. Several huge tapestries depicting hunting scenes hung from the walls. A cheery fire blazed in the large stone hearth. He rose from his chair when she stepped through the doorway, one hand outstretched in a gesture of welcome. Her gaze moved over him. Here, in her dream, he wasn't made of canvas and paint but of living flesh and blood. The light of the fire cast golden highlights in his fair hair, his deep blue eyes burned with a heat to rival the flames crackling in the hearth.

As she walked toward him, she realized she wasn't wearing her nightgown; instead, she wore a long, ice-blue velvet gown with a square neck and long, fitted sleeves that tapered to points at her wrists. The skirt swished around her ankles; a pair of matching slippers covered her feet.

She offered him her hand as though she were a highborn lady, surprised that the gesture came so naturally. His fingers were cool when they closed over hers, yet her whole body warmed at his touch. He was several inches taller than she was, his shoulders broad. Holding her gaze with his, he drew her down on a bed of thick white furs that suddenly appeared on the floor in front of the fireplace. Lying side by side, he aligned his body with hers. Even through the heavy material of her gown, she could feel the hard length of him, the heat of his arousal. He wooed her with soft-spoken words and sweet caresses, granted her every desire, fulfilled her every secret fantasy without being asked. His kisses were intoxicating, unlike any she had ever known. When he looked at her, she felt cherished. When he whispered her name, she felt loved as never before.

In the morning, Kari woke with tears in her eyes because it had only been a dream, and because he was nothing more than an attractive figure painted on canvas. It wasn't fair, she thought. She had finally met the man of her dreams, and that's all he was, a dream, a figment of her own warped imagination. For the first time in her life, she had found a man who made her feel vital and alive, a man she wanted to love, and he wasn't real. But real or not, she had to see him again.

Flinging back the covers, she grabbed her robe, then hurried downstairs, glad that it was a holiday and she didn't have to go to work.

Hurrying into the living room, she looked up at the painting. He wasn't there. Frowning, she examined the Vilnius from one side to the other, and from top to bottom. The horse was in the field, the dog was sleeping in the shade, the kitten was in the flower bed, but there was no sign of the man.

There was no sign of him after breakfast. He wasn't there at lunch. No matter how many times she looked at the painting that day, he was nowhere to be found.

Because it was her mother's birthday, Kari went to dinner at her parents' house. For a few blessed minutes, she forgot all about the mysterious man in the painting, until her mother asked if there was a man in her life. His image, and the dream she'd had the night before, brought a quick flush of heat to Kari's cheeks.

"Oh, I know that look," her mother said with a smile. "You've met someone! What's his name, what does he do, when will we meet him?"

"There's no one, Mom."

"Now, Kari . . ."

"Honest, Mom, I haven't met anyone."

Which was true enough, Kari thought later. In her dreams, she had made mad, passionate love to the man in the painting, but they hadn't exchanged names, or been formally introduced, so, technically, they hadn't met. And then there was the fact that he didn't actually exist.

With a shake of her head, Kari changed the subject.

She was feeling much better when she left for home later that evening. Spending time with her folks and her two older sisters and their husbands always grounded her in reality and was fun besides. Kari and her sisters had had their share of squabbles when they were growing up but they were all the best of friends now. Kaye was a kindergarten teacher, Kristina was a legal secretary. Kaye had a two-year-old son, Tommy; Kristina was expecting her first child in a few months.

Driving home, Kari convinced herself that the man in the painting had been nothing but a figment of her imagination created out of stress, boredom, and some kind of perverted wishful thinking. Tomorrow, she would put the painting up for sale on eBay and see if what Trish had said was true, that it really was worth a lot of money.

Humming softly, Kari parked the car in the driveway. She stood outside for a few minutes, gazing up at the starry sky. The air was fragrant with the scent of night-blooming jasmine and honeysuckle. It was a beautiful night, the kind they wrote songs about. If only she had someone to share it with.

Going into the house, she turned on the lights, tossed her handbag onto the sofa, switched on the TV, and glanced up at the Vilnius.

Her heart skipped a beat when she saw him waiting for her at the front of the painting. His gaze met hers, his smile melancholy.

If she removed the frame, would she discover the secret of how he moved from place to place? Or would he leap off the canvas? She laughed softly. No matter how handsome he was, what on earth would she do with him when he was only ten inches tall?

"You're not real," she murmured. "Do you hear me? I know you're not there, so just go away."

But he didn't disappear.

Standing there, she saw a number of small details she hadn't noticed before, like the jagged crack in one of the upstairs windows of the castle, and the gray squirrel on the branch of one of the trees. Funny, she hadn't noticed those things before. Had they always been there? Or was her overly vivid imagination sketching them in?

The man sat cross-legged on the grass, his gaze focused on her face. Sometimes she thought he was trying to speak to her, not verbally, but mentally. An absurd notion, to be sure. And yet, she had heard a voice in her mind. . . .

Sitting on the sofa, she shook the disconcerting thought away.

Hours passed but time had no meaning. There was only the man in the painting. She knew he was sad and wondered why the artist had painted him that way, and what magic canvas he had used, to give his creation the ability to move about and express emotion. Sometimes she was sure the man was in terrible pain, though she had no idea what made her think so. Or maybe it wasn't the man in the painting who was sad and in pain. Maybe what she was feeling were the thoughts and emotions of the artist. That hardly seemed likely, she mused, since she wasn't the least bit psychic or telepathic, but tonight she could believe almost anything.

Kari could hardly believe it when she looked at the clock and saw that it was after midnight. Shocked, she scrambled to her feet. She had to get some sleep. She had to go to work in the morning.

Reaching up, she pressed her palm against the glass that enclosed the painting, whispered, "Good night," and went to bed.

She dreamed of him again. Tonight, she wore a gown of pale, pale pink that made her feel like she was a princess in a fairy tale. Hand in hand, they walked through the verdant meadow. The horse trailed behind them, its white coat gleaming like liquid silver in the light of the moon. The dog frolicked at their heels, then ran ahead, sniffing the ground.

She was acutely aware that she was in the painting. Strange, that she didn't feel small or one-dimensional. Walking along, she felt a vagrant breeze caress her cheek, the spongy sod beneath her feet. She was equally aware of the man at her side, of the latent strength of his hand holding hers. Her whole body tingled at his nearness. Oddly, neither of them spoke, but there was no need for words.

When they reached the edge of the lake, she sat down on the rock and he sat beside her, his arm slipping around her shoulders as if it was the most natural thing in the world. Leaning forward, she trailed her hand in the water, surprised that it was cool and wet. It was only a picture of a lake, after all, yet, like everything else, it seemed so real.

With a shake of her head, she leaned against him, content to sit there in the moonlight with the wind blowing softly on her face. The breeze rustled the leaves of the trees and made gentle ripples on the surface of the water. She laughed softly as the dog splashed along the shore, threw up her hands when it bounded toward them and then stopped abruptly to shake the water from its fur.

She looked at the man beside her, thinking how handsome he was, and suddenly she was lying on her back on the grass, his body covering hers, his kiss gently driving all other thoughts from her mind.

With a sigh, she closed her eyes and surrendered to the magic of his touch, the exquisite taste of his kisses. A part of her knew it was only a dream, yet it felt more real than the world she had left behind.

Perhaps *this* was reality and everything else was a dream. She wished fleetingly that she could stay here, with him, forever.

She gazed into his eyes, trying to find a way to ask if there was some way she could stay with him when, suddenly, she was sitting at the castle window, alone, seeing what he saw, hearing what he heard, feeling what he felt. What he felt . . . her whole being was consumed with rage and frustration at being trapped inside a stagnant world where outside sounds were muted and the view of the universe was limited to wherever the painting was located at the time. And overall, a never-ending, all-consuming hunger unlike anything she had ever experienced. She felt it in every fiber and cell of her being, a pain far worse than anything she had ever known, an agony so great she knew it would consume her, body and soul, if she couldn't escape.

Fear rose up within her, hot and swift. She had to get out, had to get away before it was too late. She was smothering, unable to breathe, unable to move.

She woke with a start, wept tears of relief to find herself in her own bed, in her own house.

He was in her thoughts all the next day at work, whether she was talking on the phone with a client, adding the final touches to a presentation, or sending a fax. What did it say about her life that her dreams were more exciting than her reality?

She went to lunch with several of her coworkers but she was scarcely aware of the conversation around her. All she could think about was him and how wonderful it would be if he were made of flesh and blood, muscle and sinew, instead of paint and canvas.

She hurried home after work, eager to see where he would be. For some inexplicable reason, it no longer seemed odd that he should flit from place to place. It was simply the way it was. She had made a game of it on her way home from work, trying to guess if she would find him walking in the forest or sitting in the castle window or reclining near the water. She no longer wondered if she was crazy; she just accepted that she was. Not stark raving mad. Not a raving lunatic. Just a little bit insane.

At home, she put on her favorite soft-rock station, changed out of her work clothes and into a pair of comfy blue jeans and a sweater. She ate a quick dinner, then went into the living room and plopped down onto the sofa.

As always, her gaze was drawn to the man in the painting. Tonight he was riding the horse, or at least sitting on it.

She was about to get up and turn off the radio and turn on the TV when he dismounted and walked toward the glass.

Toward her.

Kari let out a startled gasp. She knew he changed locations but never before had she actually seen him move.

Mesmerized, she watched him stride toward her, his movements lithe, almost catlike. He wore the cloak tonight; it billowed out behind him, almost as if it had a life of its own. She was tempted to run out of the room, but she couldn't move, couldn't stop watching him as he drew ever closer.

He was stopped by the glass, of course. For a moment, he simply looked at her, and then he smiled that smile that was somehow warm and wistful at the same time.

Hardly aware that she was speaking aloud, she murmured, "You're so handsome. I wish I knew your name. But then, you probably don't have one, do you?"

With a shake of her head, she went into the kitchen to get a drink of water. She stood at the sink a moment, staring out the window into the darkness beyond. She hated winter, the long nights, the storms with their ominous rumblings of thunder and dagger-like streaks of lightning.

After putting the glass in the sink, she went back into the living room. It was almost ten. Maybe she would just watch the news and go to bed.

But all thought of world events evaporated when she glanced at the painting. There was another white square stuck to the glass.

This one said, *Rourke.*

Kari repeated his name in her mind, wondering if it was his first name or his last, and then murmured it out loud. "Rourke."

It was a strong name, a very masculine name, and it suited him perfectly. She said it again and then again, liking the sound of it.

"Rourke." She gazed into his eyes, eyes that no

longer looked painted. Eyes that followed every movement she made. "I'm Karinna."

He smiled, as if in acknowledgment.

His smile moved through her, warming her blood, filling her with a slow sensual heat. His gaze rested lightly on her face, lingered on her lips. Almost, it seemed she could feel the pressure of his mouth on hers. For a moment, she closed her eyes remembering her dreams, the hard length of his body aligned with hers, the touch of his lips, the taste of his kisses.

She hadn't had a date since she broke up with Ben almost five months ago. She hadn't missed him at all. In fact, she had been quite content with her own company, until now. Now, she wanted to feel a man's arms around her, to feel his body pressed intimately against her own, to taste his kisses. Only it wasn't Ben she wanted. It was Rourke, the man in the painting.

"Merciful heavens, Karinna Abigail Adams, you're pathetic!" she exclaimed. And after turning off the lights, she ran up the stairs to her room, and went to bed.

Once again, Rourke found himself staring after the woman. Karinna. He liked the sound of her name, the curve of her hips, the way her eyes caressed him. He wanted to hold her, touch her, taste her. . . . He wanted to drag her into his arms, bury his fangs in her throat, and ease the relentless pain that engulfed him with every waking moment. It was a good thing she was beyond his reach. If he ever escaped his canvas prison, the first mortal he encountered probably wouldn't survive.

He slammed his palm against the glass that imprisoned him. He wanted out! And only Karinna, with hair like ebony silk and eyes as blue as a summer sky, could say the words that would set him free.

Hands clenched at his sides, he took a deep, calming breath. Soon, he thought, soon she would call to him, and when she did, the wizard's spell would be broken.

And he would have her.

All of her.

Chapter 5

For Kari, the next four days passed in a kind of haze. Feeling like a character out of *Charlotte's Web*, or maybe *The Twilight Zone*, she woke each day to find a new message waiting for her. These messages, longer than the first, were written directly on the glass.

The one for Wednesday read, *Your hair is as black as a raven's wing.* As if in answer to her earlier question, one she had not voiced aloud, he had signed his name. *Jason Rourke.*

"Jason," she murmured, smiling. "I like it."

Thursday's message read, *You are more beautiful than Venus and Aphrodite. JR*

Friday's missive made her blush. It said, *I wish I was the cup you drink from that I might feel your lips on mine. JR*

She marveled that he was able to write the messages so that she could read them from her side of the painting.

Saturday's declaration was the most appealing of all. It said, simply, *You are my life. Rourke.*

He was waiting for her near the glass that night, a strikingly handsome man clad in a white shirt and buff-colored breeches, his fair hair framing a face that was the epitome of masculine beauty. She read his message a second time—*you are my life*—then murmured, "As you've become mine."

She was losing it, she thought with a sigh. She had dismissed all thought of selling the Vilnius. Like it or not, she was obsessed with the painting and with its mysterious occupant, Jason Rourke.

"I wish . . ." She shook her head. "I wish . . ."

What did she wish? That she had never gone into the Underwood Art Gallery? That she wasn't losing her mind? That he was real instead of just paint and canvas?

"Just my luck," Kari muttered. "There's never a genie around when you need one."

He placed one hand on the glass, his gaze intent upon her face. *"Tell me, Karinna, what would you wish for?"* His voice, speaking in her mind.

"I would wish that you were real, that you were standing here, beside me." She nodded. "Yes, that's what I would wish for."

The words had no sooner escaped Kari's lips than the earth seemed to shift beneath her feet. The air around her took on a kind of thickness and it was suddenly hard to breathe. Her pulse raced, there was a dull roaring in her ears. When the world righted itself again, she saw that the Vilnius had fallen off the wall and shattered on the hearth. Shards of glass littered the carpet, glinting brightly. And a tall man with long, dark blond hair and mesmerizing blue eyes stood in front of the fireplace. A man clad in an old-fashioned, loose-fitting white shirt, buff-colored breeches, and boots. A black cloak fell from a pair of broad shoulders.

It was him. The man in the painting.

She shook her head. No, it couldn't be, it was impossible.

"Rourke." She whispered his name and then the world spun out of control. The floor rushed up to meet her, and then everything went black.

Darting forward, Jason Rourke caught the woman in his arms. Her scent flooded his nostrils. The silk of her hair caressed his hands. The feel of her body against his reminded him, almost painfully, that he had not had a woman in three hundred years.

But it wasn't the hunger of the flesh that burned through him. It was the almost overpowering scent of the warm crimson tide flowing sweetly through her veins, the tantalizing beat of her heart. He groaned softly as his fangs brushed his tongue. He looked at the woman, his body cold and aching with need; looked at the pulse beating slow and steady in the hollow of her throat and saw an end to the pain that had plagued him for centuries.

Lowering his head to her neck, he swept his tongue across her silken skin and then, with a low growl, he closed his eyes, sank his fangs into her throat, and forgot everything but the primal urge to feed, to slake his hellish thirst, to ease the pain that had tormented him for so long. The warmth of her life's blood burned through him, turning away the chill, the emptiness, of three hundred years.

Lost in the ecstasy of the moment, he might have taken it all if she hadn't moaned softly. Lifting his head, he gazed into her eyes, deep blue eyes wide with terror and disbelief.

With a hoarse cry of fear, Kari twisted out of his embrace. Had she been able, she would have run out of the room and out of the house, but she lacked the strength to do so. With a sob, she staggered backward a few feet, then collapsed onto the sofa.

She looked up at him, her expression one of fear, hopelessness, and distrust.

Rourke stood over her, his hands clenched as he fought down the hunger that still raged through him. It would take more than the life's blood of one mortal female to satisfy his rampant hunger.

Even so, the heat of her blood sang through his veins, and with it came a renewal of his preternatural power. Colors increased in brightness and depth, his nostrils filled with a thousand scents, most of which were alien to him. He heard the harsh rasp of the woman's breathing, the erratic beating of her heart, the ticking of a clock somewhere upstairs, the drip of water. And mingled with those mundane sounds were others he could not identify.

It had been in his mind to drain the woman dry, but he realized now that he might have need of her. The world had changed since the wizard had cursed him. During his imprisonment in the painting, Rourke had seen but little of the new world, and much of what he had seen made no sense. She could explain it to him. And then there was the fact that he owed the woman a life debt for setting him free.

What kind of monster had he become, that he could even think of repaying her kindness with treachery?

Catching the woman's gaze with his own, he willed her to go to sleep, and then, filled with the exhilaration of freedom and the burning thirst of three hundred years, he opened the door and stepped out into the night.

He paused in the darkness, hidden in the shadows, his senses expanding as his power surged up within him like lava erupting from a long-dormant volcano.

A myriad of sights and sounds and smells pummeled his senses from all sides. He drew them in, sorting those he knew from those that were foreign to him. One scent overpowered all the others. The smell of prey, nearby.

Becoming one with the night, he followed the scent. It led him to a group of five boys gathered in an alley. Music blared from a black box.

Rourke watched them for several moments before they grew aware of his presence. They were an odd-looking bunch, with their baggy trousers, sleeveless shirts, and heavy boots. One had hair that resembled a rooster's tail; another had no hair at all; a third wore his hair in an unremarkable style save that it was bright green.

Rourke grunted softly. A veritable feast, his for the taking.

The boy with green hair noticed him first. "Hey, man," he exclaimed, "what do you want?"

Rourke smiled, displaying his fangs. "You."

The boy stared at him. "What the hell are you talking about, man?" Reaching behind his back, he produced a knife. "This is our turf, you freak. Get the hell out of here."

Focusing his energy on the blade, Rourke plucked it from the boy's hand and flung it into the street.

Perhaps thinking there was safety in numbers, the other four thugs moved closer together, their eyes narrowed. He could smell the stink of fear that rose from them with the realization that they were facing something completely beyond their ken.

"Who are you?" Green Hair asked, his voice little more than a whisper.

Rourke didn't bother to answer. He looked at each boy in turn, his mind holding each of theirs captive as he moved among them. Young blood, was there anything in all the world like it?

He was tempted to drain them dry, all of them. There was nothing to equal the rush of drinking a mortal dry, the preternatural strength that came with it, the all-encompassing sense of euphoria. But it was never wise to leave a trail of bodies behind and tonight he didn't want to be bothered with disposing of his kills.

He drank from them all, drank until he was drunk with the taste and the smell and the power. He could feel it flooding his being, singing through his veins, sharpening powers that had lain dormant for too long.

Releasing the mortals from his thrall, he vanished from their sight. The moon he had not seen in centuries called to him and he ran effortlessly in its light, his muscles stretching after their long confinement. He ran for miles, reveling in the touch of

the wind on his face, in his hair, the feel of the
earth beneath his feet, thrilling to the supernatural
power and strength that surged like a living, breathing thing within him. And as his strength grew, so
did his hatred for the wizard who had imprisoned
him and stolen so many decades of his existence.

The wizard, Vilnius. Did he still live? And what of
his daughter, Ana Luisa? Was she still ensnared
inside a painting, as well, or had her father taken pity
on her and released her years ago? Trapped in a
prison of his own, Rourke had vowed to destroy Vilnius for what he had done. It had been the thought
of avenging himself on the wizard that had kept him
sane during the long centuries of his imprisonment.
In his mind, he had killed the wizard over and over
again, each death more diabolically cruel, more lingering, than the last.

He swore softly. Finding the wizard. That could
prove difficult, if not impossible, after so many
years. But if the wizard still lived, Rourke would
find him. One way or another, he would find him.
The thought of vengeance would only grow sweeter
with the passage of days. In the meantime, he
would acclimate himself to this new century, this
new world.

With that thought in mind, he strolled down the
street, noting that houses had changed in both style
and architecture since he had been born over seven
hundred years ago. Cars had replaced the horse.
Walking along, he found that he preferred the pun-
gent smell of horse manure to the stink of oil and
gasoline. Fashions, too, had undergone a drastic

change. In his day, women had covered themselves from head to foot and often worn hats with veils. The women of today bared it all, apparently without thought for modesty or shame. Fashions for men had also undergone a radical transformation. He observed the flamboyant shirts, baggy pants, casual footwear, and shook his head.

He walked through the darkness for hours, savoring his freedom. He fed again, and yet again, until he could hold no more, until every fiber and particle of his being was replete. Sated, he made his way back to the woman's house.

The woman. Karinna. What was he going to do about the woman?

He stood in the shadows outside her house for a moment, enjoying the quiet of a night that would soon be over.

He was still undecided about her fate when he went inside. Standing in front of the sofa, he gazed down at her. She was quite lovely, with hair the color of ebony and skin kissed by the sun. Her scent drifted to him, reminding him again that he had not had a woman in three hundred years. An eternity to a man who was sensual by nature, one who had the power to seduce a woman with a look, a word, a touch.

He should destroy her. No mortal lived who knew what he was. He could do it now, quickly and cleanly, while she slept. Yet even as he contemplated ending her life, he knew he would not. She had broken the wizard's enchantment, and for that reason alone, he would allow her to live.

And yet it wasn't the only reason. How could he think of destroying such a lovely creature? He had known queens and highborn ladies, trollops and scullery maids, but he had never known a woman who was lovelier, or more tempting. Her skin was smooth, warm when he stroked her cheek. Her lips were soft, like the petals of a blood rose. Her figure was slender, petite and perfect. Her hair fell over her shoulders like a waterfall of rich black silk. Unable to resist, he ran his fingers through the thick strands.

"Karinna." He murmured her name, thinking it suited her perfectly. "Ah, Karinna, what am I to do with you?"

He couldn't bring himself to kill her.

He had no desire to leave her.

And no time to worry about it, not now, when he needed to find a place to hide from the sun.

He glanced at the painting visible beneath shards of broken glass. There was one thing he needed to do before he sought his rest.

It was with a great deal of satisfaction that he ripped the hated canvas to shreds.

Chapter 6

The wizard's head jerked up, his eyes narrowing in disbelief.

Jason Rourke had attained his freedom! It was impossible, unthinkable, and yet, he felt the truth of it explode through him with undeniable certainty.

He stared at the vessel in his hand, and then, muttering an oath, he threw it across the room, where it hit the wall and shattered most satisfactorily. Why had he let Ana Luisa persuade him to add an escape clause when he cursed the vampire?

He laughed softly, mirthlessly. Perhaps he had acceded to her wishes because she was his only child and he loved her as much as he was able, in spite of the fact that she was female and therefore weak and of little use. Perhaps it was time to call her forth from her prison. Time had no meaning for him; he was surprised to realize that three hundred years had passed since the night he caught her in Jason Rourke's arms. Ah, Rourke. It would not be safe to free Ana now, he thought, not when the vampire Rourke again walked the earth. She had no resistance to the creature's charm. Should Ana Luisa meet him again, she would no doubt succumb to his supernatural enchantment once more. He would rather see her dead than prey to the vampire's unholy lust.

Rourke. Where was he now? Vilnius closed his eyes and opened his wizard's Sight. In moments, the vampire's image rose in his mind, and with it, the knowledge that the creature was somewhere in America.

Perhaps, with half the world between Rourke and Ana Luisa, there was nothing to worry about. Then again, it was always better to be safe than sorry.

With a wave of his hand, Vilnius repaired the broken vessel and returned to the spell at hand.

Trapped in a painting located in a museum in Bucharest, the wizard's daughter sensed a shift in the supernatural world.

It took her a moment to realize what it was, and then she knew. Jason had broken her father's curse! A single tear slipped down Ana Luisa's cheek. Did Jason still hate her after all these years? Would her father ever forgive her for what she had done and release her from this horrid captivity? Alive and yet not alive, she had spent the last three hundred years trapped in a painting behind a wall of glass, doomed to remain frozen in time until someone called her forth. She had long ago lost any hope of that happening. Save for Jason, no one now living even knew her name. How had Jason managed to escape? Of course, he was a powerful vampire, while she was just a young witch with abilities she was helpless to use.

Three hundred years, and she had been unable to move in all that time. The painting that imprisoned her had changed hands many times in three centuries. It had adorned the wall of a citadel in Spain, a tavern in London, a palace in France. Once, she had languished in a cellar for over a century, with rats, mice, and spiders her only companions.

These days, the painting hung in a small museum near the outskirts of the city. She stared at the night watchman, who was sitting in a wine-colored wing chair, his head bent over a book. He had been a young man when the painting had first come here. Now his body was stooped with age, his face lined by the years, his hair as white as winter snow. Years ago, she had hoped he might be the one to call her forth from her prison, but he rarely looked at her anymore.

She was doomed, she thought, doomed to spend the rest of her miserable existence sitting on the back of a unicorn.

Discouragement settled over her like a shroud.

For her, there was no hope of escape, no chance of reprieve.

Chapter 7

Kari woke with a low groan. Opening her eyes, she glanced at her surroundings. Funny, she didn't remember falling asleep on the sofa. Sitting up, she stretched her arms, back, and shoulders, then ran a hand through her hair. She'd had the strangest dream. . . . She shook her head, recalling how she had dreamed of Rourke standing in her living room in front of the hearth.

It was then that she saw the broken glass. The tiny fragments sparkled on the rug like bits of ice on a winter day. Where on earth had all that glass come from? She looked up at the blank space above the hearth.

The painting! Of course. She remembered now. The Vilnius had fallen off the wall last night. The frame had broken and the glass had shattered into a million pieces.

Rising, she picked up what was left of the canvas. It was ruined beyond repair. She shook her head. She could understand the glass breaking. She could even see how the canvas might get ripped in a few places. But this? The canvas looked like it had been run through a paper shredder. Remarkably, the notes he had written were unscathed. She stared at them a moment, then slipped them into her pocket.

So much for the fortune she had hoped to make from selling the Vilnius on eBay, she thought, and then shrugged. Who was she kidding? She would never have sold it.

Going into the kitchen, she spread the tattered painting out on the table, her brow furrowing as she tried to smooth out the rough edges of the canvas. Where was he? Had he been destroyed with the painting?

Another memory rushed to the front of her mind, the memory of a man standing in her living room in front of the fireplace. A man with hair the color of old gold and vibrant blue eyes. A life-size version of the man in the painting.

She shook her head. "Don't go there," she muttered. "It was just a dream. Anything else is impossible."

Anything else was beyond impossible. The glass and the frame were just old, that was all. Old things broke all the time. But dream or not, she couldn't shake his image from her mind. Real or imagined, he had been the most amazing-looking man she had ever seen. Tall and broad and long of limb, with long dark blond hair and mesmerizing blue eyes. Even in the loose-fitting white shirt he had worn, there was no disguising the width of his chest and shoulders. Now that the painting had been destroyed, she would never see him again. The thought saddened her more than she would have thought possible.

"Really, Kari," she muttered in exasperation. "Tricia is right. You need to get a life. A real life."

Upon returning to the living room, she picked up the broken frame and the larger pieces of glass and tossed them into the trash, then pulled the vacuum from the broom closet and vacuumed the rug, wondering all the while how falling off the wall had torn the canvas to shreds.

The wall above the mantel looked naked without the Vilnius. Her house felt empty without the painting. Without him.

"You really are losing it." With that cheerful thought in mind, she put the vacuum away and went into the bedroom to change her clothes.

The rest of the day passed quickly. She went out to lunch and a movie with Tricia, went to the video store to return some videos, then to the market to pick up a quart of milk, cleaning supplies, and some fruit. She stopped at the cleaners to pick up her dry cleaning, and then, deciding she didn't feel like cooking, she made a U-turn and drove back to pick up some Chinese takeout from her favorite restaurant. One last stop at the gas station, and she went home.

The sun was setting in a spectacular blaze of crimson and gold as she pulled into the driveway. Getting out of the car, she paused a moment to appreciate the sunset. It took two trips to carry everything into the house, another few minutes to put her groceries away.

It was five minutes to seven when she carried her

dinner into the living room, intending to watch a rerun of one of her favorite shows while she ate. She remembered the time distinctly because it was at that exact moment that fantasy became reality, and her life changed forever.

"Good evening, Karinna."

She recognized his voice even though she had never heard it before. It resonated in her mind and in her heart and proved, once and for all, that she was totally insane.

Her dinner plate tumbled from her grasp, sending fried rice and sweet-and-sour shrimp skittering across the floor.

She stared up at him, at a strong handsome face and the vivid blue eyes that had haunted her day and night.

"You're not real." She shook her head in denial. "You're not real."

"No?" He held out his hand. "Touch me and see."

Kari moved toward him as if drawn by an invisible string. She reached for him, her own hand shaking as she touched the tips of her fingers to his.

He was real. She had half expected him to be made of nothing but air and daydreams, but he was solid, his skin cool and firm.

"No." She shook her head again. "It can't be true. How can you be real?" She glanced at the place over the mantel where the Vilnius had been. "You're . . . you're not here . . . it was just a dream."

She closed her eyes. She would count to three, and when she opened her eyes again, he would be gone and the Vilnius would be hanging over the mantel, where it belonged. She would take it back to the gallery first thing Monday morning and never look at it again.

She took a deep breath. "One."

Another breath. "Two. Three."

She opened one eye.

He was still there, only now he was grinning at her. His teeth were very white.

"You need not be afraid of me, Karinna," he said, amusement evident in his voice. "I am not going to hurt you."

"What . . . what do you want?"

"I want you to help me find my way around."

"Around where?"

"I am new to this place, and this time."

"What do you mean, this time?"

Taking her by the hand, he led her to the sofa and urged her to sit down.

"Who are you?" she asked tremulously. "How did you get here?"

"I am going to tell you a story."

"What kind of a story?"

"Just listen. A very long time ago, in a small village in Transylvania, a man met a woman in the local tavern. He was smitten with her beauty, but even more than that, there was something exotic about her. All the women he knew had dark hair and dark eyes, but this stranger had hair like fire and eyes like a blue flame. She spoke in riddles, teasing him, tempting him. The women of his village smelled of sunshine and fine wine, but this woman smelled of silk and mystery. Knowing it was wrong and yet helpless to resist, he met her at the tavern every night for a week until he was completely under her spell, and then late one night, she invited him to her dwelling. He refused, and yet, without quite knowing how it happened, he found himself following her to where she lived, a solitary house deep in the woods.

"She offered him wine and refilled his glass many times. And then, when he was drunk with it, and with her, she took him to her bed.

"When he woke, he was in a cave. He remembered very little of what had happened the night before and what he remembered didn't seem real. Glowing red eyes. The sharp prick of fangs at his throat. The taste of blood on his tongue.

"Feeling disoriented, he left the cave. As soon as he stepped outside, a sharp pain engulfed him. Frightened, he glanced around, wondering where he was, where the woman was.

"He was trying to find his way back to his village when the woman appeared at his side. She stilled the questions that poured from his lips with a wave of her hand and told him what had happened to him the night before.

"He listened in disbelief as she explained that he was now a vampire—"

"A vampire!" Kari exclaimed. "That's ridiculous. There's no such thing."

"Be still. She told him that he was a vampire. From now on, he would live only by night. He would need blood to survive. Human blood. She told him many other incredible things about his new condition, kissed him on the cheek, and vanished from his sight.

"Many years passed. The man didn't age, though all those he knew and loved grew old and passed away. And then one night, centuries later, he met another woman. She flirted with him shamelessly, and because he was a man, and lonely, he agreed to meet her the next night. They continued to meet, and then, one evening, while making love to her, he took a little taste of her blood. It was sweet, yet it burned his tongue like fire.

"Confused, he started to put her away from him, but it was too late. Her father burst into the room and found them lying together. Enraged, her father called down a terrible curse upon the young lovers. . . ."

Rourke paused, his gaze on Karinna's face. She was watching him intently, her eyes wide.

"What was the curse?" she asked, her voice little more than a whisper, as if she feared the answer.

"The father was a powerful wizard. He cast the woman into one painting, and the man into another. . . ."

She shook her head. "No, that can't be true."

"Another painting," he continued, "where the man stayed for three hundred years until a woman with hair like black silk and eyes the blue of the sky called him forth and broke the curse."

"What happened to the wizard and his daughter?"

"I know not, but I intend to find out."

"It's a nice fairy tale, but I don't believe a word of it." But even as she said the words, she recalled Tricia telling her that the painting was three hundred years old, the same number of years Rourke claimed to have been trapped inside. "What was the name of this wizard?"

"Vilnius."

"No." She shook her head vigorously. "No, no, no! It's impossible."

"It's very possible," he said quietly. And to prove it, he bared his fangs.

Karinna stared at him a moment, then fainted dead away.

With a sigh, Rourke carried her up the stairs and put her to bed.

Upon regaining consciousness, Kari sat up and glanced around the room, relieved to see that she was in her own room, in her own bed.

After rising, she moved cautiously through the rest of the house. He was gone. But of course he was. He wasn't real. He couldn't be real. Vampires, indeed!

Returning to the living room, she picked up the phone. Tricia answered on the third ring.

"Hello?"

"Hi, Tricia? Did I wake you?"

"No, I was just watching the *Late Show*. What's up?"

"Can you come over?"

"Now?"

"Right now."

"What's wrong? You sound . . . what's wrong?"

"Please, just come over."

"All right, I'll be there in ten minutes."

"Thanks. Bye."

Kari hung up the receiver then got to work cleaning up the shrimp and rice scattered on the living room floor.

Tricia arrived ten minutes later. "All right, girl-friend, what's going on?"

"The painting . . ."

Tricia glanced at the space over the mantel. "What happened to it? Don't tell me you sold it! How much did you get . . . ?"

"It broke."

"Broke? How did that happen?"

Kari sat down on the sofa and Tricia sat beside her.

"Is the canvas ruined?" Tricia asked. "I know an art restorer who might be able to salvage it."

Kari shook her head. "You don't understand. He broke it."

"He? He, who?"

"The man in the painting."

Tricia sat back, her brow furrowed. "Kari, what are you trying to say?"

"The man in the painting. Either he's real, or I'm going crazy."

"Well, one of us is," Tricia said dryly. "'Cause you're not making any sense at all."

Kari clasped her hands in her lap. "He was very handsome and I . . . well, I sort of talked to him some-times. And last night I was looking at the painting and I said I . . . I wished he was beside me and the next thing I knew, he was."

Pity and concern played over Tricia's features.

"I know you don't believe me. I know how crazy

this sounds, but it's true. Earlier tonight he showed up and . . . you won't believe this either, but he told me he was a vampire and . . ."

"This just gets better and better," Tricia muttered.

"And that he'd been cursed by a wizard. A wizard named Vilnius . . . and that he'd been inside that painting for three hundred years. And . . ."

"Kari, honey, have you thought about seeing a doctor?"

"You mean a psychiatrist, don't you?"

"Well . . ."

"I can prove it." Reaching into her pocket, Kari withdrew the notes Rourke had written. "Look at these," she said, a note of triumph in her voice, and handed them to Tricia.

Frowning, Tricia spread the notes on her lap, and then shrugged. "So, what does this prove?"

"They're notes. From him."

Tricia ran her fingernail over one of the pieces of paper, frowning when the ink flaked off. "This looks like blood."

Kari nodded. "I thought so, too."

Tricia shook her head. "I don't know what to say."

"He wants me to show him around."

"He does, huh? Well, that should be interesting."

With a sigh of exasperation, Kari said, "You're humoring me, aren't you?"

"Can you blame me? This all sounds so far-fetched." Tricia glanced around the room. "So, where is he now?"

"I don't know. He was here earlier." Kari shrugged. "I guess I fainted. . . ."

"Well, I can understand that!"

"When I woke up, he was gone." She lifted a hand to her neck. "I think he bit me last night."

"What?" Tricia was on her feet in an instant. "Where? Let me see."

Kari pulled her hair back and turned her head to the side, wondering how she could have forgotten such a thing. "Right here," she said, pointing.

Tricia leaned forward. Two small red marks could be seen just below Kari's left ear. "They don't look like bites, exactly. . . ." She sat down heavily. "Have you told anyone else?"

"No, just you."

"Why don't you come home with me tonight? I don't think you should stay here alone."

"So, you believe me?"

"I don't know what I believe, but I suppose those marks could be bites." She nodded. "Yes, I think coming home with me is the best thing for you to do."

"I don't want to intrude. . . ."

"Don't be silly. It'll be fun. Brent's at a convention in Chicago, and the kids are at my mom's for a few days. It'll just be the two of us."

"I've got to go to work tomorrow."

"I know, but we can go out to dinner tomorrow night. We haven't had a night out together for a while. We can go to that new Italian place. My treat."

Kari tapped her fingernails on the arm of the sofa. Maybe Tricia was right. Maybe she needed to get out of the house. "All right. Just let me get my things together."

Kari was pulling clean underwear out of a dresser drawer when she realized she was no longer alone. She looked over her shoulder, expecting to see Tricia. Instead, she saw him.

The vampire.

Jason Rourke.

Chapter 8

Rourke glanced at the suitcase lying open at the foot of Karinna's bed. "Going somewhere?"

"You're here," she murmured.

"So it would seem. Where are you going?"

"To spend the night with a friend."

"The woman downstairs?"

Kari nodded, her hands tightening nervously on the undergarments in her hand.

"Why are you spending the night away from home?"

"Because I need to get away. . . ."

"From what?"

"You, of course." Moving toward the bed, Kari dropped her undergarments into the suitcase, then went to the closet and pulled out a pink two-piece pantsuit and matching shell to wear to work. She folded them neatly into the suitcase, added a pair of low-heeled sandals, her nightgown and robe, and closed the lid. "Well, good-bye."

Rourke shook his head. "Spending the night away

from home will not change anything. I will still be here when you return."

"Fine. Wait right there. Don't move."

"What are you going to do?"

"You'll see." Kari stepped out into the hallway. "Tricia?" she called, leaning over the banister. "Could you come up here for a minute?"

"Need some help?" Tricia asked.

"In a way."

Kari returned to the bedroom, her arms folded under her breasts.

"Why have you called her?" Rourke asked, frowning. "Are you still afraid of me? Do you think she can protect you?"

"No, just wait." She turned toward the door at the sound of Tricia's footsteps.

"What do you wa . . . ?" Tricia's voice trailed off when she stepped into the room and saw Rourke standing beside the bed. "Who's this?"

"It's him, the man in the painting, who do you think?"

Tricia shook her head. "Come on, Kari, who is he, really?"

"I knew you didn't believe me!"

"Kari . . ."

"Just take a good look at him. Doesn't he look familiar?"

Moving warily, Tricia took a few steps toward Rourke, her eyes narrowing.

"Well?" Kari prompted.

"I didn't really look at him that closely the other night."

"For goodness' sake, Trish, look at what he's wearing! Who do you know that goes around wearing clothes like that nowadays?"

"I remember you," Rourke said, studying Tricia. "You were wearing a pair of blue trousers and a red shirt with little white hearts on it."

Tricia's eyes widened as he described what she had been wearing the night Kari had asked her to come over and look at the painting.

"Now do you believe me?" Kari asked.

"It's not possible," Tricia said, her voice little more than a whisper. Grabbing Kari by the hand, she backed toward the door. "Let's get out of here."

Tricia let out a shriek when she turned toward the door and saw Rourke barring the way. "How did you do that?"

"Tricia." He caught her gaze with his. "Listen to me, Tricia. I want you to go home. None of this ever happened. You were never here tonight. You have never seen me or the painting before. Nod your head if you understand."

Tricia nodded.

"Now go home."

Moving like a robot, Tricia left the room. Moments later, Kari heard the front door open and close.

Kari stared up at him. "How did you do that?"

"A form of hypnotism."

"You're real, aren't you? I didn't imagine you, did I?"

"No, I am as real as you are."

"Are you going to make me into a vampire?"

"If you wish."

"I don't!" She lifted a hand to her neck. "But you already did, didn't you? You bit me." She glanced toward the window. "And the moon is almost full."

He laughed softly. "You are confusing vampires with werewolves."

"But you took my blood. Isn't that how vampires are made?"

"I tasted you," he said, smiling. "I would have had to take much more to bring you across. Just a taste," he murmured. "And you were sweet, indeed."

"Sweet!" She made a gagging sound. "Blood isn't sweet."

"Ah, my dear, that is where you are wrong. It is the sweetest nectar you can imagine."

"Maybe to you." Kari took another step backward, sat down hard when the backs of her knees collided with the chair in the corner. "Were you really trapped inside that painting for three hundred years?"

He nodded curtly.

"It must have been awful."

"Awful?" He swore softly. "That hardly describes it. A bad harvest is awful. Bad wine is awful. Being imprisoned behind a wall of glass for three centuries was torture."

In more ways than one, he thought bleakly. It had been more than the loss of his freedom, more than the agony of being unable to slake his hellish thirst, more than his desire for a woman. It had been the blow to his pride that still rankled, even after all these years. The wizard had overpowered him, humbled him as no other ever had. Even now, the shame of it was hard to endure.

"Those notes you stuck on the glass," Kari remarked. "What did you write them with?"

"Blood."

Even though she had suspected as much, the thought made her shudder. "What was it like, being trapped like that?"

He looked thoughtful a moment. "I am not sure I can describe it. In the beginning, I had no sense of myself. There was no depth or color to my world, no sound. I could only stand there, unable to move or see or feel." He took a deep breath. He hadn't known fear often in his life, but he had felt it then in every fiber of his being. "All that changed, in time. Gradually, my strength returned. Once I could move, the painting came to life. With the return of my strength, I became increasingly aware of my surroundings. I began to hear what was going on outside my prison. I paid attention to everything I saw and heard, though much of it remained a mystery."

"You don't talk like I'd expect someone from the past to talk."

He grunted softly. "The influence of radio and television, I expect." He glanced at her TV. "The people imprisoned there, do you know the name of the wizard who enchanted them?"

"What?"

He gestured at the TV. "The name of the wizard who imprisoned them, do you know it?"

Kari stared at him for a moment and then she laughed. "There aren't any people trapped inside."

"But I see many of them over and over again, doing the same things, wearing the same clothes, speaking the same words, every time. Ricky and Lucy. Rob and Laura. Hawkeye and Colonel Potter. Niles and Frasier. It must be a powerful enchantment."

Kari couldn't help it, she had to laugh. "Those are reruns. Old television shows," she explained. "They replay every week, some for years. The people in the shows are actors playing a part. Some of the sitcoms, like *I Love Lucy*, are over fifty years old. The people have aged, but the images you see on the screen haven't."

He frowned. "I am not sure I understand. How is that possible?"

"Hang on a sec." Kari went to the hall closet. She returned a few minutes later with her video camera. "Okay, walk around the room, then stop and say something to me."

He looked puzzled but did as she asked.

"All right, that's enough," Kari said. "Come here." She held the camera so he could see the screen, and then hit PLAY. "Television is like this. Moving pictures. I can play this over and over again, and it won't change. Programs like the news are current events. The things that you watch on the news happened the day you see them, or are happening while you watch. Movies and TV are just entertainment, like stage plays back in your time, only our plays are recorded so that they can be viewed as often as you wish."

Rourke watched the short video a second time, amazed to see his image on the screen. And then he frowned.

"Truly a kind of magic," he murmured, "to be able to forever capture a moment in time."

Kari grinned at him. If you didn't understand how video worked, then it really was like magic, she thought. And as one who didn't have a clue, she viewed movies and her computer and practically every kind of modern technology as a kind of modern hocus-pocus. She had often looked at her music CDs and wondered how such a thing could record music that could be played in her portable CD player, on her computer, or in her car.

She looked at the camera in her hand, then frowned thoughtfully. Strange, that he didn't cast a reflection in a mirror, yet she could capture his image on video. It must have something to do with digital technology, she mused.

"I'll be right back." After setting the camera on her nightstand, she went in search of her cell phone.

"What are you doing?" Rourke asked when she flipped open the phone.

"Testing a theory. Smile." She took his picture, then looked at the screen, and he was there. "Amazing."

Taking a step forward, Rourke looked over her shoulder. He had not seen his own countenance in over seven hundred years, had, in fact, almost forgotten what he looked like. His brothers had all resembled their mother, but Rourke looked remarkably like his father. He had the same dark blond hair, the same striking blue eyes, the same hawklike nose and stubborn jaw.

Kari closed the phone, then sat down on the foot of the bed. "Your painting must have changed hands a lot in three hundred years."

"Yes." His prison had been owned by many people in the course of his captivity. It had hung in castles, in mansions, and once in a convent in the room where visitors waited to be announced. Though the painting had been kept in the convent only a short time, it had been a most interesting experience. Nuns both old and young had found reasons to pass through the room where his painting had been displayed. One young nun in particular had seemed particularly smitten with his image. For a time, he had hoped that she would call him forth, but the mother superior had discovered her postulant's fascination and sold the painting.

His last owner, a rather eccentric elderly woman, had tired of the Vilnius after fourteen years and consigned him to the attic. He had spent the last fifteen years there, gathering dust, until the old woman died and the painting had been sold to the gallery where Karinna had found him.

"And now you're free," she remarked.

"Yes." He looked past her, staring out her bedroom window. Mortal eyes would have seen little but the darkness beyond, but with his preternatural vision, he could see for several miles. "I have seen much and learned much of your world, but I want to see more, and I want you to be my guide."

"Why me?"

"Why not you?"

"Because I . . . because . . ."

Closing the distance between them, he stroked her cheek with his fingertips. "You have no need to be afraid of me, Karinna Adams. I will not hurt you."

She looked into his eyes, those deep blue eyes, and for some inexplicable reason, she believed him. She only hoped she wasn't making the biggest mistake of her life.

Kari's nerves were on edge by the time she got home from work the following night. She couldn't keep her hand from shaking as she unlocked the front door. Taking a deep breath, she stepped inside. Was he here?

In the living room, she dropped her handbag and keys on the sofa table. She hesitated a moment, then went upstairs to her bedroom. She kicked off her shoes and changed into a pair of comfy jeans and a warm sweater. After stepping into a pair of fur-lined boots, she turned toward the door, only to come to an abrupt halt when she saw him standing in the doorway. He was so tall, his shoulders so broad, he almost filled the opening. He was a beautiful man, though there was nothing feminine about him.

He smiled at her as if his being there was the most normal thing in the world. "Good evening."

"Hi." She forced the word past the lump of fear in her throat. She had forgotten how big he was, how breathtakingly handsome. How scary.

"Are you ready?" he asked.

She lifted a protective hand to her throat. "Ready for what?"

He arched a brow in wry amusement. "I've not come to dine on you, if that is what you are thinking. You were going to show me around, remember?"

"Oh, right." She was about to tell him that she hadn't had dinner when she realized her appetite was gone. She hoped his was, too. "I need my handbag and my keys," she said, edging toward the bedroom door.

He took a step backward and she swept past him, acutely aware of him as she headed for the stairs. In the living room, she grabbed her purse and her keys and headed for the front door.

He followed her outside.

With her nerves humming with awareness of the very male male standing behind her, Kari unlocked the passenger-side door. She expected him to get into the car. Instead, he walked around it, pausing to run his hands over the trunk, the roof, the hood, the tires, the windshield.

He looked at her over the roof of the car. "How does it work?"

Kari shrugged. "I don't know. I'm a graphic designer, not a mechanic."

"It has a motor, yes?"

Nodding, she unlocked the driver's-side door, leaned inside, and popped the hood, then stood back while he peered at the engine. Kari stood beside him, thinking that she didn't know any more about how the motor worked than he did.

"Seen enough?" she asked after a few minutes.

He ran his fingers over the engine block. "It looks complicated."

"You think?" She closed the hood, then slid behind the wheel.

After a moment, he got in beside her, his gaze

intent as he watched her put the key in the ignition and start the engine.

His hands clenched when the motor purred to life.

"Don't be afraid," Kari said as she backed out of the driveway, then wondered if vampires were capable of fear. "In case you're worried, I've never had an accident."

"Good news, indeed," he muttered.

"So, where do you want to go?"

"The mall."

Kari glanced at him. "The mall?" She wasn't sure what she had expected. A trip to the blood bank, maybe, but the mall?

"It is the place to shop, is it not?"

"Well, yeah, but how do you know that?"

"Television," he reminded her.

She grunted softly. And people said TV wasn't educational. "So, what do you want to buy?"

"Ah, yes, buy," he murmured.

"I guess you don't have any money," she remarked.

"No."

She had a feeling he expected her to pay for whatever he wanted. "So, what are we looking for?"

"New attire," he said, glancing at his shirt and trousers. "Something a little more up-to-date."

Kari nodded, though she couldn't help thinking that his loose-fitting white shirt and tight breeches suited him perfectly. She wondered what he had done with his cloak.

"Graphic design," he remarked a few minutes later. "What does that mean?"

"It's a way of communicating thoughts and ideas with graphic media. Pictures. Images."

He frowned.

"I work for a printing company. We design catalogs and brochures and corporate stationery, as well as posters and advertisements, that kind of thing. I also design Web sites on the side. There's good money in that."

He nodded, though she wasn't at all sure he understood what she was talking about.

Leaning over, she opened the glove compartment, pulled out a full-color brochure advertising a new iPod, and offered it to him. "Here's a sample of what I do."

Rourke ran his hand over the paper, then read it, front and back.

Kari glanced at him, wondering what he thought of her work.

"Impressive," he said.

"Do you know what an iPod is?"

He tapped on the brochure. "According to this, it is the best way to play music."

Kari grinned. Every job had its perks. Her cousin worked for the electric company and got a discount on his bill. The company that made the iPod 5000 had sent her one so she could try it out. Word of mouth was still the best kind of advertising.

Ten minutes later, she pulled into the parking lot of the downtown mall. It was the city's newest addition. Three stories high, it housed just about every retail store and food chain in existence.

Rourke followed her inside, his preternatural

senses assaulted by a plethora of sights and sounds and smells. There were people everywhere. Men, women, and children, old and young and in-between, in a variety of ethnic backgrounds. He smiled inwardly. A veritable feast, his for the taking, he mused. Various shops lined both sides of the vast building, selling everything from jewelry to footwear, food to fashions, cutlery and housewares and anything else a mortal could possibly want or need. Truly a remarkable place, he thought, his mind reeling as he took it all in, amazed by the wide selection and abundance of goods and services.

He followed Karinna into something called Sam's Big and Tall, which proved to be an establishment that sold men's clothing. Numerous racks held suits, coats, jackets, trousers, and belts in a dizzying array of sizes and styles. Counters and shelves were filled with dress shirts, sweaters, T-shirts, and vests in a wide array of fabrics and colors.

A tall man with a thin red mustache approached them. "May I help you?"

"We're just looking, thanks," Kari said.

"Certainly. If you need help, my name is Dirk."

Kari smiled at the man. "Thank you." She waited until they were alone, then looked at Rourke. "So, what kind of clothes do you want?"

"I have no idea. What do you like?"

She studied him a moment. "You don't seem like a jeans kind of guy," she remarked. But she liked men in jeans, so she steered him toward a rack of Levi's. She picked out several pair, then moved through the store selecting shirts, T-shirts, briefs in blue and black and white, a dozen pairs of socks in assorted colors, a pair of navy sweatpants and a matching sweatshirt, a brown leather jacket, a pair of dark brown dress pants, and a brown sports coat.

She found an empty dressing room and thrust the pile of clothing she had collected into his hands. "Go in there and try those on."

"You will be here when I come out?"

"Where would I go?" she asked with a shrug. "You know where I live."

He regarded her a moment, then went inside and closed the door.

Kari waited outside the dressing room. Standing there, she couldn't help wondering what he wore beneath his tight buff-colored breeches. She had no sooner dragged her mind away from that line of thought when she found herself imagining him standing in front of the mirror wearing nothing but a smile.

Alarmed at the turn of her thoughts, she walked briskly to the front of the store and spent the next twenty minutes looking at neckties and wallets and key rings, none of which Rourke needed at the moment.

She knew he was standing behind her even before she turned around.

"What do you think?" he asked. "Does this attire suit me?"

She could only stare. He wore a pair of snug blue jeans that outlined his long, muscular legs, and a dark blue T-shirt that emphasized his broad chest and shoulders and revealed long, muscular arms covered with fine golden hair. He was gorgeous, though that word seemed woefully inadequate to describe him. A dim corner of her mind noticed that he had kept his supple brown boots.

He canted his head to the side when she didn't say anything. "You do not approve?"

She swallowed hard. "No. I mean, yes. I mean . . ."

A slow smile spread over his face, as if he was completely aware of the effect he was having on her senses.

"Did you find anything else you liked?" she asked.

"A few things. Have you the means to purchase them?"

She would have bought the jeans and T-shirt even if it meant taking out a second mortgage on her house. She gathered the other things he had selected—the only thing he had rejected was the sports coat—and carried them to Dirk, who quickly rang up her purchases, accepted her credit card, and thanked her for shopping at Sam's. From the enthusiastic smile on the salesman's face, she figured he worked on commission.

Carrying a bulging shopping bag in each hand, Kari left the store. Rourke, attired in his new jeans and T-shirt, walked beside her, shortening his stride to match hers. She had expected him to offer to carry one of the bags, if not both, and then remembered that things had been different in his time. Women had been expected to fetch and carry, leaving the men with their hands free to draw their weapons if need be.

Strolling through the mall, Kari noticed that

almost every woman they passed slowed to gawk at Rourke. She couldn't blame them. Not only was he sinfully handsome, but he oozed testosterone from every pore!

Judging from the smug look on his face, he was not only aware of the admiring looks being sent his way, he was used to it.

Just like a man, Kari thought irritably. They all had egos the size of the Grand Canyon, whether they were genuine hunks like Rourke, or clowns built like Homer Simpson.

They were headed for the escalator when Kari saw Tricia walking toward them. Tricia noticed Kari at the same time.

"Hey, girlfriend," Tricia called, hurrying toward her. As always, Tricia was dressed to the nines, her make-up immaculate, every hair in place. There were times when she made Kari feel like an unmade bed.

"Hi." Kari glanced at the Babies "R" Us sack in Tricia's hand. "Been shopping for the baby, I see."

"Yeah, just a few odds and ends I couldn't resist," Tricia replied, her gaze zeroing in on Rourke. "Who's your friend?"

"Oh, Tricia, this is Jason Rourke. Jason, this is my best friend, Patricia McPhee."

Rourke inclined his head. "I am pleased to meet you, Miss McPhee."

"Likewise," she said, "and please, call me Tricia." She looked at Kari, her brows lifting in an expression that clearly said, *Wow, what a hunk!* "So," Tricia said, glancing from Kari to Rourke, "have you known each other very long?"

Rourke smiled. "Not long."

"Well, I'd really love to stay and chat," Tricia said, "but I'm supposed to meet Brent downstairs. We're going to the movies. Do you two want to come along? I think we're going to see the latest Sandra Bullock flick. It's supposed to be pretty good."

"Thanks," Kari said, "but I don't think so."

"Maybe another time. Call me later, girlfriend," Tricia said, her tone clearly indicating she wanted to know everything there was to know about Rourke.

Kari grinned in reply.

Tricia smiled at Rourke. "It was very nice meeting you."

"It was my pleasure, Miss McPhee."

Tricia stared at him as if she had never seen a man before.

Well, Kari could understand that. Jason Rourke was incredibly good-looking and he radiated sensuality, but enough was enough! "Tricia? Hey, Trish."

"What?" Tricia shook her head as if she was coming out of a trance. "Oh, yes, well, good-bye."

Kari stared after her friend, amused by Tricia's behavior. "Honestly, you'd think she'd never seen a handsome man before," she muttered.

"You think me handsome?" Rourke asked with a roguish grin.

Kari felt her cheeks grow hot as she realized what she'd said. "You know you are. Everywhere we go, women turn to stare at you like they're starving and you're the last chocolate chip cookie on the planet."

He shrugged as if to say it wasn't his fault, and she supposed that was true. He couldn't help it if he'd been blessed with abundant good looks and enough charisma for a dozen men.

"She really doesn't remember meeting you before, does she?" Kari asked a short time later.

"No."

"Amazing. A little creepy, but amazing." She blew out a breath. "So, is there anything else you need?" she asked, leading the way to the escalator that went up to the food court on the third floor. She didn't know about Rourke, but she needed something to eat.

"I think not." He glanced around when they reached the third floor, his nostrils wrinkling with distaste at the stink of so many bodies occupying the same enclosed space, the myriad odors and scents that emanated from the food booths. "What are we doing here?"

"I'm hungry."

"Hungry, yes," he murmured. His gaze rested avidly on the pulse beating in the hollow of her throat.

"Don't even think about it!" Kari warned. She thrust the shopping bags at Rourke and went to stand in line. When it was her turn, she ordered a cheeseburger with grilled onions, country fries, and a cherry Coke.

When her order came up, she carried the tray to a small table and sat down. Rourke sat across from her, a curious light in his eyes as he watched her eat.

"Want a bite?" she asked, offering him a taste of her burger.

Grimacing, he shook his head. "No, thank you."

"Can you eat regular food?"

"No."

Kari frowned thoughtfully. "Have you ever tried?"

"Only once."

"What happened?"

"Are you sure you want to know?"

"From your expression, I'm guessing it made you sick."

He nodded, though sick was a mild term for his body's violent reaction to mortal food.

"Why did it make you sick?" she asked curiously.

"Because I cannot digest it."

"Oh." She took another bite of her cheeseburger. "What about beverages, like coffee or tea?"

"No, although I enjoy a little wine now and then."

"Red, I'll bet," she muttered dryly.

He grinned at her. "The redder the better."

She popped a french fry into her mouth, then wiped her mouth with a napkin. "Have you killed a lot of people?"

He lifted one brow, obviously surprised by her question. "Not lately."

"But you've killed to survive?"

"As have you."

"Me? I've never killed anyone!"

"Perhaps not," he replied with a wry grin, "but that slab of meat you are eating came from a living creature."

"That's hardly the same thing!" Kari exclaimed.

"Isn't it?"

It was by far the strangest conversation she'd ever had with a man, or with anyone else, for that matter. "How old were you when you were turned?"

"One and thirty."

"How long have you been a vampire?"

"Seven hundred and thirty-six years."

She blinked at him, the burger in her hand forgotten. Seven hundred and thirty-six years. Good heavens. She did some quick mental arithmetic. He had been born in 1242, making him 767 years old! What would it be like to live such a long time? She nibbled on her lower lip. He had been trapped inside the Vilnius since 1709. You could hardly call that living.

She stared at him, her brow furrowed in thought. Was he alive? Weren't vampires dead? What was it they called vampires in the movies? Undead? She recalled one movie where the vampire had called his kind Nosferatu and said that it meant not dead. Was there really a difference between undead and not dead? If so, she had no idea what it might be. Undead, not dead—both meant not alive.

The grisly thought sent a shiver down her spine.

"Are you cold?" Rourke asked.

She shook her head. "No."

He regarded her a moment. "Afraid of me, are you?"

"No. Yes. I don't know, but I should be, shouldn't I? I mean, you're . . ." She made a vague gesture with one hand.

"Pray go on. What am I?"

"I wish I knew," she muttered unhappily.

"I am just a man."

"Yeah, right, a man who just happens to be a vampire."

"But still a man." His gaze moved over her face, slid slowly and seductively down her neck and over her breasts, and returned to her face once more. "I could prove it to you," he said, his voice low and whiskey smooth.

Imagining how he would do that made it suddenly hard to breathe. All she could think about was his mouth on hers, their bodies entwined, bare skin sliding sensuously against bare skin. The look in his vibrant blue eyes told her he knew exactly what she was thinking.

Tearing her gaze from his, she glanced at what was left of her burger, only to find that, thanks to him, she had lost her appetite for char-broiled beef.

"Let's go." She pushed the tray away and gained her feet. "Do you need anything else?"

His gaze brushed her throat. "No."

Without waiting to see if he followed, she dumped her trash, then headed for the escalator. He was right behind her. She could feel his nearness like a physical caress.

Rourke followed Karinna out of the mall, relieved to be outside, away from the bombardment of so many strident voices, the rapid tattoo of a hundred beating hearts all calling his name.

Kari opened the trunk and he dropped his packages inside. When she moved toward the car door, his hand closed over her forearm.

"Not yet," he said.

"What do you mean?" she glanced around, suddenly aware that they were quite alone. What if he . . . She clamped down on her all too active imagination. If he'd wanted to hurt her, he'd had plenty of opportunity before now.

"I have been imprisoned for three hundred years. I should like to go for a walk and enjoy my freedom."

With a shrug, she said, "So, go."

"I would like some company," he said, gifting her with a wistful smile. "I have been alone for a very long time."

How could she argue with that? She tossed her handbag into the trunk, closed it, and slipped her keys into her pocket. "So, where do you want to go?"

"No place in particular. I just feel like walking."

She fell into step beside him. "I didn't know vampires liked to walk. I thought they always just turned into bats and flew off to wherever they wanted to go."

He looked at her, one brow raised in amusement. "Is that what you thought?"

"Happens in the movies all the time," she said with a shrug.

"Ah, yes, on the television." He had seen movies from time to time. He grimaced at the memory. He had not yet been able to move through the painting the first time he had seen a motion picture about the Undead. Trapped behind a wall of glass, his only entertainment had been watching the moving pictures, some of them in black and white, some in all the colors of the rainbow. One of his former owners had spent hours in front of the screen. Rourke had watched, too, though he had not always understood what he was seeing, or hearing. Shows like *Batman, The Twilight Zone, Star Trek, The Rifleman, Gunsmoke, Voyage to the Bottom of the Sea, My Favorite Martian,* and

Laugh-In. His favorites had been *Dark Shadows* and *The Addams Family. Dark Shadows* hadn't been intended to be a comedy, but he had found the life and times of Barnabas Collins rather amusing. Rourke couldn't recall now if Collins had ever turned into a bat. It was something Rourke, himself, had never tried. He grinned, wondering what it would be like. In his time, he had transformed into mist and into a wolf, but never a bat. It seemed undignified, somehow.

"What are you smiling at?" Kari asked.

"I was thinking about turning into a bat."

"Can you really do that? Be a bat?"

"I have no idea. I have never tried."

She stopped walking, her hands fisted on her hips, her head tilted to one side. "I'd like to see it."

"Here, now?" he asked, glancing up and down the street. "Might cause quite a stir, I should think."

"Yes," Kari said, grinning, "I suppose it would. Might even make the news. 'Man turns into bat on Main Street. Film at eleven.'"

Rourke regarded her for a moment, and then he laughed. Times were different now. When he had first been made, everyone believed in vampires. Grisly steps had been taken to make certain that those suspected of being Undead didn't rise again. Heads were lopped off, hearts torn out and burned, bodies buried facedown so that if the dead tried to dig their way out of their graves, they would, instead, dig deeper into the earth. People had hung strings of garlic around their doorways and windows and displayed crosses and crucifixes in prominent places.

With a rueful shake of his head, he continued on down the street.

"I still can't believe you're really a vampire," Kari said, hurrying to catch up with him. "Are there any more of your kind?"

"I am sure there are a few, here and there."

"How can that be? I mean, how is it that nobody knows vampires exist?"

He didn't reply, merely looked at her, waiting for her to reach the obvious conclusion.

"Oh. I guess you'd rather keep it a secret." She laughed nervously. "In case Van Helsing is lurking around the next corner."

He nodded, and then wondered if there were any other vampires in the city, and if vampire hunters still existed.

"I don't believe any of this!" she exclaimed. And yet, as impossible as it seemed, she knew it was true. He was a 767-year-old vampire. "Where do you sleep during the day?"

"Nowhere in particular at the moment. Just some place out of the sun's reach."

"That's the reason I could never find you in the painting during the day, isn't it?" Her heart skipped a beat as she recalled the glowing red eyes she had seen in her dream. "You were sleeping in the cellar of the castle."

He nodded, his expression shuttered.

"I had a dream . . . at least I think it was a dream. It seemed so real. Were you . . . did you see me there, in the cellar?"

He nodded again. He recalled that night vividly.

The pain had been excruciating. He had been about to go outside and feed off the horse when Karinna appeared in the cellar. At first, he had thought she was real, but then he had realized it was only a dream. Had she been flesh and blood, he would have taken her then, taken her and drained her dry.

As if reading his mind, Kari stopped walking. "I think I want to go home. Enjoy the rest of your walk."

"You cannot be rid of me so easily, Karinna Adams."

She scowled at him. "What's that supposed to mean?"

"I like your company, and I do not know anyone else in this country or in this century."

"I'll introduce you to someone," she said with a toss of her head. "Good night."

Grinning, he watched her turn and hurry back toward her car. He wondered if she recalled the other dreams they had shared, wondered if they had been her dreams or his. They had seemed so real, perhaps they hadn't been dreams at all, yet, what else could they have been?

With a shake of his head, he continued down the street. He didn't know how he was going to find his father's sword, or locate the wizard who had stolen it from him, but in the meantime, Miss Karinna Adams was sure to provide a pleasant diversion.

Because Jason Rourke was curious to learn about the century he found himself in, Kari was soon acting as his tour guide.

Her evenings and weekends, once spent in mundane tasks, took on a new life. As soon as the sun went down, Rourke appeared in her living room, eager to explore the world around him.

She spent one evening following him from room to room while he acquainted himself with things that had not yet been invented when he was a young man. He examined the gas stove, the refrigerator, the garbage disposal, the trash compactor, the toaster, and the microwave. She thought it odd that he had such a keen interest in such things, since he didn't eat solid food, and therefore had no need of any of the kitchen appliances, but his curiosity was boundless. He poked around in her medicine cabinet, tried her blow-dryer, smelled her perfume and her toothpaste and her hand cream. He studied her while she sat at her computer, watched with some fascination as she printed a photograph from the Internet. He fiddled with the remote for the television until he figured out how it worked. He listened to the radio and to some of her CDs, then asked about her phone, her cell phone, and her fax machine.

One evening, he taught her the dances that had been popular when he was alive, and then he insisted she show him how the people of this day and age danced. Being in his arms had been intoxicating. He moved like silk, his feet hardly seeming to touch the floor as he waltzed her around the room. It was a most amazing experience.

They went to the mall again. He wrinkled his nose with distaste when she bought a bag of kettle corn. "Don't knock it until you've tried it," she said, and laughed when he scowled at her.

One Friday night, she took him to the movies. She hadn't expected him to be awed by anything as ordinary as a movie. After all, he had seen movies on television, but he stared at the movie screen, obviously captivated by the size of the screen and the characters on it.

"Truly an amazing age you live in," he remarked as they left the theater.

"I guess so."

Rourke took a deep breath. His senses had been assaulted by the numerous scents inside the theater. Popcorn and butter and salt, chocolate and soda, chips and cheese, hot dogs and mustard and relish. And overall, the scent of blood pumping through hundreds of beating hearts, playing like a sweet symphony in his mind. He shook his head, relieved to be outside, though even out here, in the open, the nearby scent of blood teased and tempted him.

When Karinna pulled her keys from inside her handbag, he plucked them from her hand.

"What are you doing?" she asked. "Don't tell me you want to take another walk?"

"No. I wish to learn to drive."

"Now?"

"Yes, now."

"But . . ." She shook her head. It was after midnight, but she supposed that was the shank of the evening to a vampire. "I've never taught anyone to drive."

"I have watched you."

"I know, but . . ."

There was no point in arguing with him. He was already opening the door, sliding behind the wheel, putting the key in the ignition.

"Wait!" She quickly got into the car and fastened her seat belt. "Be sure to look behind you before you back out," she warned. "Go easy on the gas."

Hands clenched, she watched him back out of the parking space, put the car in drive, and pull out of the parking lot onto the street. Fortunately, at this time of night, there wasn't much traffic.

To her surprise, he drove as if he had been doing it all his life.

"It is a strange sensation," he remarked. "But exhilarating."

Instead of heading for her house, he pulled onto the freeway. In the morning, it would have been backed up for miles. She was glad it was late and relatively clear.

He drove for several miles and then slowly increased the speed.

Kari's eyes widened as he hit the accelerator: fifty, sixty, seventy, eighty, eighty-five . . .

"Rourke, for goodness' sake, slow down!"

He glanced at her, his eyes alight with pleasure. "Why?"

"The speed limit is sixty-five."

He shrugged as he goosed it up to ninety.

Kari clung to the edge of her seat. Never, in all her life, had she ridden in a car going this fast.

She wasn't surprised to hear a siren coming up behind them.

She was surprised, though, when the police car drove on by.

"I can't imagine why they didn't pull you over," she said, frowning.

Rourke laughed softly. "Perhaps because they did not see us."

"What?"

"A bit of vampire trickery," he explained.

"I don't understand."

He eased up on the gas. "I veiled our presence from his sight."

"Sort of like using the cloaking device on the Enterprise."

"Ah, yes, *Star Trek*," Rourke said with a grin. "An entertaining tale."

He slanted a glance in her direction. "Very educational, television."

"Very," Kari agreed with a laugh. "Oh," she said, spying a late-night hamburger stand, "pull over there. I'm hungry."

At the drive-through window, she ordered a chili cheeseburger and a chocolate shake. Rourke wrinkled his nose as he handed her the sack containing her order. He didn't think he would ever get used to the smell of cooked meat. Hard to believe he had once eaten beef and mutton and enjoyed it. After so many years, he could no longer remember the taste or the texture, nor did he have any desire to experience it again.

Back on the freeway, he drove at a more leisurely pace. He rather enjoyed driving. He liked the quiet purr of the engine, the feeling of being in control, the speed of the machine.

From time to time he glanced at Karinna while she ate, wondering what a cheeseburger tasted like. He was sorely tempted to lick the drop of chocolate malt from the corner of her mouth, and even more tempted to take the woman in his arms and taste every inch of her from head to heel. The thought stirred his desire as he imagined burying his hands in the silk of her hair, raining kisses along the sweet curve of her cheek, exploring every delectable curve of her lush young body and then doing it all again.

Muttering an oath, he quickly drove her home. Exiting the car, he handed her the keys.

"Thank you for letting me drive."

"You're welcome." She gazed up at him, her brows drawn together. "Is something wrong?"

"No. Good night."

"Rourke . . ."

"I need to feed," he said curtly. "Your warmth and your nearness tempt me almost beyond measure. Do you understand?"

"Not really."

"Pray you never do," he said, then vanished from her sight.

Chapter 9

Rourke lingered in the shadows, keeping watch over Karinna until she was safely inside the house, and then he continued on his way.

Leaving the city behind, he ventured into the shadowy world beyond the lights. He ran effortlessly for miles, caught up in the sheer joy of being free after three hundred years of captivity. He reveled in the sting of the wind against his face, the feel of the earth beneath his feet, the rich fragrance of flowers and foliage, the heady smell of life itself.

Slowing to a walk, he ran his hands over his face, flexed his arms and shoulders. He paused to glance up at the sky, appreciating the heavenly display as never before. A full moon shone brightly; stars without number stretched away into infinity.

In spite of his preternatural powers, he felt small and insignificant as he stood there. He had often pondered what his fate would be when his existence ended. As a child, his mother had taught him that there was a power mightier than all the kings of the earth and that every man, woman, and child who ever drew breath would one day be judged by that Infinite Being. Those who believed and kept the Law would be taken to Paradise; those who rebelled against the Word would be sent to everlasting torment. There had been no mention in his religious upbringing of vampires, but from what his mother had taught him, he was pretty sure that his current lifestyle, even though he hadn't sought it, would not be viewed with approbation or forgiveness. He could think of no worse punishment for a vampire than burning in a fiery hell through all eternity.

Shaking off such dismal thoughts, he continued walking, approaching the city from the other side. The buildings in this part of town were mostly run-down, many of them boarded up and uninhabited. It was here that the dregs of the city congregated, plying whatever nefarious trade they could.

It was here that he came to feed.

He prowled among the beggars and the winos and the shysters until he found a man who was a little less drunk and dirty than the others. He took what he needed quickly, grimacing as the stink of the man's unwashed body filled his nostrils. There was no need to erase his memory from the man's mind. Even if the wastrel remembered what had happened, no one was likely to believe the ravings of a sot.

With his hunger appeased, Rourke turned his thoughts to finding a place to spend the upcoming daylight hours. He needed a lair; a secure, private place to call his own. In days long past, he had taken his rest in aboveground tombs or in caves, but neither of those options was available here. A house with a cellar would suffice. Perhaps Karinna could help him find one.

If only she could help him find Vilnius. He had no way of knowing if the wizard still lived, or where he might be, no idea how to find the treacherous sorcerer in this new world.

He glanced at the sky. It was still several hours until dawn.

"Where are you, Vilnius?" he wondered aloud, and then he frowned. If he was a witch, where would he go to find other witches? A coven, of course, but how to find one in this day and age? That was the question.

Tomorrow he would search for the answer.

Kari sat at her desk at work, her gaze fixed on her computer screen, but it wasn't the image on the screen she saw. Instead, her mind kept conjuring images of Jason Rourke. In spite of everything, it was still hard to believe he was real, and harder still to believe he was a vampire. Who would have thought that such creatures actually existed! And how had they managed to keep it a secret for so long? Of course, if she went into Charlie's cubicle and told him she had met a vampire, he would never believe her, and neither would anyone else she knew. Like Tricia. If only Rourke hadn't erased Tricia's memory, she might have been able to convince Trish that Rourke had been the man in the painting. Not only that, but she would have had someone to confide in, someone who wouldn't think she was crazy.

The thought had no sooner crossed her mind when the phone rang. In one of those spooky moments, she knew it was her best friend on the phone even before she picked it up. "Hello?"

"Hey, Kari, it's me."

"Oh, hi, Trish."

"You were supposed to call me, remember?"

"I know, but I've been really busy."

"I can imagine. Come on now, 'fess up. Who is he? Where did you meet him? Is it serious?"

Kari laughed softly, then quickly sobered. It was beyond belief that Tricia could have seen Rourke in the painting, met him in Kari's bedroom, and didn't remember a thing about it. Vampire magic, indeed!

"Kari, talk to me! My gosh, the man is gorgeous."

"Calm down, girlfriend, you're married, remember?"

"I know, I know, but I'm not dead or blind. So, come on, where did you meet him and how long have you known him?"

"I met him at that little art gallery over on Third and Pine a few weeks ago," Kari said, thinking that it was true, in a manner of speaking.

"And . . . ?"

"And what? The man is like a fair-haired angel, a gentleman unlike any man I've ever known, and really sexy."

"No kidding. So, have you . . . ?"

"Tricia! I just met the man."

"But?"

"I can hardly keep my hands off him," Kari admitted. If only he wasn't a vampire! If only she could tell Tricia the truth.

"I can understand that," Tricia said, laughing.

"Well, it doesn't matter. It's too soon after Ben, and . . . well, it's just too soon."

"He's not from around here, is he?" Tricia asked.

"What do you mean?"

"I mean, he seems like a foreigner, the way he talks, very proper, you know?"

"He's from . . . Romania."

"Really? I never knew anyone from there."

"Me neither."

"Well, all I can say is, wow, you'd better hang on to this one."

"We'll see," Kari said evasively. "Listen, Tricia, I've got to get back to work."

"All right. Talk to you soon."

"Bye."

"Bye."

Kari hung up the receiver, then stared at the phone. Darn Rourke for erasing Tricia's memories. She really needed someone she could talk to about this whole vampire thing, someone who wouldn't think she was losing her mind.

With a shake of her head, Kari changed the font of the text on the screen, then feathered the adjoining image. She smiled, pleased with the result, but, all too soon, she found herself thinking about Jason Rourke again. Would she see him tonight? Where was he now? Had he found a coffin to sleep in? She shuddered at the thought, and then she frowned.

How would he find a coffin in a strange city? He didn't have any money to buy such a thing. Would he steal one or just, heaven forbid, scrounge around in a graveyard for a used one?

After saving her work, she signed on to the Internet, clicked on Google, and looked up vampires. There were thousands of links! Real vampires, vampire history, monstrous vampires, vampires in myth and history, theatres des vampires. The list went on and on. According to one site, a vampire was a creature who rose at night to prey on others, drinking their blood to gain immortality. Reading on, she learned that drinking blood wasn't peculiar just to vampires. Apparently the Aztecs and some Native Americans ate the hearts and drank the blood of their captives in special rituals in order to obtain fertility and immortality. Some of the sites included images of vampires. She perused them with interest. Some depicted the Undead as hideous creatures with bloody fangs and red eyes; others depicted them as bloodthirsty but sensual creatures.

According to *Webster's*, a vampire was "the reanimated body of a dead person believed to come from the grave at night and suck the blood of persons asleep."

Another site put forth the theory that a person became a vampire because the earth refused to accept the body and heaven refused to accept the soul. No reasons were given for this.

None of the descriptions of vampires painted a very pretty picture. Certainly none of them described the hunky build, long blond hair, and mesmerizing blue eyes of Jason Rourke.

Kari lifted a hand to her neck. He had bitten her and taken her blood. Funny, she couldn't remember it more clearly, but maybe that was a good thing. What would it be like to have to drink the blood of others to live? She had tasted her own blood, of course, but then, sooner or later everyone did that. It was a common thing to lick your finger if you got a paper cut or a scratch. But to drink enough to live on? And someone else's? Yuck and double yuck!

She glanced at the time on her computer. It was almost five-thirty. She had been off the clock for the last twenty-five minutes.

She shut down her computer, turned off the monitor, gathered her handbag, and headed out the door.

Kari's heart was pounding erratically when she pulled into the driveway and cut the engine. The sun was down.

Where was her vampire?

Her vampire? What was she thinking?

Feeling uneasy yet filled with a strange sense of anticipation, she unlocked the front door and quickly closed it behind her. She glanced automatically at the empty space over the fireplace, thinking how bare the wall looked without the Vilnius, then glanced at the shopping bags she had carried inside last night.

She stood in the middle of the living room, listening, waiting, then sighed with disappointment.

He wasn't there. She told herself she should be relieved. But he was bound to return. After all, he had to pick up all the clothes she had bought him last night. She grinned inwardly. If they went shopping again, she'd probably have to find a second job just to pay for it all.

Going into her bedroom, she kicked off her shoes and changed into a pair of faded jeans and a baggy sweater, then went into the kitchen, where she fixed a toasted cheese sandwich and tomato soup for dinner. She ate in front of the TV, but her mind wasn't on what she was eating, or on the six o'clock news. Even though Rourke frightened her, she had expected to find him waiting for her when she got home. She was surprised at how disappointed she was that he wasn't there. Maybe disappointed wasn't quite the right word. After all, she had been obsessed with the man—or whatever he was—for over a week. Thinking about that now made her realize just how empty her life had become since she broke up with Ben. She had taken refuge at home, shunning the company of others while she nursed her broken heart. It occurred to her now that it hadn't been broken at all, merely bruised.

After carrying her dirty dishes into the kitchen and putting them in the dishwasher, she went upstairs, changed her clothes again, grabbed her handbag, and left the house. She had been spending entirely too much time sitting at home alone. She wasn't in mourning, for goodness' sake. It was time to get out of the house and return to the land of the living. She grinned. Land of the living, indeed, she thought, and wondered again where Rourke was.

She had always loved dancing, so she drove downtown to her favorite club. She had never gone there alone before, but hey, there was a first time for everything and she needed a diversion. Besides, women today were strong and independent. She didn't need a man to support her, or to give her confidence. Heck, according to a recent poll, the majority of today's women didn't even get married. She wondered what it said about her, that she hoped to become one of the minority.

As soon as Kari stepped into the club, she started having second thoughts. What was she doing here? She wasn't looking for casual sex, a one-night stand, or a meaningless relationship. She wanted what her parents had, what her sisters had, solid marriages based on mutual love and respect.

She was about to turn and head for the door when a man stepped up and asked her to dance. He was of medium height, with slicked-back sandy-colored hair and pale green eyes, not gorgeous, but not bad looking.

She accepted with a smile, wishing she was as chatty as her friend Amy, at work, who was never at a loss for words, or dates.

"Hi, I'm Jack," her partner said.

"Karinna."

"Pretty name for a pretty lady."

"Thank you."

He smiled at her. "You don't come here often, do you?"

"No, why?"

"You're uptight. Relax, honey. We're just dancing."

She laughed self-consciously, eager to be rid of him, though she didn't know why. While they danced, he told her that he was an accountant, divorced, with a six-year-old daughter. Though he seemed nice enough, there was something about the way he looked at her that set her teeth on edge and made her glad when the song ended.

She thanked him for the dance, then turned and headed for the bar. She had never been a drinker, but she thought this might be a good time to start.

Jack followed her, crowding her, making her uncomfortable. "What are you drinking?" he asked.

"Diet Coke." She had been about to order a Manhattan, but it suddenly seemed like a good idea to keep her wits about her.

"Come on, we can do better than that," Jack said, signaling the bartender. "Herk, give the lady a Sea Breeze."

"Herk, the lady doesn't want a Sea Breeze," Kari said.

Jack put his hand on her forearm and gave it a squeeze. "Come on, honey, loosen up a little."

"Get your hands off the lady."

A thrill shot through Kari at the sound of Rourke's voice. Glancing over her shoulder, she gave him a grateful smile. *My hero*, she thought.

Jack glared at Rourke. "Who the hell are you?"

"The man who is going to rip your heart out if you touch the lady again."

Kari didn't know if it was the tone of Rourke's

voice or the feral look in his eyes, but Jack got the message. He let go of her arm as if he'd been stung and practically ran out of the club.

Kari smiled at Rourke. "Thank you."

Rourke glanced around the room. It was smoky and dimly lit, filled with the scent of perspiration, alcohol, and lust. "What are you doing here?" He might be a stranger to this time and place but he wasn't a stranger to what was going on around him. Men had been pursuing women since time began.

"Nothing," Kari said. "I just wanted to get out of the house for a little while. I thought . . ." What had she been thinking? Looking at Rourke, she couldn't remember. With a shake of her head, she said, "Never mind," and then frowned. "How did you know I was here?"

His gaze settled on her face. The look in his eyes was hot enough to melt iron.

She had seen desire in a man's eyes before, but never anything like this. Everything that was female within her responded to the sheer masculine hunger in his eyes. He wanted her, there was no doubt of that.

Her throat went dry and her pulse raced as sexual awareness thrummed through every inch of her. Excitement fluttered in the pit of her stomach as every rational thought went right out of her head and all she could do was stare at the incredible creature before her.

He held out his hand. "Are you ready to go home?"

Home. Hearing the word on his lips sent a shiver

of a different kind down her spine, had her imagining a small house with a red brick chimney and roses growing in the front yard, and her with a golden-haired baby in her arms.

She took his hand. His skin was cool against hers, and yet, at his touch, warmth speared through her.

Outside, he walked her to her car, waited while she unlocked the doors. She was keenly aware of his presence behind her. Her hand trembled when she tried to put the key in the ignition, so much so that she had to try three times before the key slid into place. The interior of her car seemed smaller with him beside her, the air thicker. Tension stretched between them as she pulled away from the curb and headed for home.

Kari kept her gaze on the road ahead; her nerves were humming with anticipation when she pulled up in front of her house. It wasn't much to look at. It was old and not very big, but she loved it.

Mouth dry, palms damp, she unlocked the front door, stepped inside, and turned on the lights. She tossed her handbag and coat on the bench inside the door, then stood there, at a loss as to what to do next. Her thoughts went round and round, like a hamster running on a wheel.

She stilled as he came up behind her. He was close. So close, it was suddenly hard to breathe. If she leaned back, she could touch him.

"Karinna?"

"Y . . . yes?"

"Do you want me to stay?" His breath fanned her cheek.

"I . . . I don't know."

Placing his hands lightly on her shoulders, he turned her to face him. "Tell me what you want me to do."

Oh, my. She stared up at him. *Kiss me*, she thought, *just kiss me.*

She didn't think she had spoken the words out loud but he lowered his head and claimed her lips with his.

All rational thought fled her mind as her body quickly responded to his kiss. Her arms went up around his neck; her body moved toward his of its own accord as her eyelids fluttered down. Someone moaned softly. Had that sound, so filled with yearning, come from her? Lights and color flared behind her eyelids as he deepened the kiss. His tongue swept over her lower lip, its touch like a velvet flame, unleashing a wave of desire more intense than anything Kari had ever known. She didn't know what he was doing to her, but she hoped he would never stop.

His arms locked around her waist, crushing her body close as his hand moved restlessly up and down her back.

She wanted him, wanted him as she had never wanted another man, wanted him as she had never wanted anything else in her whole life.

She went up on her tiptoes, her hand delving into the hair at his nape as her tongue sought his. With a little cry of surprise, she drew back. When she touched a finger to her tongue, it came away bloody.

She looked up at him, her desire abruptly cooled.

Vampire! The word thundered in the back of her mind. What was she doing, standing in her living room making out with a 767-year-old vampire?

He gazed down at her, a hint of amusement evident in his eyes. "Forgive me," he murmured. "I did not mean to hurt you."

She stared at him, shocked to realize that not only had she been tempted to take a vampire to her bed, but that she had cut her tongue on one of his fangs.

"Karinna?"

"You didn't hurt me."

"What is it that troubles you?"

"Do you want the answers in alphabetical order?"

"You are upset." He looked genuinely confused "Why?"

"Why?" she exclaimed, fisting her hands on her hips. "Why do you think? You're a vampire!"

"Yes, I know," he replied dryly.

"Well?"

He shook his head. "Why is that a problem for you?"

"Because I . . . because you . . ." She stamped her foot in exasperation. "Because it is!"

His laughter added fuel to the fire of her indignation.

Kari pivoted on her heel and stomped into the kitchen, then stood there, at a loss as to what to do. When her stomach growled, she filled a pot with water for spaghetti and put it on the stove. The soup and sandwich she had eaten earlier hadn't filled her up. Besides, eating would give her something to do.

A subtle shift in the air told her that Rourke had followed her into the room.

"I guess you've had dinner," she muttered. Something warm and red and liquid.

"Yes."

She turned to face him, her curiosity overcoming her irritation. "How often do you have to . . . you know?"

"I take sustenance when I feel the need, the same as you."

"Hmm. And how often do you feel the need?"

"Every day or so, more often if I am injured, or if it has been a long time since I fed."

It occurred to her that he hadn't fed for three hundred years. Obviously, vampires didn't starve to death.

Fascinated by the turn of their conversation, Kari sat at the kitchen table. "What's it like, being a vampire?"

He leaned against the counter, his arms folded over his chest, his brow furrowed as he sought for an answer. And then he shrugged. "I do not know how to explain it."

"In the movies, it seems that vampires spend all their time running about sucking people dry or making other vampires."

Rourke looked at her a moment, and then he laughed. He, too, had seen those movies on the television. "Perhaps there are vampires who live that way."

"So, are you one of them?"

"What do you think?"

"I don't know," she replied flippantly. "That's why I'm asking."

"Before Vilnius, I lived a rather quiet life. I admit, when I was first made, I did my share of, how did you put it? Sucking people dry? But that soon passed." Once he had learned to control his hunger, he satisfied his craving by taking a little from two or three instead of draining one mortal dry. Since not all blood tasted the same, it gave him a bit of variety. Another advantage was that it left no bodies to dispose of, no mysterious deaths to arouse the suspicion of the local authorities.

"So, how did you spend your time?"

He shrugged. "In the beginning, I tried to maintain my associations with my old friends, but they soon questioned what they viewed as my suddenly peculiar behavior. They wanted to know where I went during the day and why I refused their invitations to go hunting or engage in other daytime activities. I made excuses, told them I had contracted a rare disease that made it impossible for me to go out during the day and severely restricted what I could eat."

"What about your family?"

"My father was killed in battle. My mother died soon after." He didn't mention Rissa, or how she had rejected him. He supposed he couldn't blame her, but he did.

"Did you have any brothers or sisters?"

"Four brothers. We were very close. When they started to notice that they were aging and I was not, I left home."

"That must have been hard for you."

He grunted softly. "It was a long time ago."

"I'm sorry." Relieved to have something to do, she added spaghetti to the boiling water and set the timer, then poured a jar of spaghetti sauce into another pot and put it on the stove.

Rourke watched curiously, thinking how much easier life was now than it had been over seven hundred years ago. In his time, there were no grocery stores, no malls. If a man wanted meat, he hunted it, or he raised it and butchered it. If a woman wanted a dress, she wove the cloth and made it herself. Books were rare, movies undreamed of.

He wrinkled his nose as the nauseating smell of garlic and oregano and tomatoes filled the air. Excusing himself, he left the room.

He wandered the length of her living room, pausing now and then to examine the odds and ends arranged on tables and shelves. She had a fondness for cats. Feline figures made of wood and stone and some hard material he didn't recognize crowded a wooden shelf. A picture of a fat black and white cat hung on one wall; a large ceramic cat sat on a corner of the hearth.

The clink of dishes and silverware drew his attention back to the kitchen, and the woman. He recalled the kisses they had shared and wondered where they might have led if her tongue hadn't brushed against his fangs and drawn blood. He cursed, quietly berating his inability to completely separate his hunger for blood from his desire. And desire her he did, with every fiber of his being. She was a woman unlike any he had ever known, strong yet vulnerable, feisty yet shy, and all female.

Sitting on the sofa, he picked up the remote and switched on the television, amazed anew at the images that flashed on the screen. Truly a magnificent invention, but his interest in it paled next to his hunger for the woman.

Perhaps, when Karinna finished her repast, he could persuade her to take up where they had left off.

Chapter 10

Kari picked at the food on her plate, her mind on Rourke, always Rourke. He was such an enigma and she had so many questions she wanted to ask him. How many people had an opportunity to find out what life had really been like 767 years ago, not by reading about it in books or researching it online, but by talking to someone who had actually lived it? Even more amazing than his age was the reality of what he was. A vampire. Not a movie villain. Not a creature of myth and legend. But a living, breathing vampire. Well, maybe not living. Still, it was incredible.

After carrying her dishes to the sink, she rinsed them off and put them into the dishwasher. She poured herself a cup of coffee, added cream and sugar, and carried it into the living room.

Her vampire—she rather liked the sound of that— was sitting on the sofa in front of the TV, a quizzical expression on his face as he watched a football game.

He looked up as she entered the room. "This game makes no sense to me."

Kari smiled as she sat down beside him. "Me neither." She sipped her coffee. "You can change the channel, you know."

"No." He leaned forward, elbows resting on his knees, as several players wearing red uniforms fell on top of a player wearing blue. "I like it."

The male animal, she thought. Man or vampire, there was no understanding any of them. "Can I ask you something?"

He didn't take his gaze off the screen. "If you wish."

"Were you ever married, or anything?"

He glanced at her briefly. "Once."

"Were you a vampire at the time?"

She had his attention now.

"I was turned after Rissa and I had been married for several years."

Remembering the story he had told her, Kari blinked at him. "You were married when you slept with the vampire?"

Rourke nodded, his expression unreadable.

"How could you? I mean . . ." She had thought him different, honorable, with his impeccable manners and polite speech.

"I knew it was wrong," he said quietly, "but I could not resist her." At Kari's skeptical look, he said, "Male or female, a vampire on the hunt exudes a kind of sexual glamour that mortals find hard to resist."

"Is that why I find you so . . ." Kari bit back the

last word, her cheeks warming with embarrassment at what she had almost said.

"Perhaps, in the beginning."

She frowned. If that was true, how was she to know if what she felt for him was real, or merely some kind of irresistible vampire allure? "Are you working that magic on me now?"

"No."

She studied him a moment, wondering if he was telling her the truth, and then changed the subject. "Your becoming a vampire must have come as quite a shock to your wife."

He nodded. That was putting it mildly. Once Rissa had discovered what he had become, she had refused to share his bed, refused to let him touch her again. There had been days at a time when she refused to speak to him, or even look at him.

Kari put her coffee cup aside. "Did you have children?"

He hesitated a moment, remembering his joy at the birth of his children, remembering how Rissa had done everything in her power to turn them against him as they grew older. It was a pain that lingered to this day. "Twin sons. They were ten when I was turned."

"Does it bother you to talk about it?"

"When I think of that life now, it is like it happened to someone else."

His sons had been approaching manhood when they began looking at him strangely. He knew they were wondering why their mother aged and their father did not. His brothers, too, began casting suspicious glances his way. Once, Rourke had over-heard his brother's speculating on whether he had sold his soul to the devil in exchange for good health and eternal youth. Soon other people in the village began murmuring behind his back, and when he heard whispers of witchcraft and Satanism, he packed a few belongings and left home in the dark of night, never to return. He had never seen his family again.

"Rourke, I'm sorry. I didn't mean to resurrect unhappy memories."

"As I said, it was a long time ago."

"I know, but . . ."

He covered her mouth with his fingertips. "No more about the past. It is the present that interests me now."

Butterflies fluttered in her stomach as his knuckles gently stroked her cheek.

"I have so much to learn." He leaned toward her, his eyes darkening. "So much to learn about you."

"Me?" Her heart jumped into overdrive. It was suddenly hard to breathe.

"Yes. For instance, do you like it when I do this?" he asked, his voice husky, as he claimed her lips with his.

Once again, all rational thought deserted her as he drew her down on the sofa so that they were lying face-to-face, their legs entwined. His kisses were more potent than whiskey, sweeter than honey, more addictive than dark chocolate, and she knew if he kissed her until the end of time, she would still be hungry for more.

His hands caressed her. Wickedly clever hands that seemed to know exactly how to arouse her. After a moment, she slipped her hands under his shirt and began a slow exploration of her own, reveling in the feel of his skin beneath her palms. His body was solid, with washboard abs and biceps like steel. A distant part of her mind wondered if he'd had a weight room tucked away in the castle somewhere.

The heat of his arousal pressing against her belly gave her pause. He was a vampire. He had been trapped inside a painting for three hundred years. Blood wasn't the only thing he'd had to do without during that time. It was a daunting thought. She felt her ardor cooling at the thought of being the first woman he had been with in such a long time.

As though attuned to her thoughts, he drew back.

Was it a trick of the light, or were his eyes red and glowing?

"Karinna?"

She was keenly aware of the strength of his arms wrapped around her. Would he let her go if she asked? Or slake his desires for her flesh and blood whether she was willing or not?

"What is wrong?" he asked.

"I . . . I need to, ah . . . go to the bathroom."

He regarded her for a moment, as if weighing the truth of her words, and then he nodded as comprehension dawned. "You have changed your mind."

"No, really, I just need to . . ."

"You do not have to be afraid of me." Releasing her, he sat up, putting some space between them.

"I have no intention of taking you, or your blood, against your will."

She looked up at him, her expression puzzled. "How do you do that? Read my mind, I mean. You've done it before."

He shrugged. "It is a by-product of being a vampire. I can sense strong emotions, and sometimes your thoughts."

"Well, it's very disconcerting."

"Yes," he replied dryly. "I suppose it is."

"Three hundred years is a long time for a man to go without . . . to be celibate."

He snorted softly. "You have no idea." Vampires were by nature sensual creatures. Abstaining from intimacy for more than a few weeks caused discomfort; living like a monk for the last three centuries had caused almost as much physical agony as being deprived of nourishment.

He rose and went to the window and looked out into the night. In spite of his words to the contrary, Karinna was right to be afraid of him. He had been a fool to think of seducing her. She was far too young and far too innocent for the likes of him, especially in his current state. Perhaps he should seek out a lady of the evening. They had been plentiful in his time; men being what they were, he assumed there were still women whose favors could be had for a price.

He turned away from the window to find Karinna watching him, her brows drawn together in a frown.

"Have you been in love very many times?"

Of all the questions she might have asked him, this was the least expected.

"I've never been in love." His gaze moved over her, blatantly hot and hungry. "Though I've been in lust from time to time."

His voice, the look in his eyes, sent a wave of heat rushing through her. She cleared her throat. "What about your wife? Didn't you love her?"

"No. It was an arranged marriage."

"Oh. I've heard about those."

"They were quite common in my time. Some turned out happily," he said with a careless shrug. "Many did not."

"Was yours happy?"

"It was tumultuous. Rissa was an only child, badly spoiled, with a quick mind and a quicker temper. I am afraid I had no patience for either her tantrums or her jealousy." Looking back, he knew the lion's share of his failed marriage rested squarely on his shoulders. Though he had been faithful until he met Melina, he had been too involved in looking after the estate to give Rissa the attention she needed. "And what of you?" he asked. "A woman as lovely as you are must have had legions of lovers."

Kari laughed as she imagined countless men lined up at her front door, all eager to sweep her off her feet. In truth, she'd had only a couple of serious relationships before Ben, and none since then. She'd had lots of offers, but they weren't the kind of offers that interested her. She didn't believe in casual sex, had no interest in sleeping with a man just because he had taken her out to dinner or a movie. And nowadays, with the threat of AIDS and numerous other sexually transmitted diseases, well, she wasn't interested in dying for love, either.

"That's very funny," she said. "Legions of lovers."

"I was quite serious."

She couldn't help being flattered that he thought she was fighting men off with a stick. "I've never had a lover."

"Never?" From what he had seen and heard on the television, the men and women of this day were largely immoral, jumping in and out of various beds with or without the sanction of the church, changing partners as often as they changed the sheets.

"I've had boyfriends," Kari said defensively, "and we've come close to going all the way, but . . ." She shrugged. "I always came to my senses before it was too late."

He lifted one inquisitive brow. "You are untouched?"

"I know, I know, it's practically a crime to be a virgin in this day and age, but, oh, well, that's the way it is."

His gaze moved over her, settling on the pulse beating in the hollow of her throat. A maiden. He should have known when he tasted her that first night. There was nothing sweeter or more satisfying in all the world than virgin blood. Unless it ran through a witch's veins, he amended. But Karinna, ah, her life's blood had been sweet indeed. At the thought, his thirst rose up within him, hot and quick. A thirst for her blood. A hunger for her flesh.

As though reading his mind, she stood abruptly. "It's getting late," she said, "and I have to work tomorrow."

Her insides went all shivery when he closed the distance between them, folded his hands over her shoulders, bent down, and kissed her cheek. "Good night, then."

Blast the man. His kisses went to her head like champagne. One kiss, and she was ready to grab him by the arm and drag him upstairs. Instead, she forced a smile. "Good night."

She followed him to the front door and locked it behind him, wondering how long she would be able to resist the temptation that was Jason Rourke.

He was waiting for her in the living room when she got home from work the following night.

"I suppose that's another by-product of being a vampire," Kari muttered as she swept past him. "Breaking and entering."

"I did not break anything," he replied, looking offended.

Grinning, she shook her head. "It's just an expression. How did you get in?"

"Through the front door."

"It was locked."

He lifted one brow in wry amusement.

"Oh, right."

"I need a favor," he said. "Actually, a couple of them."

"Like what?" she asked, a note of suspicion in her tone.

"I should like to bathe, and I need a place to rest during the day."

She had expected him to request something far more sinister. "There's a bathroom down the hall," she said. "As for a place to rest . . ." She thought a moment. "If you're not claustrophobic, there's a little place out back. Hardly more than a shed, really. You could put a bed or a . . . a coffin out there. The windows are boarded up, and the roof doesn't leak."

Rourke frowned thoughtfully, then nodded. It would do until he could find something more permanent, more secure. "Thank you."

"You'll find clean towels under the sink in the bathroom." She blew out a breath. "I'll just go make dinner while you, ah, clean up."

Without waiting for an answer, she went into the kitchen.

She was scrambling a couple of eggs when the shower went on in the bathroom. All thought of food was instantly forgotten as her mind quickly conjured an image of Jason Rourke shedding his clothes and stepping into the shower.

"Girl, get a grip," she muttered. "It doesn't matter how gorgeous and sexy he is. The operative word is *vampire*. Remember that. V-a-m-p-i-r-e. As in undead, bloodsucking creature of the night."

But she couldn't stop picturing him standing in her shower clad in nothing but soapsuds, with water trickling down his arms and chest and regions farther south. . . .

"Vampire, Kari," she muttered. "Vampire!"

She made toast and tea to go with the eggs, then went into the living room and sat down in front of the TV. She ate automatically, a naughty part of her mind picturing Rourke standing naked in her shower. She was surprised when she glanced at her plate and realized that even though she had eaten every bite, she had no memory of doing so.

She went suddenly still as the water went off in the bathroom and a host of new images flooded her mind.

Kari shook her head. What was the matter with her? She had seen other good-looking guys, even dated a few, but none of them had ever played havoc with her libido the way this one did. And he wasn't even human!

She felt that peculiar stir of awareness in the air when he entered the room. Setting her plate on the coffee table, she glanced over her shoulder. He was wearing a pair of tan slacks and a navy blue sweater that made his blue eyes look even darker.

He grinned at her, obviously aware that she found him attractive. It irritated her that she couldn't hide her feelings from him.

"A wonderful invention, hot running water," he remarked, sitting beside her.

She nodded. Of course, it was something she had always taken for granted, like her computer, her digital camera, and her cell phone. It was amazing to think of all the things she used on a daily basis that had been unheard of only a few years ago, things like fax machines and satellite TV, GPS systems and

CD players and iPods. Not so long ago, movies had been made in black and white, cars had running boards and ran on gas that cost only twenty-five cents a gallon, phones had rotary dials, and computers had taken up a whole room. People had listened to music on vinyl records. Televisions hadn't come with remotes or had more than a hundred channels. Her great grandmother had used a wringer washing machine, dried her clothes on a line in the backyard, and typed on a manual typewriter. Kari blew out a sigh. Such things were as foreign to her as airplanes and automobiles were to him.

"I must ask for one more favor," he said, a note of regret in his voice.

"What do you need?"

"I need to find a coven."

"A coven!" she exclaimed. "Good grief, don't tell me you're a witch, too!"

His laughter, deep and rich, filled the air. "No, but I need to find one."

Kari frowned. How on earth did you go about finding a witch? Witches R Us? "Maybe the Internet," she remarked, thinking out loud. "You can find practically anything there."

She went to her desk and sat down. After booting up her computer, she went to Google and typed in *covens.* As always, she was amazed by the number of hits. There were over three hundred thousand listings for covens, pagans, and witches, as well as related links to books and movies. One link listed covens by age groups. There was a link to a Wiccan directory, listings for Wiccan clergy, New England covens, a site that debated the pros and cons of being a solitary practitioner or joining a coven.

"That one," Rourke said, pointing at a link that listed covens in Europe. Kari clicked on the site. It opened to something called "The Wiccan Rede." It sounded like advice for witches. She read a few lines out loud.

"Cast the Circle thrice about, To keep all evil spirits out. To bind the spell every time, Let the spell be spake in rhyme. Soft of eye an' light of touch— Speak little, listen much. When the Moon rides at Her peak, then your heart's desire seek. Widdershins go when the Moon doth wane, an' the Werewolf howls by the dread Wolfs bane."

Reading over her shoulder, Rourke asked, "Does it say how to get in touch with a witch?"

Kari searched the site and came up with an e-mail address. She explained what e-mail was and then asked, "What do you want to say?"

"Ask if they know of a wizard named Josef Vilnius, and if he still lives."

"You're kidding, right? How could he still be alive after such a long time?"

"Wizards live longer than mere mortals."

"Must be nice," Kari muttered. She thought a moment, then typed her message: I'm trying to locate a wizard named Josef Vilnius. If you have any information about him or his whereabouts, please let me know. Kari.

She hit SEND, did a little more searching, sent out five more e-mails, and signed off. "All we can do now is wait."

Rourke raked a hand through his hair. He had already waited three hundred years.

Kari turned to look at Rourke. "Do you want to go and check out the shed?" she asked.

"Check out?"

"Look it over."

"Ah, yes."

He followed her outside, waited while she opened the door. As she had said, it wasn't much, just a small, square building she used for storing her patio furniture, holiday decorations, and junk she didn't need but couldn't bring herself to throw away.

She flipped the light switch but nothing happened. "I guess the bulb burned out. I'll go get a new one."

"No need."

"But it's so dark in there, how will you . . . Never mind, don't tell me. Night vision is another by-product."

Rourke grinned at her. "One of many."

He stepped inside and looked around. The floor was made of wood, there were a number of boxes piled along the walls. Two were marked "Christmas," one was marked "Halloween," another "Easter." Two others were marked "Miscellaneous Junk."

"So, what do you think?" Kari asked from the doorway.

"It will do."

"What will you, ah, sleep on? There's a twin bed in the spare room that you can use. Or do you need a . . . you know?"

"A bed will be fine."

"You could just sleep in the spare room, you know. It would be a lot more comfortable."

"This suits me well enough, although I would like to keep my few belongings in the house, if you do not mind."

"I don't mind," she said, and then wondered if she was making a mistake. What was she thinking? Did she really want a vampire sharing her living space? Did she really want to send him away? "I don't mind," she said again.

He rapped his knuckles on the door. "I will need to install a lock on the inside. Will that be a problem?"

"No, of course not."

He didn't tell her he would need to put other, paranormal wards around the building to protect him while he slept. He doubted anyone would be looking for a vampire in a shed in her backyard. People today did not believe the Undead existed, but it was always wise to be cautious. Too bad he hadn't remembered that three hundred years ago.

He took a deep breath and the scent of the woman filled his nostrils. She was warm and vibrant and alive, so alive. Unable to resist, he moved toward her.

Kari's heart skipped a beat as Rourke loomed over her. In the dark, she couldn't see him very well, but she was aware of his nearness with every fiber of her being, and then his arms were sliding around her waist, drawing her body ever closer to his.

His nearness went through her like a jolt of electricity.

"What are you doing?" she asked, her voice little more than a squeak.

"Nothing." He bent toward her, his lips lightly brushing hers. "Thank you for letting me stay."

"You're welcome."

Lowering his head to hers, he kissed her, his lips lingering on hers in a slow and subtle exploration. Her lips felt bereft when he took his mouth from hers.

"Thank you for freeing me from that accursed painting."

She swallowed hard. "You're welcome."

He kissed her again, his tongue boldly seeking hers this time. Pleasure unfurled deep within the very center of her being, unleashed by the sweet intoxication of his kiss. She should be thanking him, she thought. No one else had ever made her feel like this, as if her very bones were melting.

She blinked up at him when he took his mouth from hers, blurted, "Don't stop," and felt her cheeks burn with embarrassment. What was she thinking, letting a vampire kiss her? Worse, what was she doing kissing him back and asking for more?

His hand stroked her hair. "I need to go."

"Go?" She stared at him, confused. "Go where? I thought you were staying here."

"I need to feed." His gaze dropped to her throat. "Or I could stay. . . ."

The hunger in his eyes was evident even in the dark. It quickly cooled her desire. With a shake of her head, she lifted a protective hand to her throat. "I don't think so."

"I will not be gone long. Do you think you will get an answer to your e-mail tonight?"

"I don't know. It's possible, I guess. Depends on how often they read their mail."

"Will you be awake when I return?"

She nodded, thinking she would stay awake forever if he would just kiss her again.

His hand caressed her cheek, and then he was gone.

Kari stared at the spot where he had been. Amazing, she thought, that he could disappear so quickly.

She closed the door to the shed and went into the house. She had a vampire for a roommate. She could only wonder what kind of changes she would have to make in her lifestyle to accommodate him.

Rourke strolled along the dark streets, his thoughts centered on Karinna, always Karinna. In his day, it was practically unheard of for a woman to live alone or work outside the home. Women lived with their parents until they married, and then their husbands provided for them. A wife's only duties had been to obey her husband, warm his bed, and bless him with an heir. Poor women often had worked in the fields alongside their husbands, and it wasn't unheard of for women to give birth in the fields and then continue working.

In his day . . . He grunted softly. His day. How very long ago that had been! And how differently everything was now. Given time, he thought he might come to like this century. Time. It was the one thing he had in abundance. Time . . . how quickly the wheels turned. Everything he had ever known was gone; everyone he had ever known was dead and buried. His wife, his children, his parents, his brothers, all gone.

He wondered idly how he would have spent the last three hundred years if he hadn't been imprisoned in that accursed painting. After leaving his wife and family, he had roamed the world, explored new cultures, learned new languages. He had reveled in his preternatural powers, gloried in his strength, satisfied his lust for blood and for flesh in every clime and on every continent. To be a vampire was to be invincible, immortal. He had looked forward to each new night. There had been so much to see, so much to do, and he'd had the time to see and do it all. Until Vilnius . . .

The scent of prey scattered his thoughts of the past.

The woman was emerging from a store, a bag of groceries in each hand. Clad in a pair of white slacks and a green shirt, she was tall and thin, with straight brown hair and troubled brown eyes.

A thought took him to her side. Murmuring, "Let me help you with that," he reached for one of the bags.

"No, that's all right," she said, her voice and expression betraying her anxiety at being accosted in the parking lot by a complete stranger.

"It is no trouble." He searched her mind for her name. "Cynthia."

She stared at him, confused. "Do I know you?"

"You will."

Staying as far away from him as she could, she fumbled in her handbag for her keys, unlocked the trunk, and placed her bag inside. Rourke placed his sack beside hers.

Murmuring, "Thank you," she closed the trunk and moved quickly to the driver's-side door.

When she would have opened the car door, Rourke placed his hand on her arm. "Wait."

"Please," she said, her voice thick with fear. "Don't hurt me."

"You need not worry about that."

"I have two small children, Janie and Joey. Please, they need me. I'm all they have."

"Hush, now," he said, drawing her into his embrace. "There is nothing to fear."

She stared at him through fear-filled eyes, her heart hammering in her breast. The scent of her fear teased his nostrils and quickened his hunger. He spoke to her mind, calming her until she stood quiescent in his arms, and then he lowered his head to her neck. Anyone passing by would see only a man embracing a woman. He drank slowly, savoring the warm, rich, coppery taste on his tongue. It had been so long since he had been able to slake his thirst, so long. Strength and power flowed into him. He was immortal, invincible.

When he had quenched his thirst, he sealed the tiny wounds in the woman's neck with a flick of his tongue, then helped her into the car.

"You will go home now, Cynthia," he said, his gaze holding hers. "You will get something to drink, and then go to bed."

She looked up at him, her expression blank.

"You will forget this happened," he said, bending her mind and will to his. "You will forget me."

The woman looked at him a moment longer, and then, with a nod, she put the key in the ignition and started the engine. She sat there for a moment, and then, with a slight shake of her head, she turned on the car's headlights and pulled out of the parking lot.

Rourke watched her drive away, and then, whistling softly, he started back toward Karinna's house. A dog barked at him; Rourke stilled it with a look. A cat, sitting on a wall, hissed at him as he passed by. Rourke grinned into the darkness. You couldn't fool animals, he thought. Domesticated or wild, they all sensed that he wasn't human.

He found Karinna sitting at her computer when he arrived. He paused in the doorway, admiring the way the lamplight shone in her hair and brought out the natural flush in her cheeks. She was a beautiful woman, perhaps the most beautiful woman he had ever known.

Kari sensed Rourke's presence almost immediately. Feeling like a rabbit in the presence of a hungry wolf, she went suddenly still all over. She knew what he had been doing while he was gone; it filled her with a primal urge to run, to hide. He wasn't a wolf, of course, but he was a dangerous predator of another kind: a vampire who had been out doing what vampires did—feeding on some luckless victim to preserve his own life. She comforted herself with the knowledge that he didn't kill them.

Rourke stood behind her chair, unmoving, silent. He knew what she was thinking, feeling. The scent of her unease filled the air, and so he stood there, waiting, wondering if she had decided to ask him to leave.

The silence stretched between them.

"Karinna?"

Just her name, softly spoken, but she heard the question in his tone, knew he was waiting for her to tell him to stay or go.

Slowly, she swiveled around to face him. He looked much the same as always, though his complexion seemed a little more flushed, his eyes darker and more vibrant.

He gestured at her computer screen. "Any luck?" he asked quietly.

She blew out a sigh, and then she smiled, dissolving the tension between them. He hadn't changed. He was the same Rourke who had captivated her from the beginning.

"I was just about to check." She opened her mailbox, scrolled down until she found the e-mail she was looking for.

Leaning forward, Rourke read the message aloud: "I am acquainted with Vilnius. However, I am not in the habit of giving out personal information to unknown third parties. If you will give me your name, I shall tell Vilnius you are looking for him. Blessed be. Esme."

Kari glanced over her shoulder. "I guess it's too late to worry about it now," she muttered, "but I'm not sure I like the idea of a practicing witch having my e-mail address. I mean, what if she hexes my computer or something?" She drummed her fingertips on the desktop. "So, what should I say?"

"Nothing."

"Nothing?" She shook her head. "I don't understand. Why were you so anxious for a reply if you're not interested in talking to her?"

"I just wanted to know if Vilnius is still alive. I do not want him to know I am looking for him."

"Then how are you going to find him?"

"How, indeed. I shall have to think on that for a while." He watched her curiously for a few moments before asking, "What are you doing?"

"Backing my files up on my flash drive."

"Backing up?"

"Saving the letters and pictures on my computer that I want to keep." She shrugged. "I do it periodically anyway." She had lost everything once—her personal photos, files, music, and graphics—when her hard drive crashed. Since then, she backed up her important files every night, and everything else at least once a week.

It seemed even more important now, she thought, just in case some malevolent witch decided to send a nasty virus her way. And as soon as she finished backing up her files, she was going to delete her old screen name and come up with a new one. Maybe she was overreacting, but what the heck, better safe now than sorry later.

Rourke watched her for a moment, fascinated by the workings of the computer. It was a kind of magic far beyond his comprehension, as was the automobile and the other equally amazing machines that Karinna took for granted. Of course, he had some incredible, seemingly magical powers of his own.

But computers and cars weren't on the same level as the kind of magic Vilnius was capable of. They were just inventions made by ordinary men. Vilnius, on the other hand, was far from ordinary.

And he was still alive.

Rourke clenched his fists. Revenge, and his father's sword, were within reach at last. But before he sought out Vilnius, he had to find Ana Luisa and free her, if necessary. He had no lasting love for the wizard's daughter. She had been nothing but a passing fancy, a bit of sweetness he had been too hungry and too foolish to resist, but she was no more deserving of the punishment her father had inflicted on her than he himself had been.

Going to the window, he stared out into the darkness. He had a vast new world to explore city by city, country by country. A new beginning in what appeared to be an exciting new century. He glanced over his shoulder. A new woman. The thought of exploring Karinna Adams from north to south made him smile with anticipation. She looked to be a tasty morsel from the top of her head to the soles of her feet.

She would make a pleasant diversion while he searched for the wizard's daughter. Now that he was freed, his conscience wouldn't let him leave Ana Luisa trapped inside the painting. And after he had liberated the wizard's daughter, he would avenge himself on Vilnius and recover his father's sword.

A ripple in the fabric of time drew his gaze to the yard. There was a shimmer in the air and then he saw a woman standing on the grass, swathed in a long, dark traveling cloak.

He recognized her at once.

It was Melina, the vampire who had brought him across so many years ago.

Chapter 11

Rourke glanced at Karinna again. Still engrossed in backing up her computer files, she seemed to have forgotten he was in the room. It was just as well.

A thought took him outside.

Melina turned gracefully to meet him, a smile of welcome curving her lips.

"Jason," she murmured.

"Melina."

"I thought you had been destroyed."

"Not yet."

Rourke's gaze moved over her. Though he hadn't seen her in centuries, Melina was as vibrant and beautiful as he remembered. She had come to him every year since the night she had brought him across until Vilnius had cursed him. No matter where Rourke had been, Melina had found him and they had spent a night together from dusk until dawn. They had hunted together, and later, while making love, she had tasted him, and he had tasted her. Only a small taste, since vampires did not feed off each other, but a taste was as good as a feast. Vampire blood produced a high like no other.

"I have not felt you in three hundred years, and now, suddenly, you are here." She looked up at him through incredibly thick lashes, patiently waiting for an explanation.

"'Tis a long story."

Moving like a wisp of silvered moonlight, she flowed toward him. "'Tis a long night," she replied with a saucy grin.

"So it is."

She pressed herself against him, her slender body molding itself to his. "I have missed you these many years. It saddened me to think that you had been destroyed, that I might never see you again." She looked up at him, a faint smile teasing her lips, and he saw the gleam of her fangs. "We have many years to make up for. We can start tonight."

Before he could reply, she rose up on her tiptoes and kissed him, long and hard.

"Have you missed me, Jason?" she purred. "Have you missed me as much as I have missed you?"

Rourke considered the truth, and opted for a lie. "Of course." Saying the words, he realized it wasn't a lie after all. He had missed her. She was a law unto herself, a truly unique creature, beautiful, selfish, totally without guilt or guile. She said what she wanted, did as she pleased, and the devil take the hindmost.

"So," she said, linking her arm with his, "where have you been these past three hundred years?"

While they walked down the street, Rourke told

her of Vilnius and his wicked curse and how, at long last, a mortal woman had freed him from his prison.

"Vilnius!" Melina spat the name from her mouth. "A vile man. But you are free now, and this is our night."

Drawing him into the shadows, she wrapped her arms around him and kissed him again only to draw back, her brows rushing together in a frown when he didn't return the kiss. "Aren't you happy to see me?"

Rourke hesitated. There had been a time when he had looked forward to the one night each year that he spent with Melina. She had satisfied all his hungers, but now . . . Why did holding Melina suddenly seem wrong, as if he were betraying Karinna's trust?

"Jason?"

He looked into Melina's eyes, beautiful green eyes filled with desire, and thought of Karinna's eyes, as blue and clear as the sky he had not seen in 736 years.

Slowly, he removed Melina's arms from around his waist. "Yes, of course."

"Come then, let us go." She trailed her fingertips down his cheek. "Shall we hunt first or . . ."

He glanced down the street toward Karinna's house. "Not tonight."

"You are refusing me?" she asked in disbelief. "You *dare* to refuse me?" She followed his gaze, her eyes narrowing ominously. "Who is the woman? What has she done to you?"

Rourke shook his head. "She has done nothing but free me from that accursed painting."

"You care for her." It was not a question but a statement of fact.

"Of course I do. Did you not hear what I said? But for her, I would still be imprisoned."

"I see."

"I doubt it."

Melina glanced down the street again, her expression filled with disdain. "It sounds to me as though you have exchanged one prison for another."

"Maybe so," Rourke allowed, thinking that his sweet Karinna was a far more pleasant jailer than Vilnius had ever been.

"I could compel you to do my bidding," Melina warned. "I could bend your will to mine and make you fulfill my every wish."

"You could try."

"Impudent pup! Do you doubt my power?"

Rourke grinned at her. "Not for a minute."

"Maybe next year you'll be more willing."

"Perhaps."

It wasn't the answer she wanted. Eyes narrowed, she glared at him.

Rourke waited, wondering if it might have been wiser to humor her for one night. Her anger was a palpable thing. He was the first fledgling Melina had made; as such, he had always held a special place in her heart. Or so she had said. True or not, it was never wise to offend a woman, especially a jealous woman with unlimited supernatural powers.

"Melina . . ."

"If you've changed your mind, I don't want to know. And if you haven't, I don't want to know that, either," she said imperiously, and with a wave of one delicate hand, she vanished from his sight.

Rourke swore softly. He hadn't meant to hurt her feelings, but it was too late to do anything about it now.

Kari stood at the window, wishing she knew who Rourke was talking to outside, wishing she could hear what was being said.

Thanks to a nearby streetlight and a full moon, she could see that his companion was a woman clad in a long black cloak. Her skin was almost luminous in the moonlight; her hair fell to her waist in shimmering red waves.

Curiosity turned to jealousy when the woman drew Rourke into his arms and kissed her.

Kari shook her head. She couldn't be jealous. That was absurd. She hardly knew Jason Rourke. She had nothing to be jealous of. For all she knew, the woman could be his girlfriend.

Or his wife.

She was being ridiculous. He hadn't said anything about having married again. Anyway, he had been trapped inside a painting for three hundred years. Even if he'd had a girlfriend or a wife or a daughter, any or all of them would be long dead by now.

Unless the woman was a vampire.

Now there was a scary thought! One vampire was bad enough. Two would be . . . impossible. Still, vampires were made, not born, so it stood to reason that there had to be at least one other.

The jealousy she refused to acknowledge ratcheted up a notch as Kari watched Jason and the woman walk down the street, arm in arm.

After dropping the curtain back into place, Kari went into the living room and sank down onto the sofa. She didn't know why she was so surprised to see Jason with another woman. Vampire or not, he was gorgeous, though she couldn't help wondering how and when he'd had time to get to know another woman.

Hot tears stung her eyes and she blinked them away. She would not cry!

After what seemed like an eternity but was, in fact, only a few minutes later, she heard the front door open.

Kari stood and turned to face Rourke, her arms crossed under her breasts. "Who was that?"

He lifted one brow at the barely concealed jealousy he detected in her voice. "Her name is Melina."

"Who is she?"

"She is the vampire who made me."

Kari blinked at him. Even though the thought had crossed her mind, it was the last thing she had expected him to say. "What is she doing here?" Kari's hand flew to her throat. "She's not going to make me one, is she?"

Rourke laughed softly. "No, I will not let that happen." His gaze moved to her throat. "If anyone brings you across, it will be me." He lifted one hand as her face drained of color. "I would not turn you against your will."

Mollified by his words, Kari dropped back down

onto the sofa. "Why did she come here? What did she want?"

"She wanted me to spend the night with her. We have done so every year since she made me."

"Every year?" Once a year didn't sound like much until she realized he had been a vampire for 736 years. Of course, she supposed the last three centuries didn't count.

Rourke nodded.

"So, why didn't you go with her?" Kari asked, injecting what she hoped was a note of indifference into her voice.

His gaze moved over her from head to foot, his dark-eyed perusal like a physical caress. "Why, indeed." He had always enjoyed the time he spent with Melina, but that was before Karinna had entered his life. When he was with Karinna, he felt alive, truly alive, in a way he had not felt since Melina brought him across so long ago.

Kari stared at him. There was no mistaking the hungry look in his eyes. But did she really want to compete with a vampire for this man?

Who was she kidding? She had been fascinated with him from the moment she first saw the painting in the art gallery. Fascination had become obsession, and obsession had become . . . what? Was it possible she had fallen in love with Jason Rourke? With a vampire?

She frowned as a horrible thought occurred to her. "Are you in love with that . . . with Melina?"

"No."

"You've lived for hundreds of years. I can't believe

you've never been in love. I mean . . . why haven't you?" she asked, and then bit down on her lower lip. Maybe vampires were incapable of love.

He pondered her question for several moments. He had no good answer to give her, at least none she was likely to condone, or perhaps even understand.

"I was born into a noble family, the second of five sons. My older brother, Joseph, became a priest. My brother Paul went off to fight in the Crusades with my father. Mathias was a physician, Joshua, a merchant. It fell to me to look after the family estate, though I had no desire to do so, and no desire to marry. I am ashamed to say that I was not a good husband. My wife and children deserved better than I gave them." He paused a moment, his thoughts turned inward. "I have often wondered if becoming a vampire was some form of divine punishment. It was only after I had been turned that I realized what I had lost."

He sighed with the memory. "My father was killed in the Crusades. Paul brought him home and gave me his sword, saying it was my father's last wish that I should have it.

"I was one and thirty when Melina made me. For a time, I was able to hide what I had become but . . ." He shrugged. "As I said, as the years passed and I did not age, my family became suspicious of me. One night I took my father's sword, kissed my sons good-bye, and left home, never to return."

"That's so sad."

He shrugged. "It made me grow up. I wandered

the world, never staying long in any one place. And then, one night, I met a woman in a tavern. She was young and innocent and all the more tempting because of it. She played the wanton, tempting me, teasing me, even though I knew she had never been with a man."

He paused a moment, as though seeing it all again in his mind. "I knew it was wrong, but I was determined to have her. I took her virginity and her blood and spent three hundred years imprisoned in that accursed painting because of it." Even now, he could remember the way Ana Luisa's blood had burned his tongue. It was the taste of her blood that would lead him to her now. "You know the rest of the story."

"It all sounds so far-fetched," Kari remarked. "Vampires and wizards and evil curses. It's hard to believe that any of it's real."

"Sometimes I have trouble believing it myself."

"Did she know you were a vampire?"

"No."

"How could you take her blood without her knowing, or at least suspecting?"

"I took but a little."

"What did she say when you told her what you are?"

"I never told her."

"So, she still doesn't know?" Kari shook her head. "That's hard to believe."

Rourke shrugged.

"Do you think the wizard's daughter is still alive?"

He nodded. "I know she is." Closing his eyes,

he blocked everything from his mind and then he conjured Ana Luisa's image even as he drew upon the memory of the fiery taste of her life's blood on his tongue. He murmured her name, felt his senses reach out across endless time and space, homing in on the unique scent of her blood, the slow, steady beat of her heart.

"Rourke . . ."

"Shh." Concentrating harder now, his senses expanding, he continued to reach out, crossing land and water as he searched for that one scent, that one heartbeat.

It took several moments of intense concentration, and then, as if looking through the wrong end of a telescope, he saw Ana Luisa and the painting that imprisoned her. A unicorn with golden hooves and a golden horn stood in the midst of a field of flowers, its head raised to sniff the wind. Ana Luisa sat on its back, her long blond hair flowing down her back and over her shoulders. Clad in a long white gossamer gown, she gazed into the distance, her luminous green eyes filled with unspeakable sorrow. A single tear glistened like a drop of morning dew on one rosy cheek. He wondered if Vilnius had painted it there, or if it was one of Ana Luisa's own tears, shed the night her father had found them.

Rourke quietly cursed the wizard's cruelty. If he lived another seven hundred years, he would never understand how a man could condemn his own flesh and blood to such a horrid fate.

"Rourke? Rourke, are you all right?"

He shook his head. He would never be all right

until Ana Luisa had been freed from her prison of glass and canvas. She was so young, far younger than she had professed to be when he seduced her. Had he known she was little more than a child, he never would have touched her. But she had professed to be older and acted far more worldly wise than her years.

"I need to make a journey," he said. "And I need you to come with me."

"A journey?" Kari asked doubtfully. "Where do you want to go? And why do you need me?"

"I need to find Ana Luisa," Rourke said. "And I need you to help me find my way around. There is still much here I am not familiar with."

"But I can't just take off. I have a job, you know." She frowned. "How do you know where she is, anyway?"

"She is in Romania."

"Romania? As in Transylvania? Are you kidding me? I can't go running off to Romania."

"Karinna, I cannot do this without you." Had he been stronger, he could have flown there under his own power, but he needed time to regain his full strength, he needed added sustenance to restore his preternatural powers. In his present condition, he could never make such a long journey, let alone bring Ana Luisa back with him. He could wait until his strength and his powers were fully restored, but that might take weeks. Some might say he was being too impulsive. After all, what was another few weeks after so many centuries? But anyone who suggested such a thing had never been confined in a stagnant world of paint and canvas.

"But . . ."

"She has been trapped in that painting for three hundred years," he said quietly. "I know what she is feeling, thinking. She has no supernatural powers of her own that I know of." True, she was a witch, but if she couldn't move or speak, she had no way of casting a spell, no way of easing the torment of being immobile year after year. He shook his head. "I cannot leave her there, alive yet lifeless."

There had been a time, soon after the wizard had cursed him, when Rourke had found pleasure in knowing that Ana Luisa had also been cursed. He had blamed her for not telling him how young she was, or warning him that her father was a powerful wizard. But those feelings had soon passed and he had admitted that he was as much to blame for what had happened to them as was she, perhaps more.

"I cannot leave her there," he said again, "not when I have the power to free her."

Kari's shoulders slumped in defeat. "Where, exactly, do you want to go, and when do you want to leave?"

Chapter 12

It took Kari several days to make all the necessary arrangements. Not only did she have to get a passport, book a flight, and make reservations for a place to stay, she also had to arrange to take a week of her vacation a few months early, buy a coffin for Rourke to travel in, rent a hearse to transport it to the airport, and arrange for someone to pick it up at the other end, all of which was going to put quite a dent in her bank account.

As Kari thought about the coffin, it brought Tricia's friend Mel to mind. Maybe she could arrange to borrow Mel's hearse. It would be much easier than trying to rent one. That way, she wouldn't have to come up with a good story explaining why the body was being picked up at her house instead of at a funeral home or the morgue, and why it had to be picked up after dark.

While waiting for her passport photos, Kari learned all she could about Romania. According to a map, Romania was bordered by Hungary, Yugoslavia, the Ukraine, Bulgaria, and the Black Sea. One site showed photos of a number of impressive buildings that were located in towns with romantic and exotic names like Brasov and Oradea and Arad.

Transylvania was also located in Romania. Vlad Tepes, who was also known as Vlad the Impaler and Vlad Dracula, was perhaps Romania's most famous, or infamous, hero. It was well known that Vlad had been the inspiration for Bram Stoker's famous story. Only Rourke's destination wasn't Transylvania, but Bucharest.

One of the places that caught Kari's imagination was Bran Castle, which was located on the border between Transylvania and Wallachia. The castle, located atop a two-hundred-foot-tall rock, overlooked the village of Bran. In ancient times, the fortress had been used to protect Brasov from the Turks and later served as a customs house. The rooms and towers were built around an inner courtyard.

She grinned as she read that some of the rooms were connected by underground passageways.

"No surprise there," she muttered. Every respectable castle had the requisite underground tunnels and secret passages.

Judging from the pictures on the Web, the fifty-seven-room castle was quite spectacular. She thought it interesting that Bran Castle was often touted as Castle Dracula even though it had no real connection to Vlad Tepes save for some speculation that he had attacked and captured the place sometime in 1460.

Reading on, she learned that the castle had a fascinating history. It had originally been built by the Knights of the Teutonic Order as a stronghold in 1212. Between 1395 and 1427, the castle had belonged to Mircea the Wise, who was Vlad Dracula's grandfather. Toward the end of the thirteenth century, it had been taken over by the Saxons. At the beginning of the twentieth century, it had been the home of Queen Victoria's granddaughter Queen Marie. Marie's daughter Princess Ileana of Romania inherited the castle.

In 1950, Bran Castle had been appropriated by the country's Communist regime. After the Romanian Revolution in 1989, the castle became a tourist attraction that was especially popular during Halloween.

The castle, now a museum of medieval arts, is furnished with artifacts from Queen Marie's time, including traditional furniture and wall hangings that she had collected to showcase Romanian crafts and skills. A small park, located at the bottom of the hill, displayed examples of peasant cottages and barns that had been moved there from different parts of the country. Not surprisingly, a small market was located near the castle gates where tourists could buy a wide variety of souvenirs depicting pictures of the real Vlad Dracula, as well as images of the fictional Dracula made famous by Bram Stoker.

In 2006, Bran Castle had been returned to the rightful heir, Dominic von Habsburg, who had put it up for sale a year later.

Vlad Dracula's real castle was the Poienari Fortress located in the Arges Valley. To reach it, one had to climb fifteen hundred steps and cross a bridge. According to legend, his wife had jumped out of one of the fortress windows in order to avoid being captured by the Turks. It was said that Vlad had escaped over the mountains by riding a horse wearing shoes that left cloven hoofprints instead of the hoofprints made by a horse.

Kari couldn't help grinning when she read that, nor could she help wondering where he had found horse shoes that left cloven hoofprints.

Vlad had been a cruel master. It was said that he enjoyed watching people die while he dined, and that his favorite form of execution was by impalement. He had also had people skinned and boiled alive. Thieves and liars had been impaled. As might be expected, there hadn't been a lot of crime in Walachia during Vlad's reign. To prove how law-abiding his citizens were, he once placed a gold cup near a fountain in the town square. Anyone who wished to could use the cup to draw water from the fountain, but no one was to remove it. Fearing impalement, no one ever removed it. Despite his cruelty, his subjects had respected him for being a strong leader and for defending their country against the Turks.

Another site showed the birthplace of Vlad Tepes in Sighisoara. The building was now a restaurant. Rising above the town of Sighisoara was The Citadel, built by the Saxons in the twelfth century. It had been preserved as a museum. Another Web page displayed photos of several beautiful cathedrals, including the Black Church in Brasov. Like most of the other churches and cathedrals in the area, it had been built hundreds of years ago.

Kari next went in search of information on Bucharest. She was surprised to learn that the city had been inhabited since 500 B.C. and that, according to Romanian legend, Bucharest had been founded by a shepherd boy named Bucur. Besides being a shepherd, Bucur had played the flute and made wine, all of which endeared him to the local merchants, who had named the town after him. Even more surprising was the fact that Bucharest had once been known as "Little Paris."

The city, besides being the largest in the country, was also the capital, with a population of over two million. It boasted thirty-seven museums, twenty-two theaters, opera houses and concert halls, eighteen art galleries, as well as a number of libraries and bookstores.

While looking up hotels, Kari found a vacancy at a bed-and-breakfast in the city of Miklosvar. She was thinking she might like to stay there until she read an accompanying blog, which said, in part, that visitors to the city had to endure a three- or four-hour trip over a road made up of potholes and gravel that was guaranteed to loosen your back teeth. It went on to say that if you wanted to see a part of the country that had changed but little over the last century, Miklosvar was the place to go. Quaint farmhouses lined roads made of dirt and cobblestone, men and women still cut their hay with scythes, and cars had not yet replaced the horse and cart.

Although Dracula hadn't lived in Miklosvar, the

city was inhabited by bats and a charming count who hoped to turn the area surrounding Miklosvar into an environmental retreat and preserve the region's architectural heritage. The count and his family, descendants of the feudal overlords whose roots dated back to 1252, maintained four restored farmhouses that now served as guesthouses.

Continuing her search for a place to stay, Kari found a place that rented apartments for a short term and decided an apartment might be a wiser option than staying in a hotel. She figured there would be fewer people coming and going. With that thought in mind, she booked a first-floor apartment with two bedrooms. Next, she booked her flight. Since she had never flown before, and was pretty sure she never would again, she decided to go all out and fly first class.

When all her reservations had been made, she switched off the computer, picked up the phone, and called Tricia's friend Mel.

"Hey, Kari," he said. "What can I do for you?"

"I was wondering if I could borrow your hearse for a week or so."

"Is it Halloween already?"

Kari laughed. "No, silly."

"Well, sure, when do you want to pick it up?"

"Next Monday afternoon, around one-thirty or so?"

"No problem. Do you want the coffin, too?"

"Oh, yes," she exclaimed, pleased to have solved two problems with one phone call.

"Allrighty, then. I'll be at work Monday, but I'll

leave the hearse in the driveway. The keys will be under the mat on the back porch."

"Thanks, Mel. I'll leave the keys to my car there so you can move it or drive it."

"Right. So, what's up? Are you having a scary party or something?"

"Or something," Kari said, grinning inwardly. "And I'd appreciate it if you'd keep this to yourself."

"Will do, cupcake," Mel said. "Just keep it legal and drop the hearse off when you're done with it."

"I will. And thanks again."

Kari grew increasingly nervous as the day of departure grew closer. She had never been on an airplane before. Just thinking about it made her extremely nervous, almost as nervous as the thought of traveling with a vampire.

It gave her the creeps, thinking about Rourke lying as still as death inside a casket during the flight, dead but not dead. As near as she could figure, the flight would take something like fifteen hours. Fifteen hours. He wouldn't be asleep the whole time, but then, she supposed it wouldn't bother him to be awake inside the coffin any more than it would bother her to have to stay in bed for an extended length of time.

Her life had certainly gotten complicated, she mused. Sometimes she wished she had never bought that painting, never heard of Vilnius and his evil curse!

Needing to connect to something ordinary and uncomplicated, she went into the living room, curled up on the sofa, and called Tricia.

"Kari, hi. I was just going to call you!"

"Oh? What's up?"

"Nothing, I was just bored, and wondering how you and Mr. Tall, Blond, and Handsome were getting along."

"Just fine," Kari said lightly. "In fact, I'm going away with him for a few days."

Tricia laughed softly. "A little one-on-one time?"

"Tricia!"

"Well, why else would you be going away if it wasn't to get to know him better?"

Kari sighed in exasperation. "It's just a little vacation."

"Uh-huh. So, where are you going?"

"Romania."

"Romania!" Trish exclaimed. "Are you kidding me? I mean, Romania! Really, Kari, that doesn't sound like a very romantic place to me. Why not go to Rome? Or Paris?"

"Rourke's from Romania. Remember?"

"I know, but still . . ."

"I've been reading up on the place and it sounds fascinating. Lots of beautiful architecture and old churches, that kind of thing."

"Isn't Transylvania there?" Tricia asked, her voice betraying her lack of enthusiasm. "Isn't that where Dracula lived, or died, or whatever?"

"So they say."

"Well, stay away from those old tombs."

"Don't worry."

"Are you sure you don't want to vacation somewhere closer to home? I mean, what if you go all that way and then find out you two don't have as much in common as you seem to think, or you have a fight? You won't be able to make a graceful exit and head for home."

"I'll be fine, Trish. Sheesh. You sound like my mother."

"How soon are you leaving?"

"Tomorrow night."

"Well, since I can't talk you out of it, have fun. And be careful!"

"Yes, mom."

"I mean it, Kari," Tricia said soberly. "You haven't known him very long and now you're going off to a foreign country with him. The world's a scary place these days, so keep your eyes open and . . ."

"Be careful, I know. Don't worry, I'll be fine."

"Do you need a ride to the airport?" Tricia asked.

"No, thanks, I've got it covered."

"Well, call me as soon as you get back, and I mean the very minute."

"I will, I promise."

"Send me a postcard. Oh, and be sure to take lots of pictures."

"Right. Talk to you soon."

Taking pictures was the last thing on Kari's mind. But now that Tricia had brought it up, Kari went searching for her digital camera.

She spent the rest of the day getting ready for the trip. She packed a suitcase for herself and another one for Rourke. He had told Kari that he thought she and Ana Luisa were about the same height and build, and with that thought in mind, Kari went to the mall and bought a loose-fitting dress, a pair of low-heeled shoes, a bra and panties, a coat, and a nightgown for Ana Luisa, figuring the girl would most likely need some contemporary clothing to wear on the plane, and something to sleep in when they got back home.

She went to a bookstore and picked up a couple of paperbacks so she would have something to take her mind off the flight and the reason for it.

On the way home, she stopped at Mel's to pick up the hearse. She shivered as she slid behind the wheel and backed it out of the driveway. She had never liked scary parties, scary movies, or scary stories, and now she was living a scary story of her own, although she had to admit Rourke wasn't really scary, just a little strange.

Back at home, she checked her suitcase to make sure she hadn't forgotten anything and made sure her plane tickets and the paperbacks were in her handbag, along with a couple of candy bars. She called Pizza Joe's and ordered a ham and pineapple pizza, then went into the kitchen to clean out the refrigerator of anything perishable.

The pizza and Rourke arrived at the same time.

He wrinkled his nostrils against the stink of meat and cheese and tomato sauce as he shouldered his way past the young man delivering the pizza.

Kari scowled at Rourke as she closed the door. "Don't look like that. Pizza's very good. Have you ever tried it?"

"Of course not."

Silly question, she thought. It hadn't even been

invented when he was born. She dropped the box on the coffee table, then went into the kitchen for a soda. When she returned, Rourke was sitting on the sofa, remote in hand.

He surfed the channels while she ate.

She couldn't imagine not being able to eat pizza, or bread, or bananas. How did he survive on nothing but blood? "Don't you ever get tired of consuming the same thing night after night?"

"What is your favorite food?"

"I don't know. I have a lot of them. Chocolate, I guess."

"Do you eat it every day?"

She shrugged. "Pretty much."

"Do you ever get tired of it?"

"Of course not, but I eat other things, too. I mean, I suppose I'd get tired of chocolate if I couldn't eat anything else." Even as she said the words, she doubted it would be true.

She ate another slice of pizza, washed it down with soda, then sat back, feeling pleasantly comfortable and content until Rourke switched off the TV and turned his full attention to her.

"Have you made all the necessary arrangements?"

"Yes. We have to be at the airport at seven o'clock tomorrow night. Our flight leaves at eight."

He nodded.

"I packed everything I thought you'd need, but you might want to take a look and make sure I didn't forget anything."

He nodded again. "Have you made arrangements for Ana Luisa?"

"Yes. I bought her a dress and shoes, and a coat and a nightgown and some other things. They're in my suitcase. Does she speak English?"

"When I knew her, she did not, but she may have learned it, as I did, from hearing it spoken."

"How are we going to get her on the plane? She doesn't have a passport or any identification."

"She will travel with me."

Kari stared at him. "With you?" She tried to imagine herself alive and locked inside a coffin for fifteen hours and knew she would go stark raving mad. She shook her head. "That won't work. I read somewhere that it's, you know, like freezing in the cargo hold, and they don't pipe any oxygen in there, either. She'd suffocate."

He looked thoughtful a moment. "I will think of something."

"Yeah?" she asked skeptically. "Like what?"

He shrugged. "Do you have a better idea?"

"No, but . . ."

"It will be all right."

"If you say so. Where's her painting located?"

"It is in a museum in Bucharest."

"How are you going to get it?"

He lifted one brow. "How do you think?"

"I don't suppose you plan to buy it?"

"No."

She tried not to think of what would happen if he got caught, and then wondered why she was worried. He was a vampire, after all. If anyone saw him, he could simply disappear, or wipe his memory from the person's mind.

She felt a wave of heat when she realized he was watching her, a hungry expression in his eyes. "Have you, ah, fed tonight?"

"No."

She lifted her hand to her neck. "Maybe you should."

His gaze moved to the pulse throbbing in the hollow of her throat. The weight of his gaze was like a physical touch warming her skin. Slowly, she shook her head. "Don't."

"A taste, Karinna?" His voice moved over her like a velvet caress. "Only a taste and then I will go."

How could she refuse him when he asked so sweetly, when she could hear the yearning in his voice, see the hunger in his eyes?

With a sigh, she brushed her hair away from her neck. "Just one taste? You promise?"

"I promise." He closed the distance between them. Wrapping his arm around her waist, he pulled her up against him. "Do not be afraid."

"I'm . . . I'm not."

He smiled at her. "I can hear the rapid beat of your heart, smell your fear." He stroked her cheek. "Do not be afraid of me, Karinna."

His breath was warm against her skin, his voice low and almost hypnotic. With a sigh, she leaned against the back of the sofa and closed her eyes. A shiver of anticipation ran down her spine as he licked her skin. She remembered tasting his blood, and liking it.

His mouth was hot against her skin. There was no pain in his bite, only warmth. She moaned softly, lost in a world of sensual pleasure that spread throughout her body. Why had she been afraid? Why had she made him promise to take just a taste? Maybe, if she held very still, he wouldn't stop. . . .

She felt bereft when he let her go. He went into the kitchen, returned a moment later with a glass of grapefruit juice.

"Here," he said, offering it to her. "Drink this."

Obediently, she took the glass and drank the contents. The taste, the coolness, quickly restored her.

He was watching her carefully. "Karinna?"

"Hmm?"

"How do you feel?"

"Wonderful." She lifted a hand to her neck, her fingertips tingling as she touched the place his mouth had been. "Do you want some more?"

A wry smile tugged at his lips. "Do not tempt me."

"It should be disgusting," she remarked candidly. "Why isn't it?"

"Because I do not wish it to be."

She frowned. "What do you mean?"

"It is up to the vampire whether the experience is pleasant or painful."

Kneeling in front of her, he took one of her hands in his. A sizzle of awareness skittered over her palm and spread up her arm.

"I would never hurt you, Karinna. I owe you more than I can ever repay." He lifted her hand and kissed her palm. "And now, you should go to bed."

"Are you going out to . . . you know?"

"Feed," he said, nodding. "Is it so hard for you to accept that you cannot say the word?"

"No. Yes. I wish . . ." She shook her head. "Never mind."

"What do you wish?"

"Nothing."

"You are jealous?"

"Of course not!" It was inconceivable to think she was jealous of the women he fed on. But she was, and they both knew it.

The following morning, Kari woke with butterflies in her stomach. Her nervousness grew worse with every passing minute. She wasn't looking forward to getting on the plane. She was having second thoughts about the reason for their journey. She was ashamed and annoyed by the flashes of jealousy that plagued her whenever she thought about Ana Luisa and the witch's relationship with Rourke. She was afraid that Rourke might somehow get caught in trying to free the girl.

To pass the time, she repacked her suitcase. She called her mother. She went to the mall and had her nails done. She called Tricia. She fixed a ham and cheese sandwich for lunch, then tried to calm her nerves with two candy bars and a bowl of chocolate ice cream. It didn't help. She dusted and vacuumed and did two loads of laundry, but all she could think about was the plane crashing, or Rourke winding up in prison for breaking and entering, leaving her stranded and alone in a foreign country.

She had just washed most of her dinner down

the garbage disposal when Rourke appeared in the kitchen.

Sometimes, it was most disconcerting, the way he simply appeared out of nowhere!

"Are you ready to go?" he asked.

"Not really." She didn't think she would ever be ready.

He frowned at her. "What more do you need to do?"

"Nothing. I was just . . . never mind. The suitcases are by the front door. Just let me grab my purse and my keys."

Taking a deep breath, she put on her jacket, then grabbed her handbag and the keys to the hearse and followed Rourke out the door, wondering if she was embarking on the most exciting adventure of her life, or making the world's biggest mistake.

Chapter 13

Outside, Rourke plucked the car keys from Karinna's hand. "I will drive."

"Do you know the way to the airport?"

"No," he said with a roguish grin, "but you can give me the proper directions."

Kari couldn't help grinning back as she got into the car, partly in response to Rourke's remark, but mostly because she found it morbidly amusing to be riding through the darkness in a hearse that was being driven by a man who was, technically, dead.

When they reached the turnoff for the airport, Rourke pulled onto a side street and parked the car.

"I will see you in Bucharest," he said.

Kari nodded, thinking she would feel much better about the whole trip if he could sit beside her and hold her hand.

"Do not worry." His fingertips caressed her cheek, and then, leaning forward, he kissed her. "I will see you soon."

Nodding, she watched him get out of the car and

go around to the back. Looking in the rearview mirror, she watched him lift the lid on the casket and climb inside. She couldn't help but shudder as he closed the lid.

Shaking off her doubts about the trip and her fear of flying, she slid across the seat to the driver's side, put the car in gear, and drove the rest of the way to the airport.

A ground agent told her where to drop off the coffin. She had been told it would be X-rayed before being put on board. She smiled a sickly smile, wondering what sort of reaction vampires had to being X-rayed. But it was out of her hands now.

After dropping off the casket, she left the hearse in the parking lot and made her way into the terminal. Feeling totally out of her element, she went to check in, annoyed to see there were long lines at the check-in agent's desk. But then, you couldn't go anywhere these days without standing in line. The post office, the bank, the gas station, the DMV, Disneyland—there were lines everywhere.

When it was her turn, she handed the agent her ticket and her passport, waited while her suitcase was weighed and labeled. She smiled as the agent returned her ticket and a newly printed boarding pass with her gate number and seat number on it. The agent then pointed her in the direction of the gate where she would be boarding and informed her of the time boarding would begin.

After leaving the check-in counter, she made her way to airport security. She had heard that security was tight since 9/11; now she saw it in action. All around her, people were shedding their coats and shoes, men were emptying their pockets, removing their belts. Her shoes, purse, carry-on bag, and jacket went into a bin that gave way to a conveyer belt to be X-rayed. Barefooted, she got into line to go through the metal detector. On the other side, she grabbed her belongings and moved on. The man behind her set off the metal detector. The sound made her heart skip a beat. Was he a terrorist? She watched anxiously as a guard waved a handheld wand around the man, and finally declared the man's zipper had set off the alarm.

Relieved, she put on her shoes and grabbed the rest of her belongings. She felt like a criminal by the time she reached the international departure area for her flight.

A short time later, she made her way past the two gate agents at the entrance to the Jetway, and past a flight attendant who also checked her boarding pass and directed her to her seat.

The aisle was crowded with people shedding coats and stowing their luggage. One man was trying to shove a large suitcase into a storage compartment.

Kari put her carry-on bag in an overhead compartment that looked surprisingly like an old-fashioned breadbox turned upside down. When that was done, she noticed there was a blanket, a pillow, and what looked like a small cosmetics bag piled on her seat. Moving them aside, she sat down, her heart pounding. Over the conversation of those around her, she could hear the faint humming of the engines, which, in her imagination, grew louder and more ominous with each passing moment.

Hoping to allay her mounting fears, she glanced around the plane.

Flight attendants walked up and down the aisle, helping passengers find their seats and stow their luggage. Other attendants were taking drink orders and passing out newspapers.

One of the attendants, a grandmotherly type with pretty gray hair and silver-rimmed glasses, stopped beside Kari to ask what she would like to drink. Kari requested orange juice, then wondered if she should have ordered something stronger.

She picked up the little leather bag, rummaged inside, and found a mini toothpaste tube, mouthwash, a comb and a shoehorn, a small package of tissues, earplugs, a sleep mask, an emery board, and moisturizer. Grunting softly, she closed it and put it aside.

A dull thud signaled that the boarding door had closed. Kari took a deep breath. This was it. There was movement as the plane taxied to the runway to await its clearance for takeoff.

Kari looked up as one of the flight attendants welcomed the passengers aboard. She stated their flight number and destination, no doubt to give anyone who had somehow gotten on the wrong plane a heads-up. In a bright, cheerful voice, she advised the passengers to pay attention to the safety and emergency procedure film they were about to see.

Moments later, screens were lowered from the ceiling. Kari's heartbeat accelerated when the film began. Emergency exits were pointed out and the passengers were instructed that in the event the plane lost oxygen, oxygen masks would drop from overhead. She wasn't comforted by learning that the seat cushions could be used as flotation devices, or that life vests were located under the seats. She was feeling light-headed as instructions were given on the proper way to put on a life vest.

"Oh, Lord," she murmured. "I can't do this."

"Karinna, what is wrong?"

Startled by the sound of Rourke's voice, she looked up, expecting to see him standing beside her, but there was no one there. The man across the aisle looked at her and smiled.

"Karinna?"

Lowering her head, she whispered, "I've always been afraid to fly. I've never done it."

Again, his voice whispered in her mind. *"There is nothing to fear."*

"Easy for you to say," she thought. *"You're already dead."*

His laugh filled her mind. *"I will protect you."*

"You will, huh? Don't tell me you can fly, too."

"In a manner of speaking. If the plane should fall, I will catch you before we hit the ground."

"I'd like to know how you plan to manage that, seeing as how you're in the hold and I'm here."

"Trust me."

Kari blew out a breath. Maybe vampires were immune to sarcasm.

She swallowed hard as the captain's voice came over the PA. "Ladies and gentlemen, we have been cleared for takeoff. Flight attendants, please take your seats."

Kari grabbed the armrests and hung on for dear life as the engines revved up. She shuddered when the plane did, her knuckles going white as the plane picked up speed. Eyes squeezed tightly shut, she sent a hurried prayer to heaven that the plane wouldn't explode, that the pilot wouldn't make a mistake, that there were no crazed terrorists on board.

Startled to feel a hand squeezing hers, she opened her eyes. She was going mad, she thought. That was the only explanation for the sound of Rourke's voice in her head, the feel of his hand holding hers.

And suddenly she wasn't frightened anymore.

She glanced out the window as the plane gathered speed and lifted into the air, leaving her stomach somewhere on the ground. The plane made a long, slow curve, away from the airport. The ground seemed to be tilted sideways until the plane gradually leveled out.

Sometime later, the senior flight attendant's voice came over the PA. "Ladies and gentlemen," she said brightly, "the captain has now turned off the FASTEN SEAT BELT sign and you are free to move about the cabin. We do ask that while in your seats, you keep your seat belt loosely fastened. Thank you, and enjoy your flight."

Drinks were served again, and dinner menus were passed out. Kari ordered lasagna and a glass of soda.

After dinner, the lights were dimmed. Kari was too keyed up to sleep and opted to watch a movie.

It was hard to concentrate, though. She wondered what it was like for Rourke, riding in a coffin in the cargo hold. It was dark outside. Was he still awake? She wondered if he was having second thoughts about rescuing Ana Luisa, and if he would tell her he was a vampire. How would Ana Luisa react after he freed her from the painting, and how would he convince the girl to climb into his coffin?

She shook her head. With Rourke's preternatural powers, convincing the girl to do his bidding should be a cinch.

Yawning, Kari closed her eyes. She would just rest her eyes for a moment. . . .

In the cargo hold, Rourke knew the moment when she drifted off to sleep. Lifting the lid on the coffin, he sat up and stared into the darkness. In his day, he had been a simple man, accustomed to simple pleasures. This new world continued to astound him. Mankind had progressed in the most amazing ways. He supposed people had always dreamed of flying, but he had never expected that it would become a reality, or that he himself would actually take to the skies. He wondered how Aña Luisa would handle the changes the centuries had wrought in the world.

Only time would tell. Time, he thought, the stuff that human life and dreams were made of.

Kari felt like a seasoned, world-weary traveler by the time she reached Bucharest. She collected her luggage and made sure the coffin was loaded onto the hearse she had arranged for in advance. Rourke had told her to have the coffin delivered to the cemetery and he would take care of the rest.

Her rental car was waiting for her, and after getting detailed directions, she drove to the apartment she had rented. Thanks to a wrong turn, she had to stop and ask for directions again. By the time she checked in and unpacked, she was exhausted. Her internal clock told her it was still early, but it was almost nine-thirty P.M. Bucharest time.

She wondered where Rourke was, and if he intended to try to free Ana Luisa that night. In spite of his supernatural abilities, she couldn't help worrying that something might go wrong. What if he was caught stealing the painting? What if he couldn't free Ana Luisa? What if he freed her only to find that, after being frozen in a painting for three hundred years, the girl had gone stark raving mad?

She put the worrisome thoughts from her mind. Whatever happened now was out of her hands. Worrying wouldn't help.

She wandered around the apartment. It was small but comfortable, with a living room, tiny kitchen, tinier bathroom, and two bedrooms. The furnishings were quaint. She had booked the room for three days. She would have liked to stay longer, would have liked to see the sights while she was here, but it just didn't seem like a good idea to spend too much time in a foreign country with a vampire and a young woman whom she might or might not be able to communicate with.

Returning to the living room, she curled up on

the sofa, wondering if she dared go into the city alone at night. Back at home, she had searched the Web for information on Bucharest and learned that it was a cosmopolitan city with an active café society, elegant restaurants, historic churches and palaces, opera houses, antique shops and boutiques and shopping malls. As eager as she was to see all that, she remembered another Web site that had warned tourists to be careful and noted that Romania was one of the most corrupt nations in the world, with public, municipal, and political life supported by bribes. Of course, she had no way of knowing if that was true or not.

The same article also said that Romania's cities were among the safest in the world, with very little violent crime, as long as one avoided the "bad" areas and questionable clubs. The article went on to say that drugs were not tolerated and that users could expect to spend seven years in prison, while distributors could face life behind bars.

The article also warned visitors to be sure to take a cab from a reputable company. It went on to say that a common scam was for a cab to pick up a fare and then, a short time later, stop to help two men, one of whom would appear to be injured. After pulling over to pick up the two men, the cabby would assure the first passenger that he would take the injured man to the hospital only after delivering his paid fare to his destination first. Instead, it often turned out that it was the paid fare who would wind up in the hospital after the two men had robbed them. A further warning was for women to keep an eye on their handbags, and to avoid shoulder bags and backpacks, as there were those who made a habit of cutting the straps with razor blades and making off with the rest.

Rising, she went to the window and stared out into the darkness. She was still debating the wisdom of going out alone when Rourke appeared.

Kari pressed a hand to her heart when she turned away from the window and saw him standing there, looking as tall and gorgeous as always.

"I don't think I'll ever get used to your popping in and out like that," she muttered.

"I am sorry. I did not mean to frighten you."

Her gaze moved over him. "I see you made it through the X-ray machine all right."

He frowned. "X-ray?"

She nodded, wondering how to explain it, and then decided not to try. "So, what now?"

"Later tonight I will go to the museum that houses the painting and look around. Tomorrow night, I will free Ana Luisa and bring her here. Perhaps you can explain the new world to her. . . ."

"Oh, right, that should be a cinch!"

"Perhaps not as difficult as you expect."

Kari lifted her brows in an "oh, sure" gesture but said nothing. She wasn't looking forward to staying cooped up with a witch who had spent the last three hundred years trapped inside a painting!

"I am going for a walk through the city," Rourke said. "Would you like to come with me?"

Kari had been nervous about wandering around by herself, so she jumped at the chance to go exploring with Rourke. Grabbing a jacket and her handbag, she followed him out the door.

They walked in silence for a time. It was a lovely night, cool and clear, beneath a black velvet sky crowded with stars. Kari slid a glance at Rourke, wondering if he had dined on one of the residents of the city.

As though sensing her thoughts, he looked at her and smiled. His teeth were very white in the darkness. "I took only a little."

Kari felt her cheeks grow hot. It was disconcerting knowing he could read her thoughts. She looked up at him and frowned, remembering how she had heard his voice in her mind when she was on the plane.

"How did you do that?" she asked. "Talk to me when you were in the cargo hold?"

"I felt your fear and I simply spoke to your mind."

"But I felt your hand on mine." She shook her head. She could accept that he could read her thoughts. Many people claimed to be able to read minds. But to actually feel his hand on hers? "How did you do that?"

"I have many supernatural abilities. I have tasted your blood, and it has formed a mental bond between us."

Kari nodded, though she didn't really understand. The city was pretty by night. When they passed an old church, she glanced at Rourke, wondering if he could go inside or if he would go up in smoke if he crossed the threshold.

Her stomach growled when they passed a café.

Backtracking, she went inside and Rourke followed her. She ordered soup, a sandwich, and a cup of coffee. As usual, he ordered a glass of red wine.

It was pleasant sitting outside under the stars. Kari grinned inwardly. Never in a million years would she have expected to find herself in Romania with an actual vampire!

"I really wanted to see Bran Castle," Kari remarked when she finished eating, "but I won't have time now."

"It is a beautiful place."

"You've been there?"

He grinned. "Of course. How could I not go?"

"Right. You didn't know Vlad Dracula, did you?"

"I doubt that anyone really knew him. But I was acquainted with him."

Kari stared at him, awed and repulsed at the same time. "Are all those horrible stories about him true?"

"I cannot speak for all of them, but he was a harsh, cruel man to those he considered his enemies. That much is true. If you still wish to see the castle, I will take you there."

"Isn't it closed?"

He shrugged. "What are locks to me?"

"But . . ."

"Come." He took her hand and led her away from the lights of the city. "Hold on to me," he said. "And do not be afraid."

"What are you going to do?"

"Take you to the castle."

She looked at him suspiciously. "How are we going to get there?"

"You will see. Hold on now."

Before she could argue further, they were . . . she didn't know what they were doing. Sight and sound were lost to her and there was only a growing coldness and the sensation of moving rapidly through the night.

When the world slowed, they were standing in the castle courtyard. "How did you do that?" she gasped. "Wait . . . don't tell me. More vampire magic."

"Yes. Vampires are capable of moving faster than the human eye can follow. And now, here we are. You see that fountain, there?" he asked. "It conceals a labyrinth of tunnels."

"I suppose you've seen them, too?"

"Of course, but we will not go there."

"Good!"

Rourke worked a bit of vampire magic on the castle door and Kari found herself inside the citadel. Rourke found a candle to light their way. It was an amazing place, she thought, especially in the warm glow of candlelight.

She loved the arched ceilings in some of the rooms, the fairy-tale atmosphere that came from the mixture of Renaissance, Romance, and Gothic styles. She didn't know which room she liked the most. Queen Marie's bedroom was lovely, with its baroque rosewood bed. There were a desk and a couple of beautiful carved chairs, a long table covered in a tapestry, a vase of flowers, paintings on the walls. Then there was Queen Marie's library, with its paneled walls, dark floors, and comfortable-looking furniture. The shelves that lined the walls held plates, vases, and pitchers. She wasn't surprised to see a deer head and horns on the walls of the hunting trophies hall, or the bearskin rug on the floor. There was a council hall, a dining room decorated with large, dark furniture. The music room had carpets and another bearskin rug, a ceiling with dark wooden beams, comfortable-looking furniture, and a line of beautiful windows. All the rooms were lovely and beautifully decorated.

Outside again, they stood in the courtyard.

"Thank you for the tour," Kari said. "It was wonderful."

He inclined his head. "My pleasure."

"Do you suppose Dracula really stayed here?"

Rourke shrugged. "Who can say?"

Kari blew out a sigh, and then she grinned. "Well, there's a real vampire here now."

"Indeed." Rourke smiled at her, and then his gaze dropped to her throat, and the pulse beating there. An indrawn breath carried the fragrance of her hair and skin, the tantalizing scent of her life's blood. She was pure temptation wrapped in sweet mortal flesh. He clenched his hands into fists to keep from reaching for her when he wanted nothing more than to brush her hair away from her neck and drink and drink until he was filled with her warmth, her very essence.

As though sensing his thoughts, she took a step backward. Her next words confirmed that she did, indeed, know what he was thinking.

"I don't like that look in your eyes," she said in a shaky voice, and then her own eyes widened. "They're . . . are they glowing?"

Swearing softly, he turned his face away.

"Rourke? Are you all right? Rourke?"

When he had his hunger under control again, he met her gaze. "I want you," he said quietly. "I want all of you."

She took another step backward. "What does that mean? All of me?"

"What do you think it means?"

"I don't want to know." She crossed her arms under her breasts in a timeless gesture of self-defense. "I think we'd better go back to the apartment."

"Do you think you will be safer there?"

"Rourke, you're scaring me."

Unable to resist the way she looked in the moon-light, he moved slowly toward her, hating himself for his weakening control, for the fear that he smelled on her skin.

"Rourke." She stared up at him through fathomless blue eyes. "Don't. Please, don't."

"One kiss." He backed her against a low stone wall. He could hear the rapid beating of her heart, smell the crimson nectar that flowed through her veins, hot and sweet. "One taste."

"You won't stop at one," she said breathlessly. "I know you won't. Please, Rourke . . ."

His hands folded over her shoulders. Drawing her body against his, he took a deep breath. "I can smell your sweetness."

"Don't." She placed her palms against his chest to push him away, but it was like trying to move a mountain. "I'm afraid. . . ."

"One taste," he said again, and lowering his head, he nuzzled her neck, just below her ear.

Kari gasped as his tongue swept over her skin. She felt a familiar pressure, but no pain, and then there was only the same pleasurable warmth she had experienced before. Soul-deep, heart-stopping sensual pleasure.

She surrendered with a sigh, her arms sliding down to wrap around his waist. What had she been afraid of? He had taken her blood before; she hadn't been afraid then. But this time was different. Maybe it had been the eerie red glow in his eyes. Maybe it had been the way he said, "I want all of you." Or maybe it had been the look in his eyes when he said it.

But none of that mattered now.

Rourke groaned low in his throat. Sweet, so sweet. He had tasted the blood of hundreds of mortals, men and women alike, but none had soothed his hunger or satisfied his unearthly craving as did the woman in his arms. The heat of her body warmed his, the fragrance of her hair and skin aroused his desire, making him yearn to lay her down and bury himself deep within her.

With an effort of will, he drew back. He would have her, he thought. One night soon, he would have her. But this was not the time or the place.

Holding her close, he willed them back to the apartment.

Chapter 14

Kari tossed and turned all that night, her mind in turmoil. She was troubled by her growing affection for Rourke, frightened by the fact that his drinking her blood didn't disgust her more than it did, and even more upset by her growing curiosity about what it would be like to be a vampire. She was also worried about his plans to free Ana Luisa the next night, getting the girl back to the States with no one being the wiser, and what they were going to do with the wizard's daughter, assuming they were able to smuggle her out of Romania.

Kari wasn't sure why she was so worried about the girl. Rourke had managed to adapt to the twenty-first century pretty well; maybe she was worrying about the girl's ability to adjust to her new surroundings for nothing.

And maybe, if she was honest with herself, she would admit that she was just plain jealous of the girl. Ana Luisa was young, she was beautiful, she had been intimate with Rourke, and she was obviously infatuated with him.

With a shake of her head, Kari flopped over on her stomach and commanded herself to go to sleep.

It didn't work, of course.

Rolling onto her side, she stared into the unfamiliar darkness, wishing that she had never set foot in the Underwood Art Gallery and never seen that blasted painting. It had turned her whole life upside down. And now, like it or not, she was falling in love with a vampire. And how stupid was that? She didn't know what Rourke's plans were once they got back home, but somehow she couldn't picture the two of them settling down together in a cozy little vine-covered cottage.

She punched her fist into her pillow. It just wasn't fair!

She closed her eyes again and willed herself to sleep. She was drifting when, from out of nowhere, she found herself wondering how many other vampires were wandering around the countryside and since vampires were real, did that mean there were other mythical creatures like werewolves and zombies lurking in the shadows?

It was not a thought conducive to a good night's sleep.

Rourke wandered aimlessly through the night. He had found the museum where Ana Luisa's painting was housed without any trouble. In spite of the rigid security that protected the building, he hadn't had any trouble getting inside. He had stayed only long enough to locate the painting and determine the night watchman's routine.

And now he roamed the darkness, remembering the years he had spent in this city. Though many of the buildings remained, life as he had known it no longer existed. Filled with bittersweet memories, he found himself wondering how long it would take him to feel at ease in this century.

And what of Ana Luisa? What was he to do with her? It would probably be wiser to leave her where she was. Vilnius would know the moment the spell binding his daughter had been broken. Would he also know who had freed her? Would Vilnius come looking for her? Rourke had no desire to confront the wizard a second time, yet, in spite of that, he couldn't leave Ana to her fate, not when he could help her, even when it might mean putting Karinna's life in danger, as well.

Muttering an oath, he stalked the dark streets, inwardly cursing the streak of innate gallantry that refused to let him abandon the wizard's daughter to her fate. Though he hadn't prayed in years, he prayed that he would be strong enough to protect Ana Luisa and Karinna from the wizard's wrath, that he would emerge victorious if he and Vilnius faced each other again.

Kari spent the following day sightseeing. Overwhelmed by the intricate beauty of the ancient buildings, she found herself stopping time and again to admire one edifice after another. She bought a few souvenirs for herself, as well as a delicate teapot and six matching cups for her mother. She also picked up a Dracula shot glass for Mel, a bloodred scarf for Tricia, and numerous postcards of different landmarks, because she'd left her camera in her suitcase.

She browsed a few more gift shops, then ate lunch at a quaint sidewalk café, where she spent an hour sipping coffee and people watching. And all the while, she wondered where Rourke was spending the day.

She took a long walk, went to a movie with English subtitles, enjoyed a leisurely dinner, and then drove back to her apartment, her tension mounting with each passing moment.

Where was he? How long would he wait before he freed Ana Luisa from the painting? Was he there, even now? What would the girl's reaction be when she realized that she had been imprisoned for three hundred years? Kari frowned. What if, after all the trouble they had gone to, Ana Luisa didn't want to leave Romania? Would Rourke agree to let her stay here, alone, or would he stay to look after her?

Kari sighed. If he stayed here, her life would quickly go back to normal, as in incredibly boring and mundane, she thought ruefully. Still, it might be for the best.

Sitting by the window, Kari tried to read one of the paperbacks she had brought with her, but she couldn't concentrate on the words, could only sit there, waiting and wondering when Rourke and the wizard's daughter would arrive.

She stretched her arms and back, moved her head from side to side, then settled back in the chair again. She had never known the hours and minutes to pass so slowly. Time and again she glanced at her watch, willing the hands to move faster. She hated waiting. Why hadn't she insisted that Rourke take her with him? At least then she would know what was going on instead of sitting here waiting and wondering.

What would she do if something happened to Rourke? In spite of the complications he had brought into her life, she could no longer imagine her life without him. Yet she had no idea if he intended to stay with her once he freed Ana Luisa. For all she knew, he had plans of his own that he hadn't seen fit to share with her.

Thrusting the thought aside, she tried to concentrate on the book in her hands. She even tried reading it aloud, but it didn't help. She couldn't think of anything but Rourke and the wizard's daughter.

Rourke paced the shadows listening to the footsteps of the night watchman as he made his way from one end of the museum to the other. He had no trouble tracking the man's whereabouts.

Pausing near the back entrance, he wondered idly what it was like to be an old man, to endure the aches and pains of age, to have one's health and vigor slowly slip away. He could no longer remember what it had been like to be mortal, to be subject to physical ailments, or to endure injuries that didn't heal almost immediately.

At midnight, the old man went down into the basement to have a bowl of soup and a cup of coffee. Moments later, Rourke slipped into the museum. He could have entered the building earlier. He could have hypnotized the watchman and sent him away. Now, making his way toward the wing where Ana Luisa's painting was displayed, he wondered why he hadn't done so. Was it because he was in no hurry to shoulder the responsibility for Ana, or because he didn't want to divide his time between Karinna and Ana? Or because, deep down, he knew that, in freeing the wizard's daughter, he would have to face the wizard again?

Muttering an oath, he turned a corner and entered the wing where Ana waited. He stared at the painting for a moment, thinking how lovely she was, remembering how a few drops of her blood had scorched his tongue. He moved closer to the painting. Was she aware of his presence, or was she deaf and blind to the world around her?

Taking a deep breath, he called her by name.

"Ana Luisa, come to me."

There was a sharp crack as the glass broke in two. Rourke stared in wonder as Ana fell to the floor at his feet, a lovely young woman clad in a flowing white gown.

He knew a sharp stab of fear as she lay there, unmoving, and then, with a shake of her head, she sat up.

She stared up at him for several seconds, her expression blank, and then she frowned. "Jason?" Her voice sounded dry, rusty with disuse. "Jason, is it really you?" she asked in Romanian. "Is the nightmare finally over?"

"Aye. Come, Ana," he said, answering in her native tongue, and taking her by the hand, he lifted her to her feet. "We must go, quickly."

She didn't argue, but when she tried to follow him, her legs gave way. With a little cry, she stumbled and fell.

Muttering an oath, he swept her into his arms and transported the two of them to the apartment where Karinna waited.

She was free.

The wizard's head snapped up as he felt the curse he had placed on his daughter's painting unravel.

Vilnius felt the glass that had encased the painting split in half as if it were his own soul, knew the moment his daughter took her first true breath in three hundred years, just as he knew that it was Rourke who had summoned Ana Luisa from her prison.

Vilnius swore a vile oath, cursing the vampire for meddling in his affairs even as he vowed to avenge himself anew on the creature who had defiled his daughter. There would be no escape from his vengeance this time, not for his daughter, not for the vampire, and not for the puny mortal female who had called Rourke forth from his prison. The vampire was a creature to be reckoned with, Vilnius mused, and more powerful than he had suspected, else he would not have been able to move about within the painting. In so doing, he had given life to the other creatures, as well.

Vilnius shook his head ruefully. He had placed the same curse on both paintings, had done so to give Ana a little taste of freedom within her prison, thinking she would use her witchcraft to bring her world to life. Instead, it had been the vampire who had gathered the strength to move.

He would not make such a foolish mistake again. He would not underestimate the vampire's power this time, or be swayed by his daughter's tears.

This time his punishment would be swift and ir-revocable.

Kari couldn't seem to stop staring at the wizard's daughter. Ana Luisa was, in a word, stunning. She had luminous green eyes, the longest eyelashes Kari had ever seen, and hair that fell over her creamy shoulders in waves of honey-gold silk. She wore a long white gown reminiscent of the kind women had worn in medieval times. The material clung to every voluptuous curve of her slender figure. She looked like some fairy-tale princess come to life.

When Rourke introduced them, Ana Luisa surprised them both by speaking to Kari in English.

"Where did you learn my language?" Kari asked.

"The guard in the museum. His son married an American woman. Every night, he listened to

English-language tapes so he could learn his daughter-in-law's native tongue. I practiced, too," she said with a note of pride. "It gave me something to do."

Kari nodded, glad that the girl spoke English. It would make everything much easier, especially since Rourke wouldn't be around to translate during the day. Kari was less enthusiastic about the way the girl looked at Rourke, her eyes filled with affection. Although Kari had no idea what Rourke's feelings for Ana Luisa were, it was obvious that the wizard's daughter was hopelessly smitten with the vampire. She looked at him, touched him, and spoke his name at every opportunity. Once, meeting Kari's gaze, Rourke smiled and shrugged, obviously amused by Ana Luisa's infatuation.

Kari was not amused, nor was she looking forward to having the girl staying at her house. And she intended to tell Rourke so the first chance she got.

They spent the rest of that night bringing Ana Luisa up to speed as best they could on life in the twenty-first century. Kari wasn't sure how much the girl actually understood, but Ana Luisa stared at Rourke, hanging on his every word, her expression rapt. Kari folded her hands in her lap to keep from slapping that silly, lovesick expression off the girl's face.

But there was something else bothering Kari even more, and that was Rourke's plan to get the wizard's daughter onboard the plane with no one being the wiser. A year ago, his plan would have been impossible due to layovers, the difference in time between the United States and Romania, and the need to show proper ID and passports every time they changed planes. But now, thanks to jets that went faster and farther on less fuel, it was possible to book a nonstop flight to just about anywhere in the world, which meant fewer stops and less chance of being discovered.

And if his plan didn't work . . . Kari shook her head. She had done her part. She had gotten him this far. The rest was up to him. If he and Ana Luisa got stuck in Romania, so be it. Whatever happened from here on out was Jason Rourke's problem, not hers.

It was after midnight when the wizard's daughter curled up on the sofa and went to sleep.

Kari yawned behind her hand. It had been a long day.

"You should go to bed," Rourke remarked.

"Yes, I think I will."

"I will meet you at the plane tomorrow night." His smile caressed her, making her toes curl inside her slippers. "Try not to worry."

"Right."

Rising, he moved toward her chair. Hands braced on the arms, he leaned toward her. "Sleep well, Karinna," he murmured, and then he kissed her.

With his mouth on hers, she could believe that everything would be all right.

Kari was a nervous wreck all the next day. After explaining what a shower was to Ana Luisa, and convincing the girl to give it a try, Kari got on the phone and made sure that the coffin would be delivered to the airport as previously arranged, hoping, all the while, that Rourke was safely inside.

Later, she took the girl out to breakfast. It seemed to Kari that everywhere they went, men turned to stare at Ana Luisa. Kari couldn't blame them. Even attired in a loose-fitting dress, the wizard's daughter was a knockout.

After breakfast, they went sightseeing for a few hours. Ana Luisa's expression seemed to change every few minutes. One minute she was smiling as she saw a building that was familiar, the next she was wide-eyed and frightened as a young man went speeding by on a motorcycle. She watched the people passing by, no doubt bemused by the current trends in hairstyles and fashion.

After stopping for lunch, Kari suggested they head back to the apartment so she could pack.

Ana Luisa had hardly spoken a word the entire day. Kari didn't know if it was because she was just shy or because she was so awed by the world she now found herself in, she couldn't find the words to express her feelings.

After making sure she hadn't left anything behind, Kari checked out of the apartment and they went out to dinner.

After ordering, Kari looked at Ana Luisa. Determined to make the best of things, she smiled and said, "I guess you must be overwhelmed by all this."

"Overwhelmed, yes," the girl replied. "It is all so . . . different. Have you known Jason very long?"

Kari blinked at her, surprised at the abrupt change of topic. "Not very."

"Are you in love with him?"

The girl was nothing if not direct, Kari thought. "Excuse me?"

"Jason. Do you have strong feelings for him?"

A number of answers flitted through Kari's mind, but she decided on the truth. "Yes, I do."

"Does he have feelings for you also?"

"I think so."

Ana Luisa pushed her plate away. "I am ready to go now."

With a sigh of exasperation, Kari finished her drink and signaled for the check.

The drive to the airport was made in chilly silence. Ana Luisa stared out the window, her hands folded in her lap.

Kari parked her rental car in the space provided, grabbed her luggage from the backseat, and walked briskly toward the terminal, not caring if Ana Luisa followed her or not.

Rourke was waiting for them outside the terminal when they arrived. Kari took him aside. "The coffin?" she asked. "Did you check to make sure it's onboard?"

"Yes," he said. "Do not worry."

She glanced at Ana Luisa. "What do you think she'll do when the plane takes off?"

"She will fall asleep as soon as you board," he said confidently, "and she will not awake until the plane lands."

Kari didn't doubt him for a minute.

What happened from that point on was like something out of a science-fiction movie. She didn't know what kind of vampire mojo Rourke exerted, but no one they passed en route to the plane paid any attention to him or to Ana Luisa. It was as if neither one of them existed.

Kari didn't know if it was luck or vampire magic, but the seat next to hers was vacant. Ana Luisa sat down, Rourke leaned over and whispered something in her ear, and in a heartbeat, she was asleep.

"Amazing," Kari murmured.

"Indeed," Rourke said with a smile, then vanished from her sight.

Kari's hands gripped the armrest as the plane taxied down the runway, then lifted off. She watched the earth fall away, gradually growing smaller and smaller until it disappeared beneath the cover of the clouds. It was an odd feeling to look out the window and see only thick white clouds and a bit of blue sky. She knew the earth was still down there, but she would have been happier if she could see it.

If she had her way, she would never fly again. She was tapping her foot restlessly, wishing the flight was over, when she heard Rourke's voice whisper in her mind.

"Relax, sweeting. You will soon be home."

"Not soon enough," she thought.

The faintly amused sound of his laughter made her smile.

"Are you all right?"

"I am quite comfortable."

She shook her head, thinking no one would believe any of this.

Again, the soft sound of his laughter filled her mind. *"I have complicated your life, haven't I?"*

"In ways you can't imagine," she muttered.

The soft sound of his laughter filled her mind again.

With a sigh, Kari stared out the window. The next thing she knew, the stewardess was shaking her awake.

It was a little after noon when their flight landed. Ana Luisa woke as soon as the plane came to a halt. Again, no one paid any attention to the girl when they left the plane or when they moved through the airport. Kari picked up her luggage and loaded it into Mel's hearse, then opened the passenger door for Ana Luisa.

"Get in," Kari said.

Ana Luisa climbed into the vehicle as if it might swallow her whole.

Kari grinned inwardly. Ana Luisa didn't say a word when Kari showed her how to fasten the seat belt, or when Kari closed the door, but all the color drained out of the girl's face when Kari put the hearse in gear and pulled out of the parking structure.

Kari's next stop was to pick up the coffin.

Ana Luisa frowned as two attendants slid the coffin into the back of the hearse. "Who is in there?" she asked.

"An acquaintance," Kari replied, and left it at that. Rourke had told her that Ana Luisa didn't know that he was a vampire. As far as she was concerned, when the time came, he could tell the girl the truth and handle the aftermath, whatever that might be.

"Where is Rourke?" Ana Luisa asked. She glanced around, obviously looking for him.

"He'll join us later."

"But . . ."

"I can't explain it now," Kari said. "Don't worry. He's going to meet us at my house."

Kari was grateful for Ana Luisa's silence on the drive home. The last few days had left her feeling utterly exhausted. She couldn't wait to get home, to sleep in her own bed.

Kari let out a sigh when she pulled into the driveway. After stepping out of the hearse, she gathered her luggage and carried it up to the front door, then went back and locked the hearse. Returning to the house, she opened the front door and stepped inside. After staying in the tiny apartment in Bucharest, her house seemed huge.

Ana Luisa followed Kari inside, her eyes alight with interest as she went, uninvited, from room to room. Kari trailed behind her, answering her questions, doing her best to explain what the various appliances were and how they worked.

In the bathroom, Kari showed Ana Luisa the tub and asked if she'd like to bathe.

"Is this like the shower?" the girl asked.

"Sort of, only you do it sitting down. Didn't you take baths in your time?"

"Not often," Ana replied as she studied the tub. "And never in anything like this."

"Well, people in my time usually bathe every day."

"What if I don't wish to bathe every day?"

Kari shrugged. "I guess that's up to you. You can take a shower, if you'd rather, although I think baths are more relaxing, but it's up to you."

"I should like to bathe," Ana Luisa decided.

Kari showed her how to turn the tap on and off, added a generous amount of jasmine-scented bubble bath to the running water, then showed the girl where the towels were. While the tub filled, Kari retrieved Ana Luisa's suitcase and then showed the girl to the guest bedroom.

"Make yourself at home," Kari said, then left the room.

After returning to the living room, Kari sank down onto the sofa, closed her eyes, and immediately had a mental image of Rourke resting outside in the coffin. It would be hours until the sun set. Tomorrow, she would have to return the hearse, then go to the market and stock up on groceries. She glanced at her watch, wondering if Ana Luisa was going to spend the night in the tub.

Another thirty minutes passed before Ana Luisa emerged from the bathroom wearing the nightgown Kari had bought for her.

"I thought you'd drowned," Kari muttered under her breath.

Ana Luisa glanced around the room. "Where is Rourke? You said he would meet us here."

"I'm sure he'll be along in a while," Kari said. "Are you hungry?"

Ana Luisa nodded. "Yes."

"Well, there's no food in the house," Kari said,

"and I'm too tired to go out, so . . ." She reached for the phone and ordered spaghetti, garlic bread, a small pizza, and a salad from Pizza Joe's.

Joe's son delivered her order thirty minutes later.

Kari quickly set the table, then dished up the spaghetti. She left the pizza in the box, filled two bowls with salad and two glasses with milk, placed everything on the table, and then sat down across from Ana Luisa.

Ana Luisa regarded the food on her plate with open curiosity. After watching Kari pick up a slice of pizza, Ana Luisa did likewise. She chewed it slowly for a moment before declaring, "I like it! Can I have more?"

"Help yourself."

The girl had a little trouble winding the spaghetti around her fork. Kari couldn't remember if forks had been around three hundred years ago, but Ana Luisa got the hang of it after a few minutes and declared that spaghetti was her new favorite food.

Kari had just finished clearing the dishes when someone knocked at the door.

Kari opened it, surprised to find Rourke on the doorstep, since he usually just appeared in the house, and then she remembered that Ana Luisa was in the living room watching TV.

"Is everything all right?" he asked, glancing past her.

"Yes, we didn't have any trouble at all. You should be a magician."

He grinned faintly.

"Are you coming in?" she asked when he continued to stand on the porch.

"I must go out for a short time. I came only to make sure you had arrived safely."

Noting the faint red glow in his eyes, she said, "I guess you haven't eaten."

"No." His nostrils flared. "But you have. Pizza again. And spaghetti."

She grinned. "They're my favorites."

"Heavy on the garlic?" he said, grinning back at her.

"Sorry. Have you ever thought of . . . never mind."

"What?"

"Well, instead of going out and, uh, preying on the local population, have you ever thought of, well, getting blood from the Red Cross instead?"

He lifted one brow. "This Red Cross gives blood away?"

"Not exactly, but I saw this movie where a vampire survived on blood taken from a blood bank. And another program where the vampire survived on the blood of cattle."

Rourke grimaced. "'Tis obvious you have never been a vampire."

Kari made a face at him. "I guess neither idea appeals to you."

"No."

"Well, it was just a thought."

He caressed her cheek with the back of his hand. "You appeal to me. Will you be all right while I am gone?"

"I think I can survive without you for an hour or so," she said dryly.

His mouth quirked at one corner. "Will you not miss me even a little?"

She shook her head. "I'd say yes, but you've already got an ego the size of the Grand Canyon."

He laughed softly.

"Rourke, what are you going to do about Ana Luisa? I mean, she can't stay here with me indefinitely, you know."

He looked thoughtful for a moment, then said, "I will find her a coven. They will look after her."

Kari nodded, thinking that was probably the best thing to do.

"Thank you for your help," he murmured, and taking Karinna into his arms, he kissed her.

She swayed against him. The fate of the wizard's daughter faded away with the rest of the world as his lips claimed hers. She wondered briefly if all vampires kissed as well and as thoroughly as he did, and then she surrendered to the magic of his mouth on hers. His tongue was like a flame as it dueled with her own in a timeless dance of mating, making her yearn for more than kisses. His hands skimmed over her back, massaged her nape, delved into her hair, each touch a wish and a promise.

She was drowning in an endless sea of sensual pleasure when her tongue brushed his fangs. She drew back with a little cry of alarm.

He stared down at her, his eyes glowing with hunger and desire. "I should go," he said abruptly, then left her standing there battling a hunger of her own.

When her breathing returned to normal and her heart stopped pounding, Kari went into the kitchen, thinking a glass of ice water might cool her ardor. It eased her thirst but did nothing to quench the physical desire he had aroused in her. No other man had ever affected her the way Rourke did, she thought, and technically, he wasn't even a man. He was a vampire. She had to remember that, but somehow, with the taste of his kisses still on her lips, it didn't seem to matter.

"Was that Rourke?" Ana Luisa asked when Kari returned to the living room.

"Yes."

"I thought I heard his voice." Ana Luisa looked past Kari. "Where is he?"

"He had to go out for a little while," Kari replied. Taking a seat on the sofa, she curled one leg beneath her. "He should be back soon."

"Oh." Ana Luisa returned her attention to the TV for a few minutes, her expression one of disappointment.

Kari tried to concentrate on the program Ana Luisa was watching, but she kept glancing at the door, wondering when Rourke would return.

When the program ended, Ana Luisa yawned, then rose gracefully to her feet. "If you will excuse me, I should like to retire."

"Sure. Good night." Kari flipped through the channels until she found a movie she hadn't seen. She didn't know how long Rourke would be gone, but with each passing minute, it grew harder and harder to keep her eyes open. Trying to stay awake was a losing battle. The flight and the stress of the last few days were catching up with her.

Going into her room, Kari slipped on a T-shirt and her favorite pair of pajama bottoms, brushed her teeth, and fell into bed, wondering if she would ever be able to call her life her own again.

Rourke stalked the drifting shadows of the night, his hunger and his impatience growing as he searched for prey.

He had just turned down a dark street lined with older homes when he sensed a presence behind him. Whirling around, fangs bared, Rourke found himself face-to-face with another vampire. Startled, he could only stare. Except for Melina, he had not seen another vampire in centuries. Before Vilnius had cursed him, Rourke had wondered from time to time if he and Melina were the last of their kind. Obviously, they were not.

"Who are you?" the stranger demanded, his voice laced with arrogance. "And what are you doing in my territory?"

"Rourke," Jason replied coolly. "I was unaware that this territory had been spoken for."

"Yeah, well, now you know."

"You would do well to treat your elders with respect, fledgling," Rourke said, baring his fangs.

The other vampire reached out with his preternatural power, testing that of the stranger in his domain.

Rourke met it with a rush of his own force, grinned inwardly as the younger vampire realized, with something of a shock, that he was the weaker of the two. But he didn't back down.

"This is still my territory," the young vampire said belligerently.

"Only as long as you can keep it," Rourke retorted, annoyed by the younger man's surly attitude. "What is your name?"

"Ramon Vega."

"Are you the only other vampire in this area?"

"No, there are three others."

"Did you make them?"

"What if I did?"

In a movement so fast Vega never saw it coming, Rourke's hand closed around his throat. "I do not like your tone," he said coldly, "or your attitude. You will change both, or I will rip out your heart." His hand tightened around Vega's throat. "Do you understand me?"

Vega nodded. For the first time, there was a faint hint of fear in the vampire's eyes, along with a healthy dose of respect.

"How long have you been a vampire?" Rourke asked.

"Almost five years."

"And the ones you made?"

"I brought Maitland across three years ago. Nita about a year ago, and Jan last month."

"Where are they now?"

"Back at my place."

"Just so you know, I intend to stay here as long as it pleases me. Do you have a problem with that?"

"No, man. Hell, stay as long as you like."

With a nod, Rourke released his hold on the other vampire. "I do not want to see you again."

Vega rubbed his throat. "Don't worry, you won't," he said, and melted into the shadows.

Rourke stared after him, wondering if the vampire had meant his parting words as assurance or threat.

With a shake of his head, Rourke continued on down the street, drawn by the scent of prey.

Chapter 15

Ana Luisa stared up at the ceiling, her thoughts muddled. She was happy to be out from under her father's curse, delighted to be free again, thrilled to see Jason again. At the same time, she was frightened by a world that was totally foreign to her. Thus far, save for a few buildings in Bucharest, she had seen nothing that was remotely familiar. But then, after three hundred years, she supposed that was to be expected. Life went on, people changed, the world changed. It bothered her that she recalled so little of her past life. Would her memories return, in time, or had they been lost forever, wiped out in the void of the last three centuries?

So many changes . . .

Earlier, she had followed the woman, Karinna, from room to room, her mind spinning as she tried to understand what she was seeing. So many new things to learn. A big white box that kept food cold on one side, yet kept things frozen solid on the other. She liked the box with pictures that moved and talked, although she didn't comprehend most of what she saw or heard. There was another square box that washed and dried the woman's dishes, and other boxes that washed and dried her clothes. Truly incredible, as was the metal box that Karinna had called a stove. It had flames in small rings on the top that were used for cooking, as well as an oven that lit itself, making it unnecessary to haul wood into the house. A most amazing thing! Even more astonishing was a rectangular box that heated food in moments and cooked a meal in minutes. In the room Karinna called the bathroom, there was a small round bowl where one relieved oneself, and then, with the push of a lever, it swept everything away. Truly a kind of modern magic, she thought. Imagine, no smelly chamber pots that had to be emptied every morning. There was even special paper to use to wipe oneself. It was all so new, so different from the life she had once known. She wondered if she would ever get used to the world in which she now found herself. It occurred to her that she was trapped here, just as surely as she had been trapped in her father's painting. Only there was no escape now. Like it or not, this was her new home. She had to admit, there were things she liked. Bathing, for instance, was most pleasurable.

She turned over onto her side, thinking how nice and soft the bed was. The sheets smelled of springtime, the blankets were warm, the pillow was downy soft.

Unable to sleep, she got out of bed and tiptoed into the kitchen. She opened the cold box, pulled out a carton of milk, then poured herself a glass. She had never tasted milk like this, nor any that was so cold. She drank it all and wondered if she dared have any more, and then she frowned. Where did the milk come from? And the meat? She hadn't seen any pigs or chickens or cattle or goats.

With a sigh, she put the glass into the sink and went back to bed, marveling at the plush carpet beneath her bare feet. Snuggled under the covers once again, she thought of Jason, remembered the few nights they had shared, the way he had made her feel, as if she were the most beautiful, intelligent woman in the whole world when, in truth, she had been nothing but a foolish child who had never ventured out of the village where she had been born. In Jason's arms, she had been unafraid of the future and of her father. In Jason's arms, anything had been possible until her father found them. She would never forgive Vilnius for the way he had treated her, for what he had done. He had claimed he loved her, but what kind of father magicked his daughter into a painting and left her there for three hundred years? No, she would never understand him or forgive him.

She huddled deeper into the covers. Her father would already know that the spell had been broken. Would he come looking for her? Her magick could not stand against his. Her anger and indignation, even when fueled by three hundred years of captivity, would be no match for his wrath. There was no one to stand between her and her father's fury save for Jason. He hadn't been able to protect her last time, yet he was her only hope of salvation. She had no one else to turn to.

The thought hit her with stunning force as, for the first time, it occurred to her that everyone she had ever known save for Rourke and her father had turned to dust long ago. A wave of loneliness washed over her with the realization that her childhood friends, the sweet lady who had raised her after her mother passed away, the young boy who had delivered wood to their home, the village seamstress, the town crier, the men and women who had peddled their wares in the town square were all gone.

There was no one to help her but Jason. Where was he now? Karinna had said he would be back soon, but he had not yet returned. Was he avoiding her? A single tear slid down her cheek. He was the only constant left in her life, all that was familiar in this strange new world. Without him, she would be utterly lost.

And what of her father? Where was he now? Thinking of him made her shiver. If she had to face her father's wrath again, she wanted Jason Rourke to be there beside her.

Chapter 16

Kari slept until late afternoon. Rising, she padded barefoot into the bathroom, and took a long hot shower. Then, wrapped in a fluffy white robe, she went downstairs and put on a pot of coffee. When it was done, she sat at the table and sipped it slowly, grateful, for the moment, to have nothing to worry about.

After a time, she went into her office and booted up her computer. She went through her e-mail, replying to some, deleting others. Even with a spam filter, it was amazing how much junk she received. When she finished reading her e-mail, she began searching for a coven. She didn't think it was a good idea to contact the witch she had e-mailed before since neither Rourke nor Ana Luisa wanted Vilnius to know where his daughter was staying, and Kari heartily agreed with their decision. If there was one thing she definitely didn't want, it was an angry wizard showing up on her doorstep. She had no desire to find herself trapped in a canvas prison for three hundred years!

It took only a few minutes to find a coven located in Oak Bluff, which was about twenty miles away. Kari sent an e-mail to the contact address, informing them that she knew of a young witch who needed a place to stay, as well as instruction about life in the twenty-first century. Taking a deep breath, she hit SEND. All they could do now was wait.

After signing off the Internet, she played several hands of Scorpion. If there was a trick to winning the card game, she hadn't found it yet. Out of 386 games played, she had won only thirty-six. Not a very good record. After quickly losing four games in a row, she went into the kitchen for another cup of coffee.

Standing at the sink, Kari glanced upward wondering if Ana Luisa was awake yet, and what she was going to do with the girl come Monday morning. Leaving her home alone didn't seem like a very smart thing to do.

When she finished her coffee, Kari rinsed the cup and put it in the dishwasher and then went upstairs to get dressed. After combing her hair and brushing her teeth, she went to look in on the wizard's daughter, who was sitting up in bed, looking lovely and lost.

Kari went into her own bedroom, then returned a few minutes later with one of her dresses and a pair of panties. The dress she had bought for Ana Luisa to wear on the plane had been too large. She wasn't sure her own dress would fit the girl, she was such a tiny thing.

"Here," Kari said, dropping the clothing on the foot of the bed. "Why don't you get dressed while I fix us something to eat?"

Ana Luisa nodded. "Thank you. I am most grateful for your kindness."

Kari waved her hand in a dismissive gesture. "I'm glad to be able to help," she said, though taking care of Rourke and the wizard's daughter was turning out to be more of an expense than she had anticipated. After breakfast, she would have to take Ana Luisa to the mall and buy the girl some more clothes, underwear, and shoes. And then she needed to return the hearse, go to the market and stock up on groceries, pick up her dry cleaning, and fill her car with gas.

"Where is Rourke?" Ana Luisa asked. "You said he would meet us here."

Kari folded her arms across her chest. "I'm sure he'll be along later."

"Are you?"

"I can almost guarantee it," Kari said reassuringly.

The girl nodded but she didn't look convinced.

After a late breakfast, they went to the mall. Ana Luisa proved to have very expensive taste in both clothing and shoes, but the girl took such delight in her new attire that Kari didn't have the heart to ask her to pick out items that were less expensive. Besides, the girl had spent three hundred years wearing the same dress. It wouldn't hurt to let Ana Luisa splurge a little.

When they left the mall, Ana was wearing a black ankle-length skirt, a black short-sleeved sweater over a white tank top, and a pair of white sandals.

They stopped for lunch at Kari's favorite restaurant, where Kari introduced Ana to a triple-decker ham and cheese sandwich and a chocolate malt, both of which the girl polished off in record time.

After leaving the restaurant, Kari picked up her cleaning, then stopped at the gas station. She glanced at Ana Luisa from time to time wondering what the girl was thinking.

It was near dusk when Kari pulled into the supermarket parking lot. Shopping with the wizard's daughter was an adventure all its own. The girl followed her up and down the aisles, though she stopped frequently to examine whatever item caught her eye: a bottle of blue mouthwash, a stuffed animal, a Mylar balloon. Kari spent so much time explaining what each item was, she didn't think she would ever get her shopping done.

Ana marveled at the variety of fresh fruits and vegetables that were available. She popped a grape into her mouth, took a bite out of a carrot. She was reaching for a pear when Kari grabbed her hand.

"You can't sample the food," Kari said.

"But how am I to know if I like it?" Ana asked with perfect logic.

Kari could only shake her head as Ana ran her hands over a head of lettuce, a watermelon, a cantaloupe, a coconut.

In the bread aisle, Ana picked up one loaf after another, unable to believe that bread came baked, sliced, and wrapped in plastic. "This one is not done," she said, picking up a loaf of white bread.

Kari couldn't help smiling as she realized that Ana had probably never seen anything in her life except whole-wheat bread.

Moving on, the girl picked up boxes of cereal and cans of vegetables, stared in awe at the frozen-food section, shook her head in wonder as she picked up a carton of eggs. She stopped in front of the dairy section, frowning at the rows of milk contained in plastic bottles.

"But where are the cows?" Ana Luisa asked with a frown. "I have not seen any cows. Or sheep, or goats. Or chickens." She shook her head. "If you do not keep cows or chickens, where do the milk and eggs and butter come from? I have not seen any fields of wheat or corn, either. How do you have bread without wheat?"

Kari was doing her best to explain how bread and milk and other dairy items were delivered to various markets all over the country when she felt a familiar shift in the atmosphere. Moments later, Rourke rounded the end of the aisle. It took but one look to see that he had fed, and fed well.

Kari glanced at her watch. "You're up early," she remarked, keeping her voice low so Ana Luisa wouldn't hear.

"I was missing you."

His words, softly spoken, sent a pleasant tingle down her spine.

"Jason!" Ana Luisa hurried toward him, a radiant smile spreading over her face as she threw herself into his arms.

"Ana." He gave her a hug.

"Where have you been?" Ana Luisa asked, a note of censure in her voice.

"I had some things to take care of," he replied evasively. "You are looking well."

She beamed at him. "Thank you." She grabbed his hand. "This is the most remarkable place," she said, dragging him toward one of the counters. "Have you ever seen so much food in your life?"

"No." Glancing at Karinna over the top of Ana's head, he lifted one shoulder in a shrug that said, "What can I do?"

Kari had a few thoughts on the subject but wisely kept them to herself. She watched Rourke and the wizard's daughter indulgently as they went from aisle to aisle, wondering how she would ever get the two of them out of the store.

Although Rourke couldn't eat mortal food, he seemed as curious about the market and its contents as was Ana Luisa. The two of them trailed after Karinna, their heads together as they examined whole chickens, spareribs, fish, and hamburger in the meat department, exclaiming over the way the various items were packaged.

Rourke picked up a package containing a whole chicken, his nose wrinkling with distaste. "How long has this been dead?"

"I don't know," Kari said with a shrug. "Why?"

"It stinks."

"It does?"

He glanced at the package, then at Kari. "I thought mortals did not drink blood."

"We don't."

He lifted a package of steak. "There is blood in here."

Kari glanced at the juice in the bottom of the container. "We don't drink that," she said, thinking she would never look at meat the same way again.

Even though Kari had already visited the produce department, Ana Luisa dragged Rourke over that way, eager to show him the fresh fruits and vegetables.

Rourke had little interest in the food itself, but, like Ana, he was fascinated by the wide variety of produce that was available.

"So many choices," he mused, studying the items in Karinna's cart. So many things he had never heard of. He ran his fingertips over the edge of the metal shopping cart, the side of a box that held milk, the plastic wrap on a package of pork chops. His nostrils filled with a multitude of aromas, not all of them pleasant. Some he recognized from having smelled them in Karinna's house; others were completely foreign to him.

Ana Luisa picked up an orange and began peeling it before Kari could stop her.

"No samples, remember!" Kari exclaimed. "I have to pay for these things before you can eat them."

"But I am hungry now," Ana said, popping a segment of orange into her mouth.

"I still have to pay for it," Kari insisted. Plucking the orange from the girl's hand, she dropped it in a plastic sack and added it to the items in the cart.

Ana Luisa looked at Rourke. "There is enough food in this place to feed our village for over a year."

Rourke nodded. In his day, people had raised their own food. True, on occasion they had traded goods with their neighbors, and sometimes, in the summer, an entire village might get together to swap goods. But there had been no markets like this, nor such an abundance of produce. If their crops failed, people went hungry.

He watched Karinna as she bagged and weighed the fruits and vegetables she wanted and added them to her cart. He never tired of watching her, knew he could spend hours admiring the gentle sway of her hips, the way her hair fell over her shoulders, the pink in her cheeks, the soft glow in her eyes.

He followed her to the checkout counter, waited with Ana Luisa while Karinna paid for her purchases. He grunted softly as it occurred to him that he was going to have to find a way to earn some money to support Ana Luisa. He couldn't keep expecting Karinna to pay for the girl's food and clothing, though he had no idea what he could do in this day and age to earn a living.

Outside, he helped Karinna load the groceries into the back of her car. Ana stood nearby, looking lost and ill at ease as numerous cars and trucks pulled into and out of the parking lot. He would have to be patient with her, he mused. It was obvious she knew less about this new world than he did.

When the groceries were loaded and Ana was settled in the backseat, he plucked the keys from Karinna's hand and slid behind the wheel.

Kari couldn't keep from staring at him as he drove home, thinking how amazing it was that she knew a vampire and that he was nothing like the creatures she had read about in books or the emaciated, bloodthirsty monsters depicted in so many movies, or eluded to in myth and legend.

When they reached home, Ana Luisa went into the living room to watch TV. Ever the gentleman, Rourke carried the groceries into the house, then went to talk to the wizard's daughter.

Kari had just finished putting the groceries away when she realized she was no longer alone. She didn't have to turn around to know that Rourke was standing behind her.

"It bothers you," he said, "having her stay here."

Kari turned around to face him, her heart pounding a little faster at his nearness. "Not really, well, yes, maybe a little," she admitted with a shrug. "It's just that I'm used to living alone."

"Does that mean you want me to leave, as well?"

"No." Her cheeks warmed under his regard. "I like having you here."

"No more than I like being here." He took a step toward her, his presence seeming to fill the room.

"I found a coven not far from here. I e-mailed them and . . ." She gazed into his eyes and forgot what she was going to say next.

"Karinna?"

She shivered with delight at the sound of her name on his lips. "Where is Ana Luisa?"

"She is watching something called *Bewitched.*"

"Oh." In spite of Rourke's nearness, Kari had to smile at the thought of a real live witch watching Samantha's silly antics on TV. "What kind of magic does Ana do?" Kari asked, thinking she'd never seen the girl do anything remotely supernatural.

"Let us not think about her now."

A thrill of excitement shot through Kari's whole body when he reached for her, his arms sliding around her waist to draw her into his embrace. She went willingly, every fiber of her being yearning to be close to him, to feel his hands sliding over her skin, his mouth branding hers.

"I cannot be near you and not hold you." His voice caressed her; the look in his eyes made her stomach flutter with anticipation. "Or touch you." He cupped her cheek in one hand. "Or kiss you."

His gaze held hers as he slowly lowered his head and claimed her lips yet again.

With a sigh, she closed her eyes, giving herself over to the incomparable pleasure of his touch, the incredible sense of belonging that overwhelmed her whenever she was in his arms. She swayed against him, wanting to be closer, swallowed a gasp when she felt the evidence of his desire, although it wasn't completely unexpected. Still, she was glad her own desire was less obvious.

She lost track of time as he kissed her again and yet again, might have suggested they go to bed and be comfortable, if someone hadn't coughed softly to get their attention.

Peering around Rourke, Kari saw Ana Luisa standing inside the open doorway, her eyes shooting sparks of anger and jealousy.

Kari stared at the wizard's daughter uncertainly. She recalled Rourke telling her that he had seduced Ana Luisa. Did the girl have feelings for him in spite of what he had done? Rourke had also said Ana

Luisa had flirted shamelessly with him. She couldn't help thinking that, although Rourke seemed to have no deep feelings for Ana Luisa, the wizard's daughter, being young and impressionable, had read more into their relationship than was there.

She hated the fact that she felt guilty when there was no reason for it.

"Did you want something, Ana?" Rourke asked, his arms still holding Karinna close.

Ana Luisa stared at Rourke, her hurt a palpable thing, and then, with a harsh cry, she turned and ran out of the room.

Rourke swore softly, but he didn't let go of Karinna.

"Maybe you should go after her," Kari suggested.

"I would rather be here, with you."

His words pleased her more than they should have. She didn't want him to go, didn't want him looking after another woman, but Ana Luisa was very young. Not only that, but it was obvious she was in love with Rourke, or thought she was.

"You should go after her," Kari said again. "She's young and in a strange place, and you're the only person she knows." Kari took a deep breath before adding, "She needs you."

Rourke's gaze burned into hers. "What about your needs?"

Kari slipped out of his embrace and gave him a little push toward the living room. "I can wait. She needs you now."

Cupping her chin in his palm, Rourke kissed her gently, then left the room.

Feeling dazed by his kisses and confused by their relationship, Kari stared after him. She was sorely afraid she had fallen in love with him, and equally afraid it would only end in misery. After all, what kind of life could a mortal and a vampire have together? She was a day person; he lived by night. She would age and die; he had already lived for 767 years, with no end in sight. She liked eating food and getting a tan in the summer and taking early morning walks, none of which they could enjoy doing together.

With a sigh, she went into her office and booted up her computer, determined to get a little work done. Work, she thought. How was she going to go back to work on Monday and leave Ana Luisa in the house alone? Maybe she should take another week off. She stared at the blinking cursor, but it wasn't work on her mind. Instead, she found herself wondering what Rourke was saying to the wizard's daughter.

Chapter 17

Rourke found Ana Luisa sitting on the sofa in the living room. To his dismay, she was crying softly. Feeling like the worst kind of cad, he sat beside her and gathered her into his arms. She didn't protest, merely laid her cheek against his chest and sobbed all the harder. Karinna was right. Ana was young, so young. He couldn't turn his back on her now when she had no one else to turn to, no where else to go.

"Ana Luisa . . ."

"I thought you loved me."

"I never said that."

"But I thought . . . we made love."

"It was wrong. I took advantage of you, and I am sorry."

She sniffed. "If you do not love me, why did you come after me? Why did you bring me here?"

"Would you rather I had left you where you were?"

"No." Moving out of his arms, she wiped her tears away with her fingertips.

"I know how you're feeling," Rourke said gently.

"Everything is strange here, but I promise you that, in time, you will come to like it."

"I do not know anyone but you." She made a vague gesture with one hand. "And Karinna."

"I am working on it."

She looked up at him, her expression puzzled. "Working on what? I do not understand."

Rourke grinned. He had only been here a few weeks and he was already picking up the local slang. "Do not worry, Ana Luisa. Everything will work out," he said, and hoped he was telling the truth.

After Rourke left the room, Ana Luisa stared at the moving images on the strange rectangular box called a TV. Karinna had tried to explain the moving images to her, saying that some of the things she saw on the box were like plays and some, like news programs, were events actually happening around the world while she watched. It was all so confusing. She hadn't been happy trapped in that horrid painting, but she wasn't any happier here, in this strange place and time. She didn't belong in this new world, and she never would.

She wondered where her father was. He would know that she had been freed from the prison he had made. Was he looking for her, even now? What would he do to her, to Jason, if he found them together? She shuddered at the thought of facing her father's wrath again, and yet, who else could she turn to now that Jason no longer wanted her?

Rising, she made her way to the front door, then

hesitated with her hand on the doorknob. Was she being foolish to go outside alone? With a shake of her head, she squared her shoulders and opened the door. Even though she hadn't practiced her craft in centuries, she was still a witch. She could take care of herself.

After leaving the house, she turned left at the edge of the yard and continued walking. It was a lovely night, cool and clear. There was no manure in the road; the air didn't stink of sheep and goats.

She passed one house after another, thinking how nice and clean everything was. Sometimes she could see people through the windows. Grass grew in neat, well-tended plots. There were beds of flowers, and trees in all shapes and sizes. How different life was here, in this place, from what she was used to. There were no fields here, no sheep, no cows, no horses or goats or chickens, only dogs that barked at her as she passed by.

Those strange moving vehicles called cars moved past her from time to time. Riding in one had frightened her more than she had let Jason or Karinna know. The noise, the sense of having no control over the metal monster, the peculiar smell. Given her druthers, she would rather ride a horse.

Lost in thought, she paid little attention to her surroundings until she found herself on a dark street. There were no houses here, only buildings with broken windows and sagging doors. A shiver of fear ran down her spine. Though she was not familiar with this time or place, she knew that she was in danger here. Why had she been so foolish as to venture out at night, alone?

Chiding herself for her stupidity, she turned on her heel and quickly started back the other way. She glanced over her shoulder time and again, discomfited by the horrible sensation that she was being watched. A gasp escaped her lips when she ran into something. Something that reached out to steady her.

Something that turned out to be a stocky young man with short sandy-colored hair and shaggy brows.

He studied her through pale hazel eyes, and then a slow smile spread over his face. "Well, well," he drawled, "what do we have here?"

Ana Luisa took a step backward. Her first instinct was to run, but something told her that would be a very bad idea. Squaring her shoulders, she murmured, "Excuse me," and walked past him with her head held high.

His laughter rang in her ears like the tolling of a death knell, sending shivers of dread down her spine.

She ran then, like a frightened rabbit fleeing from a hungry fox, but it was no use. There was no place to go, no place to hide.

He caught her quickly, his hand closing around her forearm in a grip like iron. "Here, now, little lady, not so fast."

"Unhand me, sir!" she cried, trying to wrest her arm from his grasp.

"Sir?" He arched a brow at her. "I like the sound of that."

"Please, let me go."

"Not until I know your name."

"Ana Luisa. May I go now?"

"Oh, I don't think so. Not until you've paid the toll."

"What is that?" she asked suspiciously.

"A kiss and a taste."

"A taste of what?"

He smiled at her. Even in the darkness, she could see the milk-white gleam of his fangs. She tried to summon her magic, but her mind went blank as fear's icy hand coiled around her insides.

"I don't want to hurt you," he said, tightening his hold on her arm, "but I will if I have to."

"Let me go!" she shrieked, then cried out in pain when he backhanded her across the mouth. When she licked her lower lip, she tasted blood.

"Here now," a deep voice demanded. "What's going on?"

Ana Luisa looked toward the newcomer, silently pleading for help. She stumbled backward as her captor abruptly turned her loose.

"Are you all right, lady?" the newcomer asked.

She nodded, her gaze moving from one man to the other. The newcomer had tawny skin, dark brown hair, and deep brown eyes.

"Maitland," the dark-haired man said, "get the hell out of here."

Maitland's eyes glinted with resentment, but he did as he was told.

Ana Luisa shook her head. One minute the man known as Maitland had been standing in front of her, the next he was gone as if he had never been there. How was it possible? Had she imagined him?

"I'm sorry about that," the newcomer said. "Are you sure you're all right?"

Ana Luisa nodded. She couldn't stop staring at him, could scarcely resist the temptation to reach out and touch him. Until tonight, she would have said that Jason Rourke was the handsomest man she had ever seen, but there was something about this man. . . . She frowned. Even though Jason and the stranger looked nothing alike, they seemed very similar, though she couldn't say why.

"I'm Ramon Vega," the newcomer said with a wink. "But you can call me anything you like."

She looked at him but didn't say anything.

"Come, chica," he said, offering her his hand. "I'll walk you home."

Ana Luisa stared at him uncertainly, torn by the need to be cautious and the desire to throw herself into his arms. It was a most peculiar sensation.

Vega let his arm fall to his side. "Hey, I'm not going to hurt you."

"That man, Maitland," Ana Luisa stammered. "He had fangs, like a vampire."

"Yes, but you're safe now."

She blinked at him. "Are you saying he *was* a vampire?"

"Yes, but he won't hurt you."

"Why did he obey you?"

Vega shrugged. "Because he's my offspring."

Ana shook her head. The two men had looked to

be about the same age. "That is not possible! You cannot be more than a year or two older than he is."

"Do you want me to call him back, chica?"

"No! What does chica mean?"

"It means girl or young woman. Come on," he said, offering her his hand once more. "Let me take you home."

Ana Luisa placed her hand in his, only then realizing she had no idea how to find her way back to Karinna's house.

"What's wrong?" Vega asked.

Blinking back useless tears, she said, "I fear I am lost."

Kari looked up from her computer when Rourke entered the room. "So, how'd it go?"

"I tried to explain, but . . ." He shrugged. "I thought she might want to be alone for a while, so I went out."

Kari nodded. She could easily imagine how it went. It was never easy to tell someone that their love was unrequited. "Where is she now?"

"I thought she might be in here, with you."

"No, I haven't seen her."

Frowning, Rourke left the room.

He returned moments later, his expression grim. "She is nowhere in the house."

"You don't think she'd go out alone, do you?" Kari asked. "I mean, she doesn't know her way around."

"Where else could she be?"

"I don't know," Kari said, rising. "But we'd better

go look for her. It's not safe for her to be wandering the streets alone."

"I will go," Rourke said. "You should stay here in case she returns."

"All right."

Rourke pulled her into his arms. "I have complicated your life, haven't I?"

"Gee, you think?"

He frowned. "Did I not just say so?"

"I was being sarcastic," Kari said, grinning. He had complicated her life in ways she never would have thought possible, invaded her thoughts by day and her dreams by night. Her gaze lingered on his lips. It hadn't been all bad, she thought. "Don't worry about it," she said. "I'm getting used to having you around."

A slow smile spread over his face. "I am glad it was you who freed me."

"Me, too." She took a deep breath. "You'd better go."

With a nod, he kissed her quickly, then vanished from her sight.

Outside, Rourke took a deep breath, his vampire senses sifting through the myriad scents and smells that lingered in the air in front of Karinna's house until he detected a whiff of Ana Luisa's unique scent.

Moving quickly through the darkness, he reflected on the twists and turns his life had taken since Karinna had called him out of his prison. She had restored his freedom, given him a place to rest, renewed his faith in humanity. Reuniting with Ana Luisa had added a new complication to his existence.

The reality of having her in the house was something he hadn't thought all the way through. He had not realized that she thought he loved her, or that she was in love with him. He had thought her infatuated with him, perhaps. After all, vampires were notorious for their supernatural allure. But love? He shook his head.

He slowed as he sensed Ana Luisa's presence. A snarl rose in his throat when Ramon Vega's scent also reached his nostrils.

Anger burned through him when he saw Ana Luisa with Vega. If the vampire had harmed her in any way, he would pay for it with his life.

Slowing, Rourke materialized in front of Vega and the wizard's daughter.

"Jason!" Ana Luisa exclaimed. "I am so glad to see you! I went for a walk, and I got lost. Ramon was helping me find my way home."

Rourke's gaze bored into Vega's. "Is that right?"

"Back off, man," Vega said. "I don't mean her any harm."

"Jason, what is wrong with you?" Ana Luisa asked, puzzled by his rude tone.

"I do not want you to have anything to do with this man."

"I will see whoever I wish," she retorted. "I do not need your approval or your permission."

"You need a keeper, is what you need," Rourke said. "Come, I will take you home."

Tears welled in her eyes. "I have no home."

Rourke swore under his breath. "Ana . . ."

"I want Ramon to come with me."

"No."

Ana Luisa lifted her chin defiantly. "Then I am not going."

Rourke took a deep, calming breath. "Stay away from him, Ana. He's no good for you."

"You do not even know him," she said defensively.

"I know he is a vampire."

Eyes wide, Ana Luisa looked up at Ramon. "Is that true?"

"Yeah, but what's the big deal?" Vega jerked his chin in Rourke's direction. "So's your friend."

"No." Ana Luisa looked at Rourke, her eyes wide with astonishment. "I do not believe it."

Rourke took a deep breath. He had always known this moment would come. "Ana . . ."

"Is it true, Jason? It is, isn't it?" When he remained silent, she demanded, "Answer me!"

Rourke glared at Vega, then looked back at Ana. "Yes, it is true," he said quietly.

Ana Luisa stared at him. How could she not have known? Had her father known? Was that why he had been so angry? She lifted a hand to her throat. "You bit me," she said. "When we made love, you bit me. I remember now."

"This is hardly the time or place to discuss such things," Rourke said curtly. "Let us go."

With a shake of her head, Ana Luisa backed away from him. "I am not going with you." Looking at Ramon, she added, "Or with you. Leave me alone, both of you."

"Stop acting like a child," Rourke said irritably.

"I shall do as I please!" she replied imperiously.

"Be gone!" A hint of supernatural power whispered through the air, then faded away.

Rourke looked at the other vampire, his animosity toward Vega swallowed up in his exasperation over Ana Luisa's behavior. It was fortunate for both of them that she hadn't practiced her craft in hundreds of years, even more fortunate that she lacked her wand to give her focus.

Vega shrugged. "I'll leave you to it," he said with a laconic grin, then vanished from sight.

Striving for patience, Rourke dragged a hand over his jaw, then said, quietly, "Can we go now?"

"You let me love you," she accused, her eyes bright with unshed tears. "You let me think you were mortal, a man. How could you do that?"

"Dammit, I said I was sorry. What did you expect me to do? Or have you forgotten how you flirted with me that night, how you begged me to make love to you?" He felt a rush of shame for blaming her. Most of what had happened that night had been his fault.

"But I did not know that you were a vampire!"

The tone of her voice, the revulsion in her eyes, flayed him like a lash. It shouldn't have bothered him. He knew what he was, he knew that what he had done to her was wrong. Her actions did not excuse his; still, her words burned like holy water.

"I am sorry for what happened between us," he said again.

A single tear dripped down her cheek. "I spent three hundred years trapped in a painting because of you. Everything I knew, everyone I loved, is gone," she said, her voice growing softer and more plaintive. "Everyone but you."

The last three words were barely audible, but Rourke heard them clearly.

With a sigh, he drew her into his arms, one hand lightly stroking her back. "I am sorry," he said again. "It was wrong of your father to punish you for what I did."

She sniffed, her arms slipping around his waist as her anger drained out of her. "I, too, am sorry," she said. "It was not all your fault."

"Karinna found a coven not far from here," Rourke said. "She wrote to ask if they would take you in."

Ana Luisa looked up at him, her eyes shimmering with unshed tears. "You are sending me away?"

"Just for a little while. They can help you adjust to life in this place, teach you to use your magick. Protect you from your father."

"But I want to stay here, with you."

"I know, but it isn't possible, not now. I do not want you to be alone during the day."

"Karinna . . ."

"She has to go back to work soon. And I cannot protect you when the sun is up."

"What if they do not want me?" she asked tremulously.

"We will not worry about that now," Rourke said, and taking Ana Luisa by the hand, he started walking back toward Karinna's house.

The beauty of the night surrounded him. It was good to be free, he mused, to feel the breeze on his face and the ground beneath his feet, to be able to come and go as he pleased. There was much to see and learn in this new land, but he had to admit that life in his painted world had been far less complicated.

Chapter 18

Kari sat at the kitchen table, a cup of hot chocolate cradled in her hands as she wondered if her life would ever return to normal. It wasn't bad enough that she had a vampire sleeping in the shed out in the backyard, now she had a witch staying in the guest room. And she had to be back at work on Monday. Not that she minded having Rourke here, she admitted. She cared for him far more than she should, knew that, in spite of everything, she was falling in love with him.

Love . . . Could she really be in love with a vampire? Just thinking about it made her feel hot and achy all over. Heck, she thought with a grin, maybe she was just coming down with a bad case of the flu!

She sighed, thinking that her life had turned into some kind of bizarre fairy tale filled with witches and wizards and one unbelievably sexy Undead guy.

Rourke and Ana Luisa had come home late last night. It was obvious that Ana had been crying. The girl had gone straight to bed without a word to either one of them.

When Kari had asked Rourke what had happened, he had simply shrugged and said Ana Luisa was having a hard time adjusting to her new life. Kari would likely have asked him a few more questions if he hadn't taken her into his arms. One kiss and she had forgotten everything else. They had made out on the sofa until it was almost dawn, and then, with one last kiss that had left her breathless, he had gone to seek his rest out in the shed.

Kari shook her head as she recalled the hours she had spent in his arms. If she could bottle whatever it was that the man had in such abundance, she could make a fortune!

She was trying to decide if she was hungry enough to make breakfast when Ana Luisa entered the room. Even sleep tousled and clad in a pair of Kari's pajama bottoms and a T-shirt, the girl was gorgeous. With her pouty pink lips and rosy cheeks, she looked like a fairy-tale princess awaiting love's first kiss.

"Good morning," Kari said, pasting a smile on her face.

Ana Luisa nodded at her, then sat down at the table, her expression bleak.

"Are you hungry?" Kari asked. "I was just thinking about making some French toast."

"I do not know what that is."

"Well, it's bread dipped in eggs and fried, I guess you'd say. It's very good with butter and syrup or jelly. And I think I've got some bacon."

"Thank you," Ana Luisa said politely.

Kari glanced at Ana surreptitiously as she busied herself preparing breakfast. It was easy to see that the wizard's daughter was unhappy. There were dark shadows under her eyes, as if she hadn't slept much. Kari supposed she couldn't blame the girl. She was pretty sure she would be just as depressed if she suddenly found herself in a time and place that was completely foreign to her.

A short time later, Kari placed two plates on the table. "I'm having coffee," she said, "but I've also got orange juice or grapefruit juice, or I can make you a cup of tea, if you prefer."

Ana Luisa shrugged. "It does not matter."

Since it didn't matter, Kari poured the girl a cup of coffee and then sat down. Wanting to spare the girl's feelings, Kari concentrated on her breakfast.

The kitchen was silent until Ana Luisa asked, "Are you in love with Jason?"

"I don't know," Kari said honestly, "but you are, aren't you?"

Using her fork, Ana Luisa drew lazy eights in the leftover syrup on her plate. "I thought I was, until last night."

"What happened last night?"

"I found out that he is a vampire. Did you know that?"

Kari nodded. She refused to feel guilty for not telling the girl the truth. If Rourke had wanted her to know, he would have told her. "He should have told you before," Kari said. "It was wrong of him to keep that a secret from you. But it was his secret to keep."

"Yes." Ana frowned. "Although I knew there was

something different about him. Now that I know the truth, I am not sure how I feel about him. Or about Ramon."

"Ramon?" Kari put her cup on the table and leaned forward. "Who the heck is Ramon?"

"Another vampire. I met him last night."

Kari stared at Ana Luisa, her mind whirling. Another vampire? Good grief, the city was crawling with them!

"When I found out that Ramon was like Rourke, I was upset and I sent Ramon away, but now . . ." She smiled a dreamy smile. "He is all I can think about."

Kari stared at the girl, speechless. One minute Ana Luisa was in love with Rourke, and the next she was mooning over a man—a vampire, no less— she had just met.

Ana Luisa dropped her fork on her plate and looked at Kari. "I wish I knew where to find him," she said plaintively.

"I'm sorry, but I'm afraid I can't help you there." Kari carried her dishes to the sink, rinsed them and put them in the dishwasher, then poured herself another cup of coffee before sitting down again. "Maybe Rourke could help you?"

Ana Luisa shook her head. "They do not like each other."

"That doesn't mean Rourke won't help you," Kari said. "After all, he cares about you and wants you to be happy."

"No. He wants to send me away."

"But only because he's worried about you," Kari insisted. "I can't stay here and look after you during the day, and neither can he. You need someone to help you find your way around, someone who . . . well, someone who's a witch, you know?" Kari shook her head in exasperation. "I'm not saying this very well. And you won't have to stay with them if you don't like it there. There's a lot to learn about life here, you know. Like how to drive a car, and how and where to shop for things you need, and how to use our currency. . . . It just seemed like it would be easier if you stayed with someone who can help you find your way around. Do you know what I mean?"

"Yes," Ana said in a small, faraway voice. "Perhaps you are right."

After breakfast, the girl carried her coffee cup into the living room to watch TV. While she cleared away Ana's dishes, it occurred to Kari that she should probably teach the girl the rudiments of twenty-first-century housekeeping, at least the simple things, like loading the dishwasher. Of course, if things went as planned, Ana wouldn't be here much longer and someone else could teach her how to do her laundry and run a vacuum and use a phone. And probably how to read and write, as well.

After wiping off the counter and the table and running the garbage disposal, Kari went upstairs to change the sheets on her bed. If she didn't hear from the coven, she was going to have to go to work on Monday and leave Ana Luisa home alone. Of course, the girl seemed to have become a couch potato overnight, so maybe it wouldn't be so bad. Ana Luisa probably wouldn't even notice that she was home alone. Still, Kari didn't like the idea of leaving the wizard's daughter alone in the house. She had visions of the girl trying to cook something on the stove and burning the house down, or forgetting to turn off the water in the tub and flooding the house, or going outside and getting lost. Who knew what havoc a frightened young witch might inflict on the city.

Maybe she was just overreacting. Then again, it was always better to err on the side of caution.

After putting clean sheets on her bed, Kari changed into a pair of jeans and a comfy old sweater. She gathered up her dirty sheets, carried them downstairs and dumped them into the washer, then went into her office. Sitting at her computer, she pulled up the file she had been working on before leaving for Romania. So much had happened since then, it seemed as if months had passed.

As always, when her creative juices were flowing, the hours flew by like minutes. It wasn't until her stomach growled that Kari glanced at the clock, surprised to see that it was after three. After saving her work, she went into the kitchen, wondering if Ana Luisa was as hungry as she was.

Kari made tuna sandwiches for lunch. She added some potato chips to the plates, along with a slice of cantaloupe. When everything was ready, she carried the plates into the living room.

"I hope you're hungry," Kari said as she entered the room, then came to an abrupt halt when she realized the TV was still on, but the room was empty. "Ana?"

Frowning, Kari put the plates on the coffee table, then went from room to room, but there was no sign of the girl. She went upstairs, thinking Ana might have gone up to take a nap. The nightgown Ana had been wearing was on the bed but there was no sign of the wizard's daughter.

"That's just great," Kari muttered.

She hurried downstairs and went outside, but the girl wasn't in the front yard or out in the back. Kari paused by the shed, wondering if Rourke would hear her if she knocked on the door, but what was the point? Even if he heard her, he couldn't leave the shed until the sun went down. What would he say, what would he think, if Ana was still missing when he woke?

Blowing out a sigh of exasperation, Kari walked around the block, pausing to ask anyone she met if they had seen anyone answering Ana's description. No one had seen the girl. It seemed she had just disappeared into thin air.

Kari grunted softly. Maybe, like Samantha on *Bewitched,* the wizard's daughter had simply twitched her nose and taken flight.

After returning to the house, Kari stared at the phone. Was it too soon to call the police? Even though that seemed like the wisest thing to do, she dismissed the idea, afraid that trying to make a missing persons report on a three hundred–year–old witch who didn't have any identification would only cause more problems.

There was nothing to do but wait, she decided. Either Ana would return or she wouldn't.

* * *

The wizard's daughter was still missing when Rourke appeared on Karinna's doorstep that evening.

"I don't know where she went," Kari said. "One minute she was watching TV and the next she was gone."

"It is not your fault."

"Then why do I feel so guilty? I should have made her feel more welcome. I should have . . ."

"Shh." He drew her into his arms. "Do not worry. I will find her."

"If anything happened to her . . ."

Closing his eyes, Rourke rested his forehead against Kari's for a moment, then muttered an oath. "She is with him."

"Him?"

"Vega."

"Ramon Vega? The vampire? How on earth did she find him?"

"I am thinking he probably found her."

Out of the frying pan and into the fire, Kari thought. "Are you going after her?"

"Yes, in a moment." Rourke's gaze held hers. "But not yet." He cupped her face in his hands and kissed her, tenderly at first and then with deepening intensity.

As always, his kiss drove everything else from Kari's mind. She leaned into him, wanting to be closer. Her pulse raced, then slowed as her heart beat in time with his. Her tongue dueled with his, then carefully explored his fangs, wondering how they could appear and disappear so quickly, wondering if it caused him pain when they popped out. She wondered about so many things. . . .

She moaned a soft protest when he drew away.

"I will not be gone long," he promised. One more kiss, and then he was gone.

Not in a puff of smoke, exactly, but one minute he was holding her and the next he was nowhere to be seen. She wondered how he did that, too.

Rourke had no trouble finding Ana Luisa. He wasn't surprised to find her in Vega's house—he had expected that. He was surprised when she refused to heed his call.

"Ana Luisa!" he shouted, his frustration and rage evident in his tone. "Come to me."

"Go away. I do not want to go stay with a coven. I do not want to live with people I do not know, people who have no reason to care for me, or protect me. I have decided to stay here, with Ramon." Her voice softened. "He said he will look after me."

Cursing softly, Rourke studied the vampire's house. It was a single-story dwelling made of solid red brick. From where he stood, he could see that there were iron bars on all the windows. The front entrance was protected by a wrought-iron security door. Not that the barred windows and door would keep him out, but the threshold, that was another matter. He had never tried to enter the home of a vampire uninvited, had no idea if the threshold of one vampire would repel another.

Angry and curious, he gained the porch and

yanked the security door from its hinges, but when he tried to open the front door, he was repelled, not only by the preternatural wards set by the other vampire, but by the sharp sting of witchcraft.

Rourke took a step backward, surprised by Ana Luisa's power. He had misjudged the girl, he mused. She was stronger than he had expected.

"I am sorry," Ana Luisa called, "but I feel safe here. With the wards around the house, my father will not be able to find me."

"I found you," Rourke reminded her. Of course, it was possible that the blood link he shared with Ana was stronger than the bond she shared with her father; then again, maybe not. Still, Vilnius might be able to track her using his magic. At the moment, it was a moot point.

There was a moment of silence, leaving Rourke to wonder if she was reconsidering.

"Thank you for helping me," Ana Luisa called. "I can never repay you for coming after me, but I am staying here."

Rourke muttered an oath. Right or wrong, he felt responsible for the girl. He had freed her and brought her to this country. It galled him to leave her in the care of another, but he couldn't force her to leave with him. She had most assuredly proved that.

"Very well," Rourke said. "Have it your own way." Raising his voice, he said, "Vega, if any harm comes to her, if you turn her against her will, I will know it, and you will answer to me."

Rourke waited a moment, and when there was

no reply from the other vampire, he turned away from the red-brick house. As the saying went, Ana Luisa had made her bed; now she could lie in it.

Karinna was waiting for Rourke in the living room when he returned.

"Did you find her?" she asked. "Is she all right?"

He grunted softly. "I found her," he said, "and she is all right, though I cannot say for how long."

"What do you mean?"

"Vega has already worked the Dark Trick on three humans. Two of them are female."

"Oh. Oh! You don't think. . . . He won't make her a vampire, will he?"

Rourke paced the floor in front of the fireplace, his hands clenched at his sides. "He will regret it if he does so against her will."

"Well, there's nothing you can do about it now," Karinna remarked. "Come, sit here with me and relax."

Muttering an oath, he dropped down beside her, his expression bleak.

"Do you like being a vampire?" she asked. "I asked you before what it was like, and you said you couldn't explain it, but do you like it?"

He stared into the distance a moment, then nodded. "All things considered, yes, though the Dark Sleep took some getting used to."

"What's that like, or can't you explain that, either?"

"It is like dying every night."

The words conjured a morbid image that made her shudder. "I don't think I'd like that part."

He laughed softly. "One has to be careful where one takes his rest. I was traveling one night centuries ago and neglected to find a proper resting place. I stopped at a tavern and requested a room. Sometime during the day, the tavern owner's wife entered the room, perhaps to clean it, perhaps to rob a sleeping guest. She mistook me for dead."

"Oh, no! What happened?"

"They buried me."

Horrified, Kari stared at him. She couldn't envision anything worse, couldn't imagine how awful it would be to wake up and find yourself in a coffin and realize you had been buried alive. She had heard stories of such things happening in the past, had seen it dramatized in movies, but Rourke had lived it. "What did you do?"

"At first, I panicked. And then I realized there was nothing to be afraid of. I dissolved into mist and materialized above ground. I never made that mistake again."

Kari shook her head. It was unbelievable. He was unbelievable. Yet there he sat, solid and whole beside her, his muscular thigh pressed intimately against hers, his deep blue eyes watching her intently. Not for the first time, she wondered why she wasn't repulsed by him, by what he was. Vampire. Undead. Nosferatu. A creature of the night. She tried to tell herself that she was being foolish, that her life was in danger every minute she spent in his presence, and yet, looking at him now, being close to him, none of that seemed to matter. He was here, and she wanted him.

As if reading her mind, he slipped his arm around her shoulders and drew her closer.

Whispering his name, she closed her eyes and waited for his kiss.

She didn't have to wait long. His mouth descended on hers, as light as fairy dust, as warm as a summer day. It was a gentle kiss, long and slow, as if they had nothing else to do the rest of their lives but perfect this one sweet kiss. His tongue teased her lower lip and she opened for him willingly, her whole body tingling as his tongue dueled with hers.

He withdrew a moment, then captured her mouth with his once more. This kiss was neither slow nor gentle but quick and hot, his tongue like a streak of fire. He stretched out on the sofa, drawing her down beside him, holding her body tight against his own. The evidence of his desire pressed intimately against her belly, awakening an answering desire deep within her.

He wanted her.

She wanted him.

But, unwanted, the word *vampire* whispered in her mind, cooling her ardor. As much as she loved him, wanted him, she wasn't ready to become the bride of Dracula, no matter how appealing and desirable he might be.

He felt her emotional withdrawal instantly.

Wordlessly, he put her away from him and gained his feet.

Kari stared up at him, her body aching with

unsatisfied need. His face was impassive as he gazed down at her. She wondered why she felt like she should apologize when she hadn't done anything wrong.

"Rourke . . ."

He held up his hand, staying her words. "I will bid you good night."

"But . . ."

He was out the front door before she could ask him to stay, to let her explain. It was just as well, she thought glumly, since she had no idea what she would have said.

Rising, she went to the window and drew back the curtains. Where was he? She told herself he had gone for a walk or to take his rest, but deep inside, she was terribly afraid that he had gone looking for a woman who would accept him for what he was.

Chapter 19

With a sigh, Ana Luisa rested her head on Ramon's shoulder. Earlier, he had ordered her a pepperoni pizza for dinner. She had liked it very much. Now, they were sitting on the sofa watching something he called football on the television. It made no sense to her, but he seemed to like it, and she was happy just to be with him. Perhaps she was being foolish, trusting her safety and her life to a vampire she hardly knew, but Ramon made her feel safe in a way that no one else ever had. Running off to find him had been the most impulsive thing she had ever done, yet nothing had ever felt so right.

She curled up against him, wondering if Jason would ever forgive her, wondering if what she had told him was true—that her father wouldn't be able to find her here. Just thinking about her father sent a cold chill down her spine. For as far back as she could remember, she had been afraid of him. She vividly remembered the looks of pity that people had turned in her direction when they learned that

Vilnius was her father. The townspeople had often come to him, seeking magical cures for their aches and pains, a charm to guarantee a good crop, an incantation to ensure the health of their sheep or cattle, yet he had been feared by everyone. She had known it, and so had he.

She pressed closer to Ramon. Vilnius was a cruel man, one who enjoyed knowing that the people who came to him for help were afraid of him. He had done nothing to make them less afraid. He had, in fact, seemed to draw power from their fear. She had seen him do awful things, unspeakable things. To this day, she was certain he had killed her mother, though she had never dared voice her suspicion aloud to a living soul, or consider it in his presence.

She recalled the look on his face when he had magicked her into that painting, his black eyes blazing, his thin lips pulled back in a feral snarl as he spoke the evil incantation. He had bound her to that painting without a hint of sorrow, had left her there without a word or a thought for three hundred years.

A single tear slipped down her cheek. But for Jason, she would still be imprisoned. Jason. She had thought she loved him, had thought he loved her in return, until she saw him with another woman.

The first time she had seen the way Jason looked at Karinna, she had been tempted to turn the other woman into a hop toad, or banish her to some faraway, ice-bound realm for all eternity. She might have done it, too, if she herself hadn't been the victim of an angry witch's curse.

And now she was here, with Ramon. When she had left Karinna's house earlier that day, she'd had no idea how to find Ramon again. She tried to remember the path she had taken the night she met him, and had ended up horribly lost in a strange part of town.

She had been frightened when a tall, gray-haired man wearing an official-looking uniform approached her. She must have looked as lost as she was, because he had asked her kindly if she needed help. She had told him that she was looking for the home of Ramon Vega and that he lived on Shadow Brook Lane. The gray-haired man had smiled and told her she was a long way from Shadow Brook Lane, and then he had offered to drive her there. She had been reluctant at first, until he explained that he was a police officer. When he had asked for the house number, she had confessed she didn't know what it was, so he had driven her to the street and dropped her off when she pointed out Ramon's house. She had thanked him profusely for his kindness. He had patted her shoulder and warned her to be more careful in the future. Sitting on Ramon's doorstep, Ana had waited for the sun to go down, and then knocked on the door, realizing only then that Ramon might not be as anxious to see her as she was to see him. He had been surprised to see her. Fortunately, he had also been pleased. He had welcomed her into his home and his arms, and she never wanted to leave.

She had known him only a short time, she thought with a sigh, yet it seemed as if she had always known him, as if she had been waiting her whole life to hear his voice, see his smile, feel his touch.

His house was like he was, warm and bright. The walls were painted in vivid hues, the furniture was casual and comfortable. He had told her all about his past, how he had been turned into a vampire five years ago by a man who had once been his friend.

The fact that he liked being a vampire surprised her. How could anyone like such a thing? He had turned three of his friends into vampires, including the man Maitland. Ramon had assured her that she had nothing to fear from Maitland, and she believed him.

How quickly her life had turned upside down! Ramon had promised to take her shopping tomorrow night. He had told her she could buy anything she wished. She smiled inwardly. If there was one thing she liked about this new world, it was shopping. She had never seen clothes so fine, or in so many styles and colors. And the undergarments that Karinna had bought her. Why, they were hardly more than a scrap of lace that barely covered the private parts of her anatomy. She had been shocked when Karinna had first shown them to her, but now . . . Her cheeks grew warm as she thought of undressing for Ramon. Would he be pleased, or shocked?

"Ana Luisa?"

She looked up, her gaze meeting his.

"Are you all right, kiddo?"

"Kiddo?"

"It's a term of affection," he explained with a grin.

"Oh." She sighed heavily. "I have so much to learn."

His hand cupped her breast. "And I'll be right here to teach you."

She had told Ramon all about her father, warned him that his life might be in danger if he helped her, but he had only laughed.

"I stopped being afraid of the future the night I became a vampire," Ramon had said, ruffling her hair. "Since then, I take each night as it comes. But you . . . ah, I never expected to find anything like you wandering in the dark."

With a sigh, she snuggled against him once again, praying that he would never have cause to regret taking her in.

A tingle of awareness threaded through her when she felt his lips move in her hair. Tilting her head back, she curled her hand around his neck and drew him closer, all thought of Jason Rourke, her father, and the future dissolving like morning mist when Ramon lifted her into his arms and carried her to bed.

Chapter 20

Back at work on Monday morning, Kari poured herself a cup of coffee, then booted up her computer and read her e-mail. As she sat at her desk, immersed in mundane tasks, everything that had happened in the last few weeks seemed like some kind of distant fever dream. It was hard to imagine that not only was Rourke made of flesh and blood, but he was also a vampire, and even harder to believe that she had made a hurried trip to Romania and managed to smuggle Ana Luisa out of the country. And that now, in addition to a sexy 767-year-old vampire, there was a witch who was over three hundred years old living in the city. Not to mention the vampire who had made Rourke, and the vampire with whom the wizard's daughter was currently residing.

Kari glanced around thinking that the people she worked with would never believe any of it.

By noon, she could scarcely believe it herself. Caught up in fonts and hues and page layouts, it was hard to imagine that there were vampires sleeping

somewhere in the city, or that one of them was
taking his rest in the shed in her backyard. At least
she thought he was. She hadn't seen him since last
night, when they had made out on the sofa. This
morning, she had been tempted to peek into the
shed to see if he was there, but the thought of seeing
him while he slept filled her with trepidation. And
even if she'd had the nerve, it would have been
impossible, since she knew he locked the door from
the inside.

She met Tricia for lunch at the coffee shop on the
corner and they spent a pleasant hour getting caught
up. Kari was dying to tell her friend everything. She
needed someone to confide in, someone she could
trust who could keep her grounded in reality, but the
last time she had told Tricia about Rourke, he had
wiped the memory from Tricia's mind.

Kari picked up a French fry, wondering just how
he had managed that, and if he had ever wiped anything from her own mind. That was a scary thought,
even scarier than his ability to do so. He might have
erased one memory or a hundred and she would
never know it!

The rest of the day passed quickly. She finished a
project for one of her major clients, spent two hours
on the phone with another client who had decided,
at the last minute, that he wanted to change his
whole presentation.

Lost in her work, she didn't have a chance to
think about who would be waiting for her at home.

Jason Rourke's image jumped to the forefront of
her mind as soon as she drove out of the parking lot.

A fair-haired angel, Tricia had called him. Ha! Angel, indeed! She was sure he had more in common with fallen Lucifer than Gabriel.

Would Rourke be waiting for her at home? Did she want him to be? She knew it would probably be better if he just disappeared from her life, but she couldn't bear the thought of never seeing him again even though she couldn't see that they had much of a future together. She was twenty-five, he was 767. She slept at night, he slept by day. She liked food and sunshine and vacations at the beach, he drank blood and hunted the shadows for prey. She would grow old, he would stay forever the same.

At the front door, she took a deep breath and then put her key in the lock, wondering whether she would feel relief or regret if he wasn't there.

She found him in the living room watching the six o'clock news, the daily paper scattered at his feet. A wellspring of happiness bubbled up inside her when she saw him there. He looked so normal, sitting in front of the TV clad in a black T-shirt and a pair of blue jeans, just like any other man relaxing after a hard day's work. Only he wasn't an ordinary man, and he didn't have a job.

He looked up as she entered the room. She frowned, perplexed by the intensity of his gaze. Was he angry? Had he come to take her by force, or tell her good-bye? He couldn't be angry, she thought, smiling inwardly, not after last night. Still, her stomach knotted as she waited for him to say something.

"Good evening, sweeting."

Relief swept through her as his voice washed over her. He definitely wasn't angry.

"Hi." She dropped her handbag on the sofa table and kicked off her shoes.

He held out his hand, and when she took it, he drew her gently toward him, pulling her down onto his lap. "How was your day?"

"I was busy playing catch-up all day. How was yours . . . never mind."

One corner of his mouth lifted in a wry grin, and then, cupping her nape in one hand, he drew her head down and kissed her, his breath mingling with hers, his hands lightly skimming over her shoulders and down her back, sliding seductively over her hip and along her thigh.

"Rourke . . ."

He kissed her again, longer, deeper. Heat flowed from his mouth to hers. Her stomach quivered as his tongue teased the corner of her mouth, then slid inside, tasting, teasing, evoking sensations that Kari felt in the very core of her being. She moaned softly, yearning toward him, longing to feel the long, hard length of his body stretched out beside hers, a part of hers. . . .

With a soft cry of protest, she drew away and gained her feet, surprised that her legs were strong enough to hold her. Her insides felt like Jell-O, her legs like limp spaghetti.

Rourke looked up at her, his eyes narrowed thoughtfully. "I want you," he said in a voice like honeyed velvet. "You want me. Why do you continue to fight the attraction between us?"

She stood there, feeling foolish and confused. She wanted him and they both knew it, but deep down inside, though she was loath to admit it even to herself, she was afraid of him, afraid of his preternatural powers, afraid that letting him make love to her would, in some way, steal her free will and make her his slave. He had erased all memory of himself from Tricia's mind. How did she know he wasn't planting ideas in her mind now? What if he had been manipulating her? What if her feelings weren't even her own? Maybe he was making her think she wanted him, but what would be the point? If he wanted her, all he had to do was take her. She was no match for him, physically or otherwise.

He held out his hand, palm up. "Come to me, sweeting."

His voice, so soft and sensual, was filled with gentle persuasion.

She waited, wondering if he was playing with her mind, relieved when she was able to resist.

"No." She shook her head even though she wanted nothing more than to be in his arms again. "No."

He rose, towering over her. "Why do you continue to deny yourself what you want?" he asked, and there was no mistaking the fine edge of anger and frustration in his tone.

"Because I've never...I mean, I don't...I mean . . ." It was one of the reasons she had broken it off with Ben. He had hurled insults at her, his voice filled with disdain as he had accused her of being old-fashioned, frigid, a cold fish, because she wouldn't sleep with him. People didn't wait until

they were married these days, he had said angrily.
What was she trying to prove? Did she want him
to beg?

She had tried to explain it to him, had tried to
make him understand that it didn't matter what
everyone else was doing, that she wanted to wait, to
make sure that the first man she slept with would
be the last. He had laughed at that. No one stayed
married forever anymore, either, he had said, his
voice laced with scorn. Until Ben had spoken those
words, she had hoped they would be able to work it
out, but what chance did a marriage have when one
partner had already decided it wouldn't last?

"You are untouched," Rourke said, a note of
wonder in his voice.

"Yes." She lifted her chin defiantly. "So what?"

His knuckles caressed her cheek. "It is an ad-
mirable quality, rare from what I have seen of the
women of this century. Forgive me."

She looked up at him, at the desire shining in the
depths of his eyes, and felt her determination
weaken just a little as she imagined herself in his
arms, in his bed.

He lifted one brow. "Be careful," he said, amusement evident in his tone, "lest your thoughts betray
you."

Heat flooded her cheeks with the realization that
he was reading her mind.

"Stop that!"

"I want only what you want," he said with a roguish
grin. "You, naked in my arms. You, naked in my bed."

His bed, or his coffin? She grimaced at the

thought, her desire extinguished like a flame drenched in cold water.

"Go back to what you were doing," she said, moving toward the stairs. "I'm going to change my clothes and then get something to eat."

She hurried up the steps, every fiber of her being acutely aware that Rourke was watching her every move.

He stared after her. She was unlike any woman he had ever known. She was afraid to fly, yet she had agreed to accompany him to Romania so he could free Ana Luisa. She was afraid of him, of what he was, yet she had offered him a place to stay. She wanted him as deeply as he wanted her, yet she clung to her principles of right and wrong as fiercely as any ancient warrior. He admired her for that most of all.

Rourke shook his head. What was he to do with her? The smart thing would be to move on. He had familiarized himself with this century. He had freed Ana Luisa from her painting. As far as he was concerned, his debt to Ana was fulfilled. It was time he fulfilled the oath he had made to himself time and again in the last three hundred years.

Rourke dragged a hand over his jaw. He should bid Karinna farewell, go after Vilnius, retrieve his father's sword, and find a place for himself in this new world.

He glanced at the staircase as Karinna descended, a raven-haired angel in a pair of faded blue jeans and a red sweater that lovingly hugged every curve. What man in his right mind, dead or Undead, would leave such a delectable creature?

He had waited three hundred years to avenge himself on Josef Vilnius. What difference would another year or two or even ten make?

Kari paused at the foot of the stairs, trapped by the intensity of Rourke's gaze. She didn't have to be psychic to know what he was thinking. It was evident in the taut line of his body, in the fire blazing in the depths of his hooded eyes. She could feel the heat arc across the distance that separated them. If he moved toward her, if he touched her, she knew she would go up in flames. . . .

Feeling as though she were rooted to the spot, she shook her head, silently pleading with him to go away and leave her alone because she was afraid, so afraid, that her ability to deny him, to deny herself, wouldn't last much longer.

Step by slow step, he moved toward her like some wild jungle cat stalking its prey.

She stared up at him, unable to speak, unable to move. His preternatural power washed over her, leaving her feeling vulnerable, helpless. Doomed.

"Karinna." His voice poured over her, warm and sweet, like melted chocolate. His knuckles caressed her cheek. "What am I to do with you?"

She blinked up at him. She was at his mercy. He could do anything he desired; there was nothing she could do to stop him, and they both knew it.

"You are so lovely." His fingertip moved back and forth over her lower lip. "Your skin is like fine silk, your eyes as blue as the sky I have not seen since I was a young man. Your body . . ." His gaze slid down, lingering on her breasts, her belly, her hips, before returning to her face. "Your body is like a symphony waiting to be played."

Lowering his head, he kissed her. He didn't close his eyes, and neither did she. She saw him then, saw him as he truly was, a man who possessed unbelievable power, who could easily take her against her will, a man who could devour her body and soul. She knew a moment of stark, unreasoning fear, and then it was swept away in the sure knowledge that he would never do anything to hurt her.

She saw something else, as well, a soul-deep loneliness unlike anything she had ever imagined. The depths of it, the pain of it, brought tears to her eyes.

Rourke drew back, a frown creasing his brow as he caught one of her tears on the tip of his finger. "Why do you weep?"

She shook her head, afraid he would laugh at her. After all, it was ludicrous that a mere mortal should shed tears for someone such as he, a being of untold power, one who had lived for hundreds of years and would live for hundreds more. What was a little loneliness compared to the centuries of discovery that lay before him? And yet, how much longer must the years seem when you had no one to share them with, when you were doomed to lose everyone you knew, everyone you loved, over and over again?

Unaccountably touched by her tears, he said, "You need not weep for me, sweeting."

"I can't help it."

With a sigh, he drew her into his embrace, his hand running lightly up and down her back. Though he could easily bend her will to his, or take her by force, he wanted her to surrender willingly, to give herself to him because it was what she wanted.

"Ah, Karinna," he murmured. "You tempt me almost beyond my control."

She clung to the word *almost*, knowing it was her salvation, even as she wondered if she really wanted to be saved.

His hand stroked her hair. "What do you want of me?"

"What do you mean?"

"I want you," he said. "In my life, in my bed. What do you want? Are we to remain strangers to each other? Do you wish me to leave? Tell me what you want."

She gazed up at him. What did she want? Slowly, she shook her head. "I'm not sure."

"Perhaps it would be best for me to leave."

"No!"

"You do care, then?"

"You know I do." She frowned at him. "How can you say we're strangers?"

"Are we not?"

"I don't think so."

His knuckles slid down her cheek. "I do not know you nearly as well as I want to."

His words made her stomach quiver. "I'm just not ready for that. I mean, it's a big step and we're . . . we're so different."

He pulled her closer. "Not so different. Feel how your body molds itself to mine, as if we had been de-signed for one another."

She nodded, too breathless to speak.

"I feel your yearning, your hunger. It is the same as mine." His hand slid down her back to cup her bottom, drawing her up against him, leaving no doubt that he wanted her. "You hesitate because of what I am, do you not?"

"Yes." Her voice was barely a whisper.

"But I am still a man, sweeting, capable of loving you, of protecting you, if need be. Be my woman." His lips brushed hers. "Be my wife."

"Wife? Are you asking me to marry you?"

"So it would seem."

Caught by surprise, she stared up at him. She had been expecting a completely different kind of proposal. She knew he wanted her. She had been on the brink of surrendering to the desire she saw in his eyes, to the need she heard in his voice. If she was totally honest with herself, it was what she wanted, as well. But to be his wife? Who would have thought that the Undead got married? What would it be like to be married to Rourke? Would she even survive the honeymoon? Mrs. Jason Rourke. It had a nice ring to it, but what would it be like to have a vampire for a husband, a man who could share only half of her life, who would be forever young and virile? What would her life be like without him?

"You need not answer now," he said.

"I never thought . . . I don't know . . . are you sure this is what you want?"

"I would not have asked otherwise." He brushed a kiss across her lips. "It is a big decision for you, I know."

That was the understatement of the year!

He laughed softly when her stomach growled. "You need to eat," he said, "and so do I." He kissed her again. "I will not be gone long."

She nodded, blatantly reminded yet again of the vast gulf between them.

Chapter 21

Vilnius closed his traveling bag, then took a last turn around his dwelling place. He had taken care of everything here at home. Tomorrow, he would go after his daughter. It was time to bring her home, time to avenge himself once and for all on the vampire who had despoiled his only child. He intended to destroy Rourke this time, thereby ensuring that Ana Luisa would never again succumb to the creature's lust. As for Luisa, he would be generous this time. He would forgive her for her past sins and bring her home. He would allow her to take her place at his side once again, and he would continue her education. She was a powerful witch, far more powerful than she knew. He had been careful to keep such knowledge from her and would continue to do so until she was older, wiser. Until she had her emotions under control. Until she knew her place.

He had but one more thing to do before he left home.

At midnight, he went down into the basement,

where he practiced his magick, and closed the door, figuratively shutting out the distractions of the world. Magick could be done by day or by night, but late at night was the most opportune time for scrying, since it was easier to avoid the excessive psychic vibrations generated by the confusion of everyday living. Not only that, but he preferred the darkness.

Scrying was an ancient method of divination often used by witches and magicians. An old legend stated that the goddess Hathor had carried a shield that reflected all things in their true light. From this shield she had purportedly fashioned the first magic mirror.

The Ancient Greeks and Celts had used beryl, crystal, black glass, polished quartz, and water. Gypsy fortunetellers generally used a crystal ball, but the purpose was the same: to see into the future, or to find that which was lost. Other objects had been used through the ages. The Egyptians had used fresh blood or ink, the Romans had used shiny objects or stones. Mirrors were often used, as well, but Vilnius preferred living water.

He opened the cupboard where he kept his magical implements and the tools of his trade and withdrew several fat white candles, which he placed on the altar located in the center of the floor. He waved his hand over the wicks and the candles sprang to life, filling the room with iridescent light.

After drawing a piece of black chalk from his pants pocket, he drew a circle on the floor. Next, he filled a large black cauldron with water and placed it on the table between the candles.

Head bowed, he summoned his power, felt it gathering around him like a dark shroud. When the water settled, he focused his gaze on the mirror-like surface.

Lifting his hands at his sides, palms up, he chanted softly, "Eye of water, eye of fire, show me that which I desire."

Most people saw only shadows and patterns of light when scrying, but Vilnius was not like most people. He was a wizard without equal.

Slowly, the water began to shimmer. All the colors of the rainbow swirled across the surface, mixing, mingling, until the face of Jason Rourke stared back at him.

Supernatural power flowed through the room as Vilnius slowly stretched his arms over his head. He held them there a moment before slowly lowering them to his sides. "Eye of water, eye of creek, show me the lair of the one I seek."

Rourke's image blurred and disappeared, and in its place Vilnius saw a two-story dwelling. The numbers 3235 were visible on the front of the house.

"Eye of ice, eye of snow, the city and state I would know."

The candlelight flickered on the walls, the house disappeared, and a map of a small town in northern California appeared on the dark surface of the water. A star indicated the name of the street he sought.

Vilnius muttered, "Blessed be," then emptied the cauldron into the sink, broke the circle, and blew out the candles. He had the information he needed. All he needed now was a suitable place to exact his revenge. When he had that, Jason Rourke's future would be numbered in days instead of centuries.

Leaving the house, Vilnius locked the front door

and set the wards. After tossing his luggage in the backseat of the Ferrari, he slid behind the wheel. He sat there a moment, enjoying the scent and feel of fine leather before he started the car. He loved being behind the wheel of the convertible, loved the low rumble of the powerful engine, the sense of exhilaration that came from being in control of such a finely crafted vehicle.

With the top down and the wind whistling in his ears, he paid no heed to traffic signals as he sped down the highway. Every light turned green as he approached.

He spent the night at a country inn. The next day, at the airport, he magicked his way on board, bypassing the endless lines and security checks. He loved flying. Indeed, he had embraced every new luxury and invention that mankind had discovered in the last four hundred years. The cleverness and ingenuity of the human race never failed to amaze him. He pitied the poor mortals who lived only a short span of years. They missed so much!

Settling back in his seat, he looked out the window. It had been years since he had been to America. Perhaps he would do a little sightseeing before he dispatched the vampire and went after Luisa. No doubt she would be angry with him at first, but, in time, she would come to understand that he had done what was best for her. If not . . . He closed his eyes. If not, he was certain he could find a way to persuade her to change her mind.

Chapter 22

Ana Luisa opened the oven door, slipped her hand into an oven mitt, and withdrew the cookie sheet. She took a deep breath, smiling as her nostrils filled with the scent of freshly baked sugar cookies. After placing the cookie sheet on the counter, she turned off the oven and closed the door.

She was enchanted with the appliances of this new world. Baking, which had been something of a drudgery in her time, was now a pleasure. In the last two days, she had baked an apple pie, two cakes—one chocolate and one strawberry—and dozens of different kinds of cookies. Since she couldn't read English, Ramon had drawn pictures of the directions for her. Her only regret was that he couldn't share the sweet treats with her. She hated to throw the un-eaten desserts away, but there was no way she could consume all of them. When she mentioned it to Ramon, he told her not to worry about it.

Truly, this was a wondrous time in which to live. She found the washing machine and the dryer fascinating and washed her clothes even when they weren't dirty. The hot running water in the shower and the sink was a never-ending pleasure. And the soap—it came in so many colors and scents.

She loved watching TV, even though she found some of the programs confusing. She also loved listening to the music on the stereo. Never had she heard such music. Often, she didn't understand the lyrics, but that didn't diminish her pleasure, and Ramon was always there to explain anything she didn't understand.

Electric lights were a marvel. Imagine, light at the flick of a switch. Ramon had promised to teach her how to read and write English; he had already shown her how to play some of the games on his computer. There had been so many changes in the world while she had been trapped in that painting, and she wanted to embrace them all, to see everything, learn everything, experience everything.

And then there was Ramon. . . . Thinking of him made her smile. She wanted to know everything about him, as well. He was a most amazing man, strong yet gentle, powerful yet tender. She didn't care that he was a vampire. She had, in fact, been giving serious consideration to asking him to make her what he was. She rather liked the idea of staying forever young, of never being sick. Of course, being a witch, she could expect to live a good long life, but she loved Ramon, and she wanted to share her whole life with him.

She also liked the idea of possessing the same kind of supernatural powers that he did. He could read her mind, compel people to obey his will, vanish into mist, hover in the air, walk up the side of a building like a spider. He could control the weather and move so fast it was as if he simply disappeared. Not only that, but he was incredibly strong. True, she could also do some amazing things, but he accomplished his without the need to cast circles or spells. She imagined the power she could have if she could combine her magical abilities with those inherent in being a vampire. She would never have to be afraid of her father again.

The idea had great appeal.

Perhaps tonight she would ask Ramon to bring her across.

"Are you sure about this?" Ramon asked. They were lying on a blanket in front of the hearth, sharing a glass of wine.

Ana Luisa traced his lower lip with the tip of her finger. "I thought it would make you happy."

He took her finger into his mouth and sucked gently, then pressed her hand to his heart. "It does. I'm just surprised."

"Will it hurt?"

He caressed her cheek. "A little, but I'll be with you the whole time."

She tilted her head to the side. "Your eyes are red. And glowing."

He nodded. "Does it frighten you?"

"Not really," she decided. "But why are they glowing?"

"It happens sometimes when I get excited, or when I'm on the hunt."

A slow smile spread over her face. "Are you excited now?"

Cupping the back of her head, he drew her closer and kissed her. "You have no idea."

"Do it, Ramon," she murmured.

Leaning forward, he kissed her gently. "Are you sure about this?" he asked, his gaze searching hers. "You've only thought about it a few days, chica. Once it's done, there's no going back."

"I'm sure." Turning her head to the side, she brushed her hair away from her neck. "Do it now, Ramon. Make me what you are."

With a low growl, he gathered her into his arms. His tongue laved the skin beneath her ear, arousing her, lulling her. She gasped, her body arching upward, when his fangs pierced her throat. Panicked, she clutched at his shoulders, and then, with a sigh, she surrendered to his dark kiss, content to let him take whatever he wanted.

To take it all . . .

High in the skies over the Atlantic Ocean, Josef Vilnius woke with a start. He stared out the window of the plane, a sudden emptiness stealing over him as his connection to his daughter abruptly disappeared, severed as cleanly and thoroughly as if someone had cut the magical bond that bound them as surely as blood.

His hands tightened on the armrests until his

knuckles went white. Only death could break the bond between the two of them.

He gazed into the vast nothingness of the heavens, surprised by the soul-deep pain her passing left in its wake. He had raised Luisa single-handedly, taught her about the world and her place in it, looked after her when she was sick, applauded her accomplishments. It grieved him to realize that their last words to one another had been filled with anger and recriminations.

It occurred to him that he had never told Luisa that he was fond of her.

He would never have the chance now.

He had waited too long.

Everlastingly too long.

Chapter 23

Rourke grinned as he laid his last card on the table. "I believe that's zero for me and twenty-six points for you, since I just . . . what did you call it?"

"You call it winning," Kari said. "That last hand put me over five hundred. And don't gloat!"

He had just learned how to play the game, and he had already beat her three games in a row. Kari glared at him, and then she frowned. Of course he was winning. He could read her mind!

"You're cheating!" she exclaimed. "Admit it, you know what cards are in my hand and what I'm going to play before I even do it."

He lifted one brow. "In days gone by, accusing another of cheating at cards often led to swordplay."

"Well, I don't have a sword," she said with some asperity. "And don't change the subject! Have you been reading my mind?"

Talk of swords brought Vilnius to mind, but Rourke shook the wizard from his thoughts. He was enjoying his time with Karinna far too much to ruin it by thinking about Vilnius now.

"Rourke? Hello? Earth to Rourke."

"Forgive me," he murmured. "What did you say?"

"I asked if you were reading my mind."

"Ah. Would you believe me if I said no?"

"Yes." She replied without hesitation, knowing in her heart of hearts that he was too honorable a man to take advantage of her.

"I have a good memory for what cards have been played," he remarked as he shuffled the deck.

Kari sighed. He didn't seem to have any trouble concentrating on the game. She wished she could say the same thing, but she spent more time watching him than paying attention to what cards had been played. He wore a pair of black jeans, and a dark green shirt with the sleeves rolled up, revealing muscular forearms. She had never known a man who exuded such raw sensuality. Even doing no more than sitting across from him, she was acutely aware of his every movement, of the attraction that hummed between them whenever their eyes met. Sometimes, when he looked at her, she felt it like a physical caress. Would it be so bad to let him make love to her? She was a big girl. Maybe it was time to leave her morals behind and have a fling with a wildly handsome, dangerous man. Maybe it was time to stop thinking so much and give in to her deepest desire.

She drew her gaze from his. What was she thinking? There was no commitment between them. True, he had proposed, but she hadn't said yes. And as tempting as marriage was, what was the point? He was a vampire. Sooner or later, he would tire of her and move on. Who needed a marriage that wouldn't last? If they made love, no matter how casually she approached it, she knew it would break her heart when he left. Of course, she was afraid she was in for some serious heartache sooner or later whether they made love or not.

With a shake of her head, she put such thoughts out of her mind. Even if Rourke had been just an ordinary man, it was way too soon in their relationship to be thinking about making love, at least where she was concerned.

Rourke was dealing a new hand when he stopped middeal. He swore softly, his eyes narrowing.

"What's wrong?" she asked.

Muttering another oath, he tossed the cards into the center of the table. "Vega has turned Ana Luisa."

Kari blinked at him, wondering if she had heard right. Vega lived on the other side of town. How could Rourke possibly know what was going on there?

When she put the question to him, he simply said, "I know."

He said it with such conviction, she had to believe it.

Kari shook her head. Poor Ana Luisa. First, she had spent three hundred years trapped in a painting, and now she was a vampire, doomed to prey on humanity and walk in the shadows for the rest of her existence. Given her druthers, Kari thought being trapped in a painting might be the lesser of two evils.

Rourke clenched his fist and brought it down on the table. "If he turned her against her wishes, I will destroy him."

"He must have," Kari said. "I mean, why would anyone ask to be a vampire?"

Rourke grunted softly. "Why, indeed."

Kari bit down on her lower lip. "I didn't mean to offend you."

"You did not offend me, sweeting." He rose, then drew her to her feet and kissed her. "I will be back as soon as I can."

"You wouldn't really kill him?"

"No. He is already dead."

"You know what I mean," Kari said. Kill him, destroy him, it amounted to the same thing.

Rourke didn't answer her question. Instead, he kissed the tip of her nose, and then he was gone.

Kari stared at the spot where he had stood, wondering if she would ever get used to his disappearing like that. Probably not, she decided. She would have to ask him how he accomplished it. Did he turn invisible, or just magically transport himself out of the room?

With a sigh, she went into the kitchen for a cup of coffee.

A thought took Rourke to Ramon Vega's house. He pounded on the door, his anger building with each passing moment.

Vega opened the door, a fleeting look of surprise flitting across his face. "What do you want?"

"Where is Ana Luisa?"

"Resting."

"I want to see her."

Vega propped his hand on the opposite door frame, blocking Rourke's entrance to the house. "Why?"

"You insolent pup, I know what you have done!"

Vega shrugged. "I did only what she asked."

"I do not believe you."

"Then ask her yourself." Vega glanced over his shoulder. "Ana, you have company."

She appeared behind him a moment later. "Jason," she murmured. "What are you doing here? Is something wrong?"

Rourke's gaze moved over her. She appeared a little disoriented, but that was to be expected. Already, subtle changes were taking place in her appearance. There was a telltale hint of red in her eyes, a richer luster to her hair. When she rose tomorrow night, she would be a full-fledged vampire, gifted with the preternatural senses and other abilities peculiar to their kind.

"Is this what you wanted, Ana?" he asked.

She blinked at him. "How did you know?"

"I have taken your blood in the past. It formed a link between us." He took a deep breath. "You did not answer me, Ana. Was this your choice?"

She nodded. "The most amazing thing has happened. I am no longer bound to my father."

Her smile was brilliant, her teeth blindingly white. "I am free."

Rourke grunted softly. He had not realized that the wizard and his daughter shared a bond. If Ana Luisa felt free, what was Vilnius feeling?

Rourke fixed his gaze on Vega. "Take good care of her. If you hurt her . . ."

"Yeah, yeah, I know," Vega said, draping his arm around Ana Luisa's shoulders. "You'll destroy me."

"Never doubt it," Rourke said coldly. "And it will be slow. And painful."

Ana Luisa glanced from Rourke to Vega. "Can we not all be friends?" she asked quietly. "After all, we are all the same now."

"It's okay by me, kiddo," Vega said. "Your friend's the one making all the threats."

"They are not threats," Rourke muttered.

"Please, Jason," Ana Luisa said. "For the first time in three hundred years, I am happy. I feel like I am where I was meant to be."

Rourke dragged a hand over his jaw. "If this is what you truly want, then so be it," he said, and offered Vega his hand.

The other vampire hesitated only a moment.

Ana Luisa smiled as the two men she loved most in the world shook hands. Rising on her tiptoes, she kissed Jason on the cheek, and then she kissed Ramon. "Thank you," she said. "Both of you."

Rourke took both of her hands in his. "If he ever hurts you, if you ever need me . . ."

"I know. Thank you, Jason, for everything."

He nodded. With a last warning glance at Vega,

Rourke turned and headed for home. He grunted softly. He had no home, no place to call his own save the shed in Karinna's backyard, and that wasn't really his. He needed to find a more secure lair, perhaps some kind of employment, though he had no idea what kind of work he could do in this day and age. Still, he wasn't the kind of man to let a woman support him. He had allowed Karinna to provide him with clothing and shelter, partly because it was necessary, and partly because he wanted to be near her, but it was unfair to expect Karinna to continue to provide for his needs. He had every intention of repaying her for what she had spent on him, and on Ana Luisa, as well.

As a young man, he had been in charge of his family's estate. He had looked after the land and the livestock, managed the family finances, settled whatever disputes arose, but that had been 736 years ago.

Muttering an oath, he turned down a dark street in search of prey. It took only minutes to find what he sought. Bending over the woman's neck, he wished it was Karinna in his arms, Karinna's essence filling him, warming him.

Karinna . . . She wanted him, he thought, but not enough to accept him for what he was. The thought saddened him even though he could understand her apprehension, perhaps better than she understood it herself. For the first time in his life, he was in love, really in love. Ana had found someone to love. The fact that Vega was a vampire hadn't kept her from loving him. Ana had wanted to be with him and she had taken the steps necessary to join her life with his.

Rourke swore softly, annoyed with himself for envying Ramon and Ana Luisa, angry with Karinna because she couldn't love him as wholeheartedly as Ana loved Ramon Vega.

Releasing the woman in his thrall, he sent her on her way.

Heading for Karinna's house, he wondered how he could overcome her innate wariness of what he was and win her to his side.

He shook his head. Perhaps she needed some time to herself. Perhaps it was time for him to go to the house of Vilnius and retrieve his father's sword. It was all Rourke had left from his father, the only physical possession that he had owned that was important to him after he had been turned. It represented his father's love, his home and his family, and all that was forever lost to him.

Maybe it would be wiser to let Vilnius keep the sword, he mused as he turned down yet another dark street. Maybe he should just forget who he had been and where he had come from. That man was dead. And yet, it was because the sword reminded him of who and what he had once been that he refused to let it go. It would be all too easy to lose himself in what he had become, to let go of his tenuous hold on what was left of his humanity, to become what so many others of his kind became—merciless hunters who preyed on mankind as if men and women and even children were no more than so many sheep, put on the earth for no other reason than to provide nourishment for his kind.

Muttering an oath, he turned the corner and headed back toward Karinna's house. He needed a place of his own, he thought again, a lair where he could take his rest in more comfortable surroundings than the wooden shed in Karinna's backyard.

Chapter 24

Vilnius rented a car at the airport. It was amazing how much had changed in the fifty years since he had last been to America. He didn't remember the freeways being so crowded, the buildings so large or so numerous. Of course, there had been similar changes in the rest of the world, as well. Houses springing up where there had once been only acres of green fields. Highways snaking their way through towns and cities, over mountains and along the coasts.

He had always admired the ingenuity, resourcefulness, and endless optimism of the people of America, but he much preferred his own land, where life was slower and not so crowded.

He stopped at the first hotel he came to. The clerk informed him that there were no rooms available without a reservation, but five minutes and one quick spell later, Vilnius was relaxing in the bridal suite on the top floor, a bottle of expensive champagne and a basket of fruit awaiting his pleasure.

Americans, he thought, *they certainly know how to live.* He glanced out the window, surprised by the sense of lethargy that tugged at him. He had expected to be eager to confront Rourke; instead, he found himself thinking of Luisa, wondering how she had died, and if she had suffered. He was even more surprised to find himself grieving her loss. He had scarcely thought of her in three hundred years. Now that she was gone, he could think of little else. He had once had plans for his daughter. He had intended to free her from the painting at some future date and continue her instruction in the art of magic, perhaps even teach her the Dark Arts. What a pair they would have made.

He was mourning, he thought, with no small measure of astonishment, mourning for his only child, mourning for what might have been had she not sacrificed her innocence to that bloodsucker.

Turning away from the window, he moved restlessly through the room. He had never been one to do anything halfheartedly. His only daughter was dead and he would mourn her after the manner of his people. For the next seven days, he would sprinkle ashes on his clothing and deny himself food and water. Each night, he would light a candle to commemorate her life.

And when his period of mourning was over, he would destroy the man who had defiled her.

Chapter 25

Ana Luisa woke with the setting of the sun. Opening her eyes, she saw Ramon lying on the bed beside her, the sheet pulled up to his waist. Propped on one elbow, he smiled at her when he saw she was awake.

"Were you watching me sleep?" she asked.

He wrapped a lock of her hair around his finger. "Maybe."

"Why?"

He shrugged. "I like looking at you."

"Even when I am sleeping...." Her voice trailed off. "It is not really sleeping, is it? I did not fall asleep. One minute I was awake, and the next, darkness enveloped me. I did not dream...." She looked at him, her expression troubled. "It really is like death, isn't it?"

"You'll get used to it." Leaning forward, he kissed her cheek. "You're not sorry I brought you across, are you?"

"No, it is just different than I thought it would be.

I think there will be more things to get used to than I expected."

"You'll get used to everything, in time," he said. "I promise." He kissed her again, longer, deeper. "And time is something we've got plenty of."

"Have you been a vampire a very long time?"

"Five years, give or take a month or two," he replied with an easy grin. "In the vampire world, I'm just a baby."

"Do you like being a vampire?"

"Yeah, I do."

"All of it?" she asked.

"All of it," he said with conviction. "And you will, too."

"Even the blood part?" she asked dubiously. "I did not really think much about that."

He laughed softly. "Even the blood part."

"How did it happen? Did you want to be a vampire?"

"Not at the time. I had a good friend who started acting strange, you know? He stopped hanging around with our crowd, wouldn't talk to anyone. I went to his place one night and asked him what was wrong. He didn't want to tell me, but I kept buggin' him. Finally, he said, 'You wanna know what's wrong with me? I'll tell ya. Hell, I'll show ya!'"

Ramon shook his head. "He showed me, all right. Showed me his fangs, and then buried them in my throat. I don't remember much after that. When I woke up the next night, I was in his house, but he was gone. I never saw him again."

"How awful! You must have been terrified."

He grunted softly. "You could say that. I didn't know what to expect, or what to do, but I figured it out."

She considered that a moment before asking, "Do you have a family?"

"Sure. They live in Mexico. My old man owns a fishing boat. My two older brothers work with my father. I have an older sister who lives in San Francisco, and a younger sister who lives in Fresno."

"Do they know what you are?"

"No."

"Do you see them very often?"

"We all go home every year or so and spend a few days with our folks." He winked at her. "My mother will be happy to meet you. She was beginning to think I'd never settle down."

Ana wasn't sure she wanted to meet his family. What if they didn't like her? Then again, what if they did? It would be nice to be part of a large family. It had been lonely growing up as an only child. She'd had no one to play with, no one to confide in. Her father hadn't allowed her to play with the children in the village; considering her parentage, she doubted if the children would have been allowed to play with her, either. As a child, she had wished for brothers and sisters, aunts and uncles and cousins.

"Are you very rich?" she asked.

"Who, me? Not hardly."

"But you do not work."

"Sure I do. I'm on vacation right now. I don't have to go back to work for another two weeks."

"What do you do?"

"I'm the night manager at the local market."

She pondered that a moment, thinking that she really didn't know very much about him, and then she smiled. She had years to learn everything there was, she mused, and then frowned. "Do I look the same?" She ran her hands over her face and down her throat. Never again would she see her reflection in a mirror.

"More beautiful than ever."

"Do you remember what you look like?"

Ramon lifted one brow, as if amused by her question, and then frowned. He hadn't seen his reflection in over five years.

"I have pictures to remind me," he said, and knew a moment of regret that he hadn't taken Ana's photograph, but then realized it wasn't necessary. If she wanted to remember how she looked, he would take her to a studio and have her portrait painted. Hell, they could have one painted every year if she liked.

Ana smiled when he told her about having her portrait painted. "Maybe we can have one made of the two of us," she suggested.

"Sure, whatever you want."

"Will people know what I have become?" she asked, then answered her own question. "They will not. I did not know you were different when first we met. Yet now . . ." She stroked his cheek, ran her fingertips down his arm. "Now, I see it so clearly."

Ramon brushed a kiss across her cheek. "Things will only get better. You'll be amazed at what you can do. Every sense is heightened, every touch magnified." He laughed softly as her eyes widened. "Yes, making love will be better than ever."

"I cannot imagine that," she said with a shy smile.

"Shall I . . ." He frowned as someone knocked on the front door. Reaching for his jeans, he muttered, "Who the devil can that be?"

Ana Luisa shrugged, then offered him a seductive smile. "Do not be gone long."

"Don't worry." With a wink, Ramon zipped his fly and went to answer the door.

Ana Luisa stretched languidly, then sat up at the raucous sound of male laughter. Curious to see who had come calling, she got out of bed and pulled one of Ramon's T-shirts over her head.

Entering the living room, she found Ramon talking to two women she didn't recognize, and a man she recognized all too well. It was Maitland, the man who had threatened her in the alley. What was he doing here?

"Ramon?"

He turned to her with a smile. "Ana, these are friends of mine. . . ."

"How can you bring him here?" she exclaimed, glaring at Maitland.

Ramon moved to her side and slipped his arm around her shoulders. "Calm down, chica. You can't blame Maitland for putting the moves on a pretty woman. . . ."

"Is that what he was doing?" Ana Luisa demanded. She shook her head. "I do not think so. I think I would be dead now if you had not interfered. I do not want him here."

"Now, listen, Ana—"

"No, you listen. I do not trust him."

Ramon looked at Maitland, a clear warning in his eyes. "He won't hurt you. You have my word on that."

"How can you be so sure?" Ana demanded.

"Because he knows if he so much as lays a finger on you, I'll destroy him."

At Ramon's words, tension thrummed through the air like lightning about to strike. The two female vampires glanced at each other and then looked at Ramon, as if waiting for him to say something, do something.

Ana Luisa looked up at Ramon, her head tilted to one side. "Would you?" she asked. "Would you destroy him?"

Ramon nodded. "No one will ever hurt you or scare you again. I swear it."

Ana Luisa smiled, touched by his words and the conviction in his voice. "I believe you, but I still do not want him here."

Ramon grunted softly. "Sorry, Maitland, but you heard the lady."

Maitland's eyes narrowed in disbelief. "You're throwing me out?"

"Looks that way." Ramon smiled at Ana. "She's the lady of the house."

Maitland threw an angry glance at Ana Luisa, then turned on his heel and stomped out of the house, slamming the door behind him.

Ana Luisa nodded and smiled as Ramon introduced her to Nita and Jan, but her mind was on Maitland and the malicious look in his eyes. Perhaps she had been too rash in denouncing the man. She bit down on her lower lip, wondering if what she had just done would somehow come back to haunt her.

Before she could worry about it too much, a sharp pain speared through her. With a gasp, she looked at Ramon. Had something gone wrong? He hadn't told her there would be pain.

Ana saw Jan and Nita exchange knowing glances. What did they know that she didn't?

"It's all right, chica," Ramon said, taking her by the hand. "The hunger is always worse the first night after the change. Come, it's time to go hunting."

Chapter 26

"You're leaving?" Kari stared at Rourke, unable to believe what she was hearing. "What do you mean, you're leaving? Why? When? Where are you going?"

"To retrieve my father's sword."

"But . . . I thought . . ." She frowned, then shook her head in disbelief. "You don't mean to go after Vilnius, do you? Are you crazy? Have you already forgotten what happened to you the last time you crossed him?"

"The sword is mine," Rourke said adamantly. He stood and began to pace the floor. "It is all I have left of my father. All I have left of my old life. Vilnius has stolen three hundred years from me. I will not let him take the sword, as well."

"But . . . I . . . how soon are you leaving?"

"Tomorrow night."

"Tomorrow night! I can't possibly get time off from work again so soon." Kari sat up, her fingers drumming on the end table. "That's not near enough time to book a flight or find a hotel, or . . ."

"That will not be necessary this time."

"Oh," she said, then frowned. "Why not?"

"I can get there under my own power."

"You can? How?"

"Preternatural flight, I suppose you could call it."

"Why didn't you go to Romania that way?" she asked, then shook her head. "Never mind. I think I know the answer. You needed my help in getting Ana Luisa here."

Rourke nodded. "I can never repay you for that."

"It was nothing. I was glad to help."

"It was a very great imposition on your funds and your time. I will never forget your kindness, or your generosity."

Kari blinked back the sudden urge to cry. Was he leaving for good? Was this his way of saying good-bye?

Lifting her from the sofa, he drew her into his arms, one hand cupping her cheek. "Nor can I ever thank you enough for freeing me from that wretched painting."

"Rourke . . ." She looked up at him, her heart aching, her thoughts torn. There was so much that she wanted to say to him, and yet, if he was leaving, the words in her heart were best left unsaid.

He smiled faintly, and then he lowered his head and kissed her, a gentle kiss that flowed through her like sun-warmed honey, thick and hot and sweet. She moaned softly when he deepened the kiss, his tongue dueling with hers as his arm drew her closer.

Her body responded immediately, every nerve

ending sparking to life. She wanted him and now he was leaving. She was sorry they had never made love. For a fleeting moment, she was tempted to surrender her will to his, to let him take whatever he wanted. Even knowing he was leaving and that she might never see him again, she was sorely tempted to beg him to make love to her, though judging from his arousal, she wouldn't have to beg very hard.

"Rourke . . ."

He looked down at her, his eyes dark with desire. Her skin tingled where his hands touched her. Her lips still felt the heat of his kisses. Her body ached for the fulfillment only he could give, and yet, as much as she wanted him, needed him, she couldn't say the words. It was bad enough that he had her heart. She could already feel it breaking at the thought of never seeing him again. If they made love and he left her, never to return, she knew she would never recover.

"I'll miss you," she said, her voice little more than a whisper.

"Will you?"

She nodded, her eyes swimming with unshed tears.

There was nothing to be gained by prolonging the moment, or by promising that he would return. Though it pained him to leave her, he knew it was for the best, for Karinna and for himself. It was time to remember that he was a vampire and she was prey. Expecting them to have a life together didn't make any more sense than putting a sparrow in a cage with a tiger and expecting them to live happily ever after. It just wasn't going to happen.

"Ah, Karinna."

"Will I ever see you again?" She hadn't meant to speak the words aloud. They made her sound weak, needy, pathetic. She wished she could call them back, but it was too late.

He gazed down at her, and though he didn't speak, she saw the answer in his eyes, tasted it in the tender kiss he brushed across her lips. He murmured her name again and then vanished from her sight.

Kari stared at the place where he had stood only seconds before, thinking he had gone out of her life as quickly as he had come into it.

With a sigh, she went up to bed, only to lie there wondering if things would have turned out differently if she had surrendered to him. If they had made love, would his last kiss have been a promise to return instead of good-bye?

A tear slid down her cheek. She'd never know the answer now.

After leaving Karinna's house, Rourke stalked the dark streets in search of prey. He fed long and often, feeling his power increase with each feeding, whether it was from a homeless man, a slightly intoxicated woman, or a young punk who was out looking for trouble and found more than he could handle.

Rourke drank from them all and sent them on their way. He needed to be strong for his upcoming journey, but, more than that, he drank for the sheer pleasure of it. He hadn't told Karinna how much he had missed the warmth of it, the taste of it, the tantalizing scent of it, or how it filled all the cold, empty places inside him. Remembering how he had longed for nourishment when it had been denied him, Rourke drank until he was replete.

He had spent three hundred years in that accursed painting, and not a night had gone by that he hadn't berated himself for being a fool, not only for going to Ana Luisa's house, but for letting the taste of her blood, her virgin blood, cloud his senses. Only when he had felt the sting of her blood on his tongue had he realized she was not only a witch, but a virgin, but by then, it had been too late. Weakened by the taste of her blood, he had been helpless to protect himself when Vilnius had stormed into the room.

But he would meet the wizard again, and soon. Vilnius would not find him such an easy mark this time!

Hours later, his hunger satiated at last, he made his way to the shed in Karinna's backyard. As he sank into the darkness of oblivion, his last conscious thought was that once he had retrieved his father's sword he would have to find a new lair.

Kari woke early after a long and restless night. She had dreamed of Rourke again, dreamed that he was back inside the painting, and that she was trapped there with him. In her dream, the castle had been warm and cozy instead of cold and forbidding. The walls had been painted a cheery blue, Oriental carpets had covered the stone floors, velvet draperies had hung at the windows. The kitchen had contained the latest state-of-the-art appliances. She had enjoyed wandering through the forest, sailing in the boat, and riding the horse, but most of all, she had enjoyed spending her nights in Rourke's arms. Instead of being frightened or eager to escape the painted world they inhabited, she had been perfectly content to remain there with him.

Now, lying in bed staring up at the ceiling, she wondered if the dream held some deeper meaning, though she had no idea what it might be. Nor did she have time to worry about it. She didn't have the luxury of lying about analyzing her dreams. She had a busy day at work ahead of her.

Throwing off the covers, she headed for the bathroom and a hot shower.

It wasn't until she turned off the water and stepped out of the stall that she realized she was crying.

Chapter 27

Standing in the moonlight, Rourke gathered his power, felt it flowing into him and through him, spreading through every fiber and cell until it hummed through his body. He focused his energy, felt himself rise into the air as if he had wings.

It was exhilarating feeling the rush of the wind against his face as he picked up speed and left the earth behind.

He reached his destination just before dawn. Drifting down, he landed in a fallow field behind the wizard's chateau, then quickly went to ground to await the night.

He rose with the setting sun. As always, he was somewhat bemused by the fact that none of the dirt or debris clung to him or his clothing when he emerged from the bosom of the earth.

The first order of business was to ease his thirst, which he did quickly and efficiently. With his hunger satisfied, he made his way to the chateau.

Set amid a copse of trees and surrounded by a

high, white rail fence, it was a lovely old place with weathered gray walls, a blue tile roof, and tall, leaded windows. A faint breeze carried the scent of damp grass and vegetation. Somewhere in the distance, Rourke heard the rush of water flowing over stones.

He frowned as he drew closer to the chateau. The house was closed and shuttered. No lights shone in the windows. No smoke rose from the red brick chimney.

"So, Vilnius," Rourke mused aloud. "Where have you gone?"

He paused briefly at the front door. Under other circumstances, he would have needed an invitation, but not now. Three hundred years ago, Ana Luisa had invited him into her home. No one had ever rescinded that invitation.

At a wave of his hand, the heavy oak door swung open, and he stepped inside.

The interior of the living room was cold and dark, the furnishings rich but austere, from the dark brown leather sofa and matching chair to the wrought-iron lamps and glass-topped mahogany tables. Expensive paintings lined the walls, an Oriental carpet covered the floor. There were few decorations in the room: a graceful Chinese vase, a carved box made of onyx, a large jade elephant.

Rourke moved unerringly through the dark room and down a hallway until he came to the back parlor. This room was also richly furnished. Looking around, Rourke could see that this was the room where the wizard spent most of his time. A big-screen TV took up most of one wall. There were a comfortable-looking overstuffed chair and a couple of side tables. A tall bookcase held a wide variety of books, everything from dictionaries and comic books to the works of William Faulkner, Thomas Aquinas, Tolkien, and Voltaire. But it was his father's sword, hanging above the marble fireplace, that held Rourke's attention.

For a moment, he simply stood there, staring at the elegant lines of the ancient weapon as he remembered the man who had been his father. Thomas Rourke had been a stern and forbidding man, unbending in his beliefs, fiercely loyal to his king and his friends, merciless to his enemies. But he had also been a loving husband and father, one who had always found time to spend with his wife and children.

With a feeling of reverence, Rourke lifted the sword from its place over the mantel. Was it only his imagination, or did the hilt of the sword seem to warm to his touch? He turned the blade this way and that, marveling at the stark beauty of it, the way it fit into his hand as if it had been made for him and no other. Power shimmered along the blade, and with it he heard the deep bass of his father's voice assuring him that he could do anything he desired.

Holding the sword in front of him with both hands, he touched his forehead to the slender blade, silently renewing his vow to avenge himself on Josef Vilnius.

And then he settled down to await the wizard's return.

* * *

Ana Luisa ran through the night, reveling in the sting of the wind against her face, the way she flew over the pavement, her feet scarcely touching the ground. She loved being a vampire, loved the sense of power and exhilaration that filled her body upon waking from the Dark Sleep. She thrilled at the hunt. It was such an amazing feeling calling mortals to her, bending their will to hers, knowing she held the power of life and death in her hands.

As a witch, she had enjoyed some of the same abilities—she could move objects with her mind, pass, unseen, through crowds, float in the air—but those abilities had not been as strong or allowed her to feel the exhilarating power that engulfed her now.

So far, she had not taken a life. From childhood, she had been taught that all life was sacred and not to be wasted or taken lightly. Ramon teased her about it, calling her Little Miss Mercy because she always left her prey alive. She knew he sometimes killed those he hunted, but he never took a life when he was with her. Once, she had almost asked him how many people he had killed, but at the last minute, she had decided she didn't really want to know.

It was only when she slowed to gaze at a shooting star that she realized she was no longer alone.

The knowledge came too late. Before she could defend herself, a body slammed into her, driving her down to the ground. She felt the rip of fangs at her throat as Maitland drank and drank. She tried to fight him, but she was no match for his greater strength.

If only she hadn't insisted Ramon send him away, she thought dully, but it was too late now. She could feel herself slipping away. Just before she lost consciousness, she thought she heard Ramon's voice.

"Maitland! What the hell do you think you're doing?"

Maitland looked up, his mouth covered with blood as he crouched over Ana's body like a lion guarding its kill. His eyes blazed red as he glared at the vampire who had sired him.

Ramon swore a vile oath as he glanced from Maitland to Ana Luisa. Her face was fish-belly white. She didn't seem to be breathing. He swore again as a vagrant breeze carried the scent of her blood to his nostrils.

Ramon glared at Maitland. He had only minutes to get to Ana and close the wound before she bled out. Although vampires were virtually immortal, the bite of another vampire intent on destruction could sometimes be fatal.

"Dammit, Maitland," he hissed. "Back off!"

Fangs bared, Maitland rose to his full height, a challenge in his eyes.

"So," Ramon said. "That's how you want it."

"It's been coming for a long time," Maitland said. "I intend to end it now, tonight." A low growl rumbled in his throat as he sprang forward.

At the last moment, Ramon darted to the side. Pivoting on his heel, he grabbed a handful of Maitland's hair and gave a hard yank. Maitland stumbled backward, his arms flailing. Ramon threw him to the ground and in one vicious movement ripped the other vampire's heart from his chest.

Maitland kicked once and lay still, like a balloon gone flat.

Ignoring his fallen fledgling, Ramon hurried to Ana Luisa's side. Lifting her into his arms, he ran his tongue over the wound in her throat, his saliva quickly sealing it. Next, he tore a gash in his wrist, then held the bleeding wound to her lips.

"Drink, Ana," he pleaded urgently. "You must drink."

For a moment, he thought she was beyond saving, but then, with a low moan, she licked a drop of his blood from her lips. A shudder wracked her body, and then, grasping his forearm, she took what she needed.

"That's it, chica," Ramon murmured. "Take what you need." And so saying, he closed his eyes and surrendered to the ecstasy of nourishing the woman he loved.

Chapter 28

Kari stared at her computer wondering how it was possible for time to pass so slowly. It had been two weeks since she had last seen Rourke, but it seemed as if months had gone by.

In an effort to put him out of her mind, she had started taking her work home with her at night so she would have something to keep herself busy while he was gone, and when that didn't help, she called some old friends that she hadn't seen in a while. The day before yesterday, she had gone out to lunch with Cindy Lewis, and last night, she had gone to the movies with Cindy and her twin sister, Sandy. She had called her mom for a long chat, and phoned her best friend, Tricia, at least three times a day.

Nothing she did really helped, because, sooner or later, she was alone and missing him again, as she was now. Going into the living room, she sank down onto the sofa, then picked up her cell phone and called Tricia.

After the usual pleasantries, Tricia said, "All right, hon, what's wrong?"

"Nothing," Kari replied with forced cheerfulness. "What makes you think there's anything wrong?"

"Number one, it's Saturday afternoon. Number two, I just saw you at lunch an hour ago. Number three, this is like the sixth or seventh time you've called me since last night. You haven't called me this many times since you broke up with Ben. What happened? Did you have a fight with Mr. Tall, Blond, and Dreamy?"

"No, we didn't have a fight." Kari sat back on the sofa, idly running her fingertips along the edge of one of the throw pillows.

"Did you break up?"

"There was nothing to break, Trish," she said quietly. *Nothing except my heart.*

"Uh-huh. So, are you going to tell me what's going on, or are you going to keep me guessing?"

"Nothing happened. I . . . he . . . I just haven't seen him for a while."

"And you miss him." It wasn't a question.

"Yes. But it's probably just as well that he's gone."

"Why? Honestly, Kari, you should hang on to that one."

"If I tell you something, will you promise not to laugh, or tell me I'm crazy?"

"Well, sure, that's what friends are for."

"He's a vampire."

"I knew you shouldn't have got to Romania!"

"Trish, listen to me. I'm serious about this."

"Serious, yeah, right," Trish said, snickering. "Come on, Kari. A vampire?"

"Please, just listen." Kari took a deep breath, striving for calm. "I know you can't remember, but I bought a painting a while back by an artist named Vilnius . . ."

"You've got a Vilnius!" Tricia exclaimed. "Good grief, girlfriend, did you win the lottery or something? Where is it? Why didn't you tell me? When can I see it?"

"You've already seen it, and I don't have it anymore—"

"Don't tell me you sold it before you even showed it to me!"

"Trish, please, just listen. I bought a Vilnius. It was called *Man Walking in the Moonlight*."

"Yes, I've heard of that one," Tricia said, and Kari heard the frown in her voice.

"Yes, you told me about it when I first brought it home. Can't you remember? You told me all about Vilnius, and how he painted only a handful of canvases, and how everybody thought the one I bought was one that had been lost—"

"Yes, that's right. Three of them were lost or destroyed. One of them, *The Wizard's Daughter,* is somewhere in Romania. Everyone assumed *Man Walking in the Moonlight* had been lost, as well."

"It wasn't lost. Rourke was trapped in it. When he got out, he destroyed it, I guess. Anyway, it's gone now. *The Wizard's Daughter* has been destroyed, too."

"Another vampire?"

"No. Long story short, Vilnius caught Rourke in

bed with his daughter. Naturally, Vilnius, who is also a wizard, was upset. He trapped his daughter in one painting and Rourke in another—"

"Kari, really, no one would believe any of this."

"I know that. But it's the truth. You saw the *Man in the Painting* at my house. And you saw Rourke after he escaped from the painting, but he made you forget everything."

There was a long pause, then, "How did he get out of the painting?"

"I said I wished he was with me, and the next thing I knew, the painting fell off the wall, the glass cracked, and he was standing there, as big as life."

"Honestly, Kari, with an imagination like that, you should write science fiction."

"This is so frustrating! I wish you could remember!"

"There's nothing to remember. . . ."

"Tricia, what's wrong?"

"My head hurts."

Kari's heart skipped a beat. Could Tricia's memory be coming back? "Try to remember. The night you came to see the painting, you were wearing jeans and that red T-shirt with the little white hearts on it. You came over after the painting broke, too, and I showed you the notes he'd written to me. You said the ink looked like blood—"

"Oh, Lord," Tricia said with a groan. "I do remember."

Kari sank back against the sofa, suddenly weak with relief. Tricia knew. Tricia believed her.

"But a vampire . . . Really, Kari, what makes you think he's a vampire?"

"Because that's what he is. Tricia, he drank my blood."

"What? Are you . . . Good Lord, don't tell me you're a vampire, too!"

"No, of course not."

"Well, he was gorgeous and he seemed to make you happy, so I can understand why you miss him, but, as you said, you're better off without him."

"I didn't say that. I just said it's probably best that he's gone."

"You didn't fall in love with him, did you?"

"Yes, I'm afraid I did."

With a sigh, Tricia said, "Well, Kari, you know those romances never turn out well in the movies. Someone always comes along and drives a stake through Dracula's heart."

Kari laughed in spite of herself. "Thanks, Tricia, I needed that."

"Well, that's what friends are for. Is there anything I can do?"

"You've done it. I just needed someone I could talk to, someone who knew the truth."

"Well, I'm here for you anytime."

"I know, and I appreciate that. I'll talk to you later."

"I'm sure you will," Tricia said, chuckling. "Bye for now."

"Bye."

Kari hung up the receiver. Nothing had really changed. Rourke was still gone. She still missed him. But she felt better just the same.

Later that evening, curled up in a corner of the sofa with a cup of peppermint tea, she tried to concentrate on the video she had rented earlier that day, but it was no use. She could think of nothing but Rourke. Where was he tonight? Was he thinking about her? Or was he off with the beautiful, red-haired vampire she had seen him with not so long ago? Maybe they were off somewhere making up for the night they had missed out on because Rourke had been with her. The thought that he might be making love to another woman was like a knife twisting in her soul.

She was blinking back tears when the doorbell rang. With her heart in her throat, she put the cup on the table and hurried to answer the door. *Please,* she thought, *please let it be him.*

Taking a deep breath, she turned the lock. A breath of cold air assailed her when she opened the door, but it was nothing compared to the disappointment that swept through her when she saw it wasn't Rourke standing on the porch, but a frail-looking man with papery-looking skin, long gray hair, and the blackest eyes she had ever seen.

For a moment, she couldn't speak, couldn't seem to catch her breath. Finally, she managed a weak, "May I help you?"

"I am looking for Jason Rourke. I was told I could find him here."

"I'm sorry, he's not here." *Nor likely to be anytime soon,* she thought glumly.

"When will he return?"

"I don't expect him back."

A muscle worked in the stranger's jaw. His black eyes narrowed.

Kari took a step backward, chilled by the stark expression in his eyes.

"Who are you?" he asked.

"Who are you?"

The stranger didn't move, yet he seemed to become more than he was. "I am Josef Vilnius."

She stared at him thinking that, on some deep, subconscious level, she had known it all along.

"And you . . ." His gaze bored into her. "You are Karinna."

"Yes." The word was drawn from her throat as if he had reached inside and forced it out.

"You care for him?"

"Yes."

"Does he care for you?"

She tried to deny it, but again, she found herself saying, "Yes," remembering, as she did so, that the last woman who had cared for Rourke had ended up trapped inside a painting for three hundred years.

The wizard nodded, and the night seemed to grow darker, colder.

Kari shivered. Unable to draw her gaze from his, unable to retreat into the house, she wrapped her arms around her middle and waited.

Vilnius studied her for several minutes the way a scientist might study a newly discovered species.

She studied him in return. He wore a pair of expensive-looking dark gray slacks, and a light gray jacket over a crisp white shirt. A tiny diamond stud winked in his right ear; his left hand sported a ring set with a blood opal.

Something froze deep inside her when he nodded. "Yes," he said, his voice sounding the way she imagined a snake would sound if it could talk. "Yes, I think you might be useful. For a while."

She didn't like the sound of that at all, and liked it less when she tried to shut the door in his face and discovered that she couldn't move a muscle, couldn't even blink.

A slow smile spread over the wizard's face. "Useful, yes," he repeated.

And then everything went black.

Chapter 29

Rourke stood on the sidewalk in front of Karinna's house. He hadn't intended to return to America until he had settled his score with Vilnius, but he had spent two weeks at the wizard's home waiting for him to return, but to no avail. As much as Rourke yearned for revenge, his need to see Karinna again had been stronger, and so he had abandoned his quest for revenge, for the time being, and come home.

Rourke grinned faintly. Home, he thought. For him, it wasn't a place, but a woman. He hadn't seen Karinna for a fortnight and he had missed her more than he would have thought possible. He hadn't found a secure lair before he'd gone in search of Vilnius, so he had spent the day before resting in the ground, and while Mother Earth offered a refuge from the sun, he preferred to take his rest in a bed on a firm mattress. He had considered spending the day in Karinna's shed, but, for some reason he couldn't quite fathom, it hadn't seemed right.

Using his preternatural powers, he had obtained

a hotel room the night before, which had provided him with access to a shower and a place to change his clothes, though he hadn't dared to take his rest there. It might have been safe, but he felt too exposed in the room. There were too many windows, too many unknown people coming and going at all hours of the day and night. It had, however, provided him with a new hunting ground.

His hunger stirred, and with it, his desire for Karinna. Ah, Karinna. Not only had he missed the woman herself, but he had missed the creature comforts of her house, the sense of homecoming he had felt whenever he entered her abode, the friendly warmth of a fire in the hearth, the casual evenings they had spent watching the television together, or playing cards.

He glanced at the windows downstairs, wondering if she was home. No lights shone from inside. He knew she had to go to work tomorrow, but surely she hadn't gone to bed so early. Had she gone out for the evening?

He was stalling, and he knew it. He was a vampire with remarkable powers, yet the thought of facing one mortal female filled him with trepidation. Would she be angry with him for leaving so abruptly? Would her eyes be filled with silent reproach? He could withstand her anger, he thought, but not her tears.

Angry or not, he had to see her. If he had learned one thing in the past two weeks, it was that his existence wasn't worth living if he couldn't share it with her.

Muttering an oath, he walked quickly to the front

door. He was about to knock when his preternatural senses told him the house was empty. He was trying to decide whether to wait inside or come back later when he caught a familiar scent on the freshening wind, a scent that raised the short hairs along his nape and filled him with a quiet sense of dread.

Vilnius.

Rourke opened the front door with a wave of his hand. Stepping over the threshold, his gaze swept the darkness, coming to rest on a folded sheet of paper propped on the mantel.

He read it quickly, then read it a second time.

Rourke, I have the woman. Call me when you read this if you hope to see her alive one last time. . . .

There was no signature, no date, just a phone number under a boldly scrawled *V.* When had Vilnius been here? How many days had Karinna been at his mercy?

Rourke moved unerringly through the darkness toward Karinna's office. Each breath carried her scent to his nostrils, reminding him of the nights they had spent together, the fervent kisses they had shared. If anything happened to her, it would be all his fault. He swore softly. He should have realized that the wizard would know when the curse was broken, should have known that Vilnius would come after him. Had the wizard also found his daughter?

Picking up the telephone, Rourke listened for the dial tone the way Karinna had showed him, then punched in the wizard's number.

Vilnius answered on the first ring.

"Where is she?" Rourke asked curtly.

"Ah, Mr. Rourke. She is here, with me."

"If you hurt her . . ."

"Spare me your empty threats."

"Where are you?"

"There is a house for sale on the corner of Willow and Wade streets. I will be waiting for you there."

Rourke swore softly as Vilnius broke the connection. A thought took him to the corner of Willow and Wade. Standing in the shadows across the street from the house, Rourke closed his eyes, his preternatural senses reaching out, searching for her. He caught a hint of the wizard's presence, but nothing to indicate that Karinna was inside.

Muttering an oath, Rourke dissolved into mist, crossed the street, floated down the chimney, then hovered near the ceiling.

Below him, Vilnius paced the living room floor, his long gray robe flowing behind him like the breath of Satan.

But Rourke had little interest in the wizard. He had come to make sure Karinna was safe, but where was she? Rourke drifted from room to room. He checked the closets, the walk-in pantry in the kitchen, but there was no sign of her, no sense of her presence in the house. Save for a tall, three-legged stool in one corner of the front room, the interior of the house was empty. The drapes were drawn across all the windows.

He returned to the living room wondering what game Vilnius was playing. He had been certain Vilnius would keep Karinna close by. Had he been mistaken? And then he saw that the house wasn't empty, after all. A large painting of a still, blue lake set in the midst of a deep green forest hung on the wall just inside the front door. A small cottage bathed in early morning sunlight stood off to one side of the lake. A blue sailboat, with its white sails unfurled, floated on the placid surface of the water.

Rourke was about to turn away from the painting when he saw Karinna. Clad in an emerald green gown, she was seated in the bow of the boat, a look of horror etched on her countenance.

If he could have spoken, he would have uttered every curse word he had ever known. If he had been in his own form, he would have smashed something, preferably the wizard's arrogant face.

Instead, he hovered near the ceiling unable to look away from Karinna. He had brought her to this, he thought. He had insinuated himself into her life and now she was in the wizard's power, caught in the same kind of hell that he himself had endured for so long.

Was she aware of what had happened to her? How would an ordinary mortal react to being imprisoned in such a fashion? If he could free her, would she be the same woman he had known, the woman he loved more than his very existence, or would being entrapped in such a way forever shatter her hold on reality?

He had to get her out of there, but how?

In his present condition, he was helpless. He had intended to destroy Vilnius. He knew there was a

possibility that Vilnius would defeat him, but it was
a chance he had been willing to take. But now . . .
Dammit, now it wasn't only his own existence that
was at risk, but Karinna's life, as well.

He was still trying to decide what action to take
when Vilnius suddenly stopped pacing. Head cocked,
his eyes narrowed, he glanced around the room.

Fearing that the wizard had sensed his presence,
Rourke made a hasty exit. Resuming his own form
outside, he paced the darkness, his mind in turmoil. He was tempted to charge in and confront
Vilnius and to devil with the consequences, but his
concern for Karinna's welfare, his love for her, demanded caution. Assuming he won the battle with
the wizard, there was always a chance that Vilnius
had worked a different enchantment on this painting and that calling Karinna to his side wouldn't
work. He couldn't kill the wizard until he knew how
to remove the spell and free Karinna.

He needed an edge . . . but what?

Rourke dragged a hand across his jaw. He needed
some backup, he thought, then grinned, thinking
that he sounded like a character on one of the cop
shows Karinna sometimes watched on the television.
Backup . . . Ramon Vega quickly came to mind. If he
could persuade the vampire to help him, he might
have a chance to overpower the wizard.

Ramon Vega answered the door wearing a pair of
faded jeans low on his hips, and nothing else. He

looked understandably surprised when he saw Rourke standing on the porch.

"Well, well," Vega muttered. "Look who's here. I guess you want to see Ana."

"I came to see you. I need your help."

Vega's eyes narrowed suspiciously. "My help? Doing what?"

"Ramon, who is it?"

Glancing over Vega's shoulder, Rourke saw Ana Luisa walking toward them. She wore a pair of white shorts that made her legs seem three yards long, and a bright red halter top that left little to the imagination. Rourke whistled softly, thinking she had quickly adapted to the somewhat shocking fashions of the time.

Vega slid his arm around Ana Luisa's waist in a blatantly possessive gesture that clearly said, "She's mine."

"Jason," Ana Luisa said, surprise evident in her tone. "What brings you here?"

"I came to ask for his help," Rourke said, frowning, "but maybe I'm asking the wrong vampire."

"What are you talking about?" Ana asked.

"Your father is here."

Ana Luisa's eyes grew wide. "He's here? In America? Are you sure?"

"He's in the city," Rourke replied. "And yes, I am sure."

"What does he want? Does he know where I am?" She moved closer to Vega. "You didn't tell him where to find me?"

"Of course not," Rourke said.

Vega smiled reassuringly at Ana Luisa. "Don't be afraid, chica. I won't let him hurt you."

"You do not know," she said, her voice tight. "You do not know what he is, what he can do."

"Well, suppose you tell me."

"He is a powerful wizard," Ana Luisa said. "More powerful than you can imagine."

"Bring him on," Vega said arrogantly. "I'm not afraid of him."

Rourke grunted softly. "Then you are a bigger fool than I first thought. Vilnius is a wizard to be reckoned with."

"More powerful than a vampire?" Vega asked skeptically.

"Powerful enough to trap me inside a painting for three hundred years," Rourke said curtly. "And his daughter, as well."

"What do you mean, trapped?"

"I mean he cast an enchantment on the two of us, one that was only recently broken."

Vega looked at Ana Luisa again. "Is that true?"

She nodded, her eyes bright with fear.

"Why didn't you ever tell me?"

"I do not like to think about it."

Vega's attention shifted to Rourke. "So, what kind of help are you looking for?"

"Vilnius has Karinna."

"Oh, no," Ana Luisa murmured.

"Come on in," Vega said, taking a step back. "Ana, why don't you get us something to drink?"

Rourke followed Vega and Ana Luisa into the house. The place didn't look like much from the outside, but it belied the luxurious interior. Rourke didn't know if Vega had decorated the place himself, or hired someone do it, but the results were remarkable. A curved, plush brown sofa flanked by glass-topped end tables was situated in front of a massive red brick fireplace. The walls were off-white, the floors were polished hardwood, and there was a cathedral ceiling. A grand piano occupied one corner of the room.

Vega gestured at the sofa. "Make yourself comfortable."

With a nod, Rourke took a seat.

Vega sat at the other end of the sofa.

A moment later, Ana Luisa appeared carrying a tray with a bottle of red wine and three crystal glasses. Sitting between the two men, she filled the glasses, handed one to Vega, and one to Rourke.

Rourke swirled the liquid in his glass, his nostrils filling with the scent of cherry, plum, and vanilla.

Vega took a drink and smiled. "Not a bad Pinot, fine acidity."

Rourke nodded. It was an excellent vintage. Vega was apparently a connoisseur and accustomed to the best money could buy. Given their long life spans, many of the ancient vampires managed to acquire a good deal of wealth. Rourke, himself, had once been a fairly wealthy man, though his holdings were all gone now, lost to others while he languished in that damnable painting.

"So," Vega said, settling back against the sofa, "have you got a plan for rescuing Karinna?"

"Unfortunately not."

"I cannot believe he's here." Ana's hand trembled as she lifted her glass. "I had hoped never to see him again."

Vega regarded Rourke for several moments before asking, "How do you suppose he found you?"

"A spell of some kind, I should imagine. It's strange that he hasn't contacted you, Ana," he mused. "I would have thought he would have come to you first."

Vega shrugged. "Maybe he doesn't know where she is."

"Perhaps not, but why not? If he could find me . . ." Rourke frowned. "Ana, you said the bond between the two of you was broken when Vega brought you across, is that right?"

"Yes."

"Can you feel it now?"

She closed her eyes a moment, then shook her head. "No, there is only emptiness."

"Evidently, the bond was broken when you died as a mortal," Rourke mused. "Your father is not looking for you because he believes you are dead."

Vega looked at Ana Luisa, his head canted to one side. "So, chica, do you know how to do magic, too?"

"Yes, although I am not nearly as proficient as my father. I have seen him do things you would not believe. Impossible things." She shuddered. "Cruel things."

Vega studied the wine in his glass, his expression thoughtful. "I should think that two vampires and a witch would be able to take on one wizard, even a powerful one."

"One can only hope," Rourke muttered darkly. "Ana, what do you think your father's reaction would be to seeing you again?"

"I do not know."

"Maybe it'll scare the life out of him," Vega remarked with a grin.

"Only one way to find out," Rourke said. "Are the two of you with me?"

Chapter 30

Kari wanted to cry, to rail at Fate and unleash her fear and helplessness in a primal scream of rage, but she couldn't move, couldn't even blink, she could only stare at the blank wall on the far side of the room. It was a terrifying sensation, being able to think but unable to move or speak. She had no sense of time passing, no idea how many days or hours had ticked into eternity since Josef Vilnius had shown up on her doorstep. Had it been only yesterday, or a year ago?

Now and then, the wizard passed in front of her, his long gray robes swirling around him like smoke. Sometimes she saw his lips moving, but she couldn't hear what he was saying. Was he conjuring another foul spell, talking to himself, or making a new deal with the devil? She wouldn't put the latter past him. Josef Vilnius was a cruel and vindictive man. It showed in his features, and in his soulless black eyes. Hard to believe that such a man had fathered Ana Luisa. The man was truly a monster, to have inflicted torture such as this on his own flesh and blood. She wondered if Ana's mother was still alive. It was hard to imagine that any woman had willingly married such a man, let alone taken him to her bed.

Karinna focused all her attention on her right hand in an effort to make her fingers move, but to no avail. It was getting harder and harder to think clearly. She had no sense of her physical self. She was neither hot nor cold. She didn't know if her heart was beating. She didn't seem to be breathing. How could she be alive and not take a breath? Was this what it was like to be in limbo, to be caught in that netherworld between life and death?

How had Rourke endured three centuries of such a wretched existence? It was worse than death. Of course, he had eventually gained the power to move about in his painted world. But he possessed supernatural powers and abilities that she didn't have, would never have. No matter how much time passed, she would be forever trapped as she was now, unable to speak, unable to move.

Help me! Somebody please, please, help me!

She screamed the words in her mind even though there was no one to hear her.

Help me!

Somebody, anybody, please.

Help me. . . .

Chapter 31

Ana Luisa took a deep breath as they approached the red brick house located on the corner of Willow and Wade streets. From the outside, the house looked dark and empty. Going closer, she peered through a break in the curtains covering the front window, felt a rush of anger when she saw the man sitting on a tall, three-legged stool in the far corner of the room. He wore a long gray robe over a white shirt and black trousers. His hair, once as brown as the earth of their homeland, had gone completely gray since last she had seen him. For the first time, she wondered just how old her father was. She had asked him about it once, soon after her mother died, but he had refused to tell her, saying only that she needn't worry about losing him, too, because he would be around to care for her for many years to come. Wizards, he had assured her, enjoyed a very long life span.

It no longer mattered to her now. Whatever love she had once held for the man who had fathered her had died centuries ago, suffocated behind the glass wall of her painted prison.

Ramon touched her arm. "Are you ready, chica?"

She nodded.

"We will be nearby if you need us," Jason assured her.

She nodded again. Jason had suggested that surprise might be the only thing in their favor. Vilnius would be expecting Rourke, or possibly the police, should Jason have been foolish enough to involve them. He would not be expecting his daughter.

Taking a deep breath, she opened the door and stepped into the house.

It was obvious from the astonished expression on her father's face that Jason had been right. She was the last person her father had expected to see.

"Luisa!" He slipped off the stool, one gnarled hand pressed over his heart as all the color drained from his face. "Luisa, is it really you?"

"Surprised to see me, father dear?" she asked in a voice laced with acid.

"I thought. . . ." He took a step backward, knocking the three-legged stool to the floor. "I thought you were dead."

"Did you? Three hundred years, father," she said. "Three hundred years and you never once came to see how I was."

"But I knew," he sputtered, his face growing even more pale. "Of course I knew."

"Liar!"

"Luisa . . ."

She advanced on him like an avenging angel. His

fear was a palpable thing now, vibrant and alive. It darkened his aura and quickened her hunger. She felt the prick of her fangs against her tongue as his heart began to beat faster.

Ana Luisa stabbed a finger toward the picture on the wall behind him. "What mischief is this?" she demanded, her voice little more than a hiss. "What did she do to you to deserve such a terrible fate?"

"Nothing." Vilnius shook his head. "She's merely a pawn, if you will, a bit of bait to catch . . ." His eyes narrowed as his voice trailed off. He regarded her for a moment before asking, "How can you be here? I felt you die."

Ana Luisa smiled, but there was no warmth in her eyes and none in her voice. "Did you?"

"I knew the vampire freed you. I felt your body fill with breath, and then, after a time, there was nothing, and I knew you were dead."

"I am dead," she replied, and let him see her fangs.

He stared at her in horror. "Rourke! This time I will kill him!"

"It was not Jason, father, and you are not going to kill anyone ever again."

He stared at her a moment, and then, drawing himself up to his full, impressive height, he lifted his arms overhead and began to summon his power.

When Ana realized what he was doing, she quickly called upon her own power, power made stronger because she had fed well earlier that night, not only on the blood of a mortal in his prime, but on Jason, as well. Her own magic, combined with Jason's ancient blood, flowed through every fiber of her being. She was strong, invincible, and for the first time in her life, she was unafraid of the man who was her father.

"Who is the woman in the painting?" Ana Luisa asked, though she already knew the answer.

"No one of importance."

"Call her forth. After what you put me through, I cannot bear to see her held there."

"You could call her yourself," Vilnius remarked, "if you but knew her name." His initial surprise and fear had receded, replaced by a growing sense of indignation that his only child dared to treat him with such disrespect. "Perhaps you would like to join her?"

The thought of again being trapped behind a wall of glass filled Ana Luisa with a terrible rage. Eyes red, hands curled into claws, she lunged at her father. Nothing but the sight of his blood on her hands could atone for the centuries she had been imprisoned.

But she had underestimated the man who was her father. The instant she touched him, she was flung backward.

A moment later, he was standing over her. "Ungrateful slut," he said with a sneer. "No better than the whore who brought you into the world."

Ana Luisa stared up at him, his words flailing her like a lash.

"No pretty painting for you this time," he said as he pulled his wand from inside one voluminous sleeve. "No hope of release." He leaned toward her. "You remember the statue in the arbor, the one you always thought looked so much like your mother?" His eyes were mere slits now, his face florid with rage. "I think it is time you joined her there." His laughter was cruel. "I'm sure she will welcome the company."

Ana Luisa shook her head. "No, it can't be." Her voice was little more than a shocked whisper. Ava Vilnius had disappeared on the night of her daughter's sixth birthday. Ana had been told that her mother had come down with some contagious disease and been taken away during the night lest she infect others of the household. Now, thinking back to that terrible time, Ana realized that the statue of the beautiful woman in the arbor had appeared the very next day. "No," she said again. "Not even you could be so heartless."

"You think not? There is no escape for her, and this time, there will be none for you."

Lifting his wand, he began the incantation.

Before Vilnius had spoken more than a word or two, Vega burst through the front door, his eyes blazing like the fires of hell's deepest pit, his fangs bared.

Vilnius whirled on the newcomer, an oath escaping his lips as he delved into his robe with his free hand, only to reappear clutching a large bottle of holy water. He pulled the cork with his teeth and threw the contents in Vega's direction.

Vega danced sideways, eluding most of the bottle's contents, and vanished in a swirl of dove gray motes.

With her father's attention focused elsewhere,

Ana Luisa rolled to her feet and grabbed the wand out of his hand.

Roaring with outrage, Vilnius lunged forward. He captured his daughter's arm with one hand even as he reached into his robe yet again and withdrew a narrow-bladed dagger. Eyes gleaming with triumph, he plunged it to the hilt into her heart.

With a shriek of pain, the wizard's daughter staggered backward, one hand clutching at her chest. Dark red blood oozed between her fingers and sprayed over her face like crimson mist as she slowly sank to the floor.

Vilnius took a step toward her, only to come to an abrupt halt when a dazzling shimmer of silver-hued motes rose up in front of him.

Before the wizard could make sense of what he was seeing, Rourke materialized between Vilnius and his daughter.

"You!" Hatred contorted the wizard's countenance.

Rourke nodded as he fought to keep his own loathing under control when all he wanted to do was wrap his hands around the wizard's throat and slowly choke the life from his body.

"Luisa." Tears swam in the wizard's eyes. Wailing, "What have I done?" he darted to the side and threw himself over his daughter's body, and then, with a savage cry, he yanked the dagger from her chest. Her blood stained the weapon; a single drop clung to the point of the blade. Vilnius stared at it a moment, and then, with an exultant shout, he sprang to his feet and whirled to face Rourke. With the blade held high, he lunged forward.

Acting on pure reflex, Rourke stepped to one side, his hand clamping over the wizard's wrist. His gaze met the wizard's for one stretched moment of eternity, and then, forgetting everything but the three hundred years he had spent in captivity, Rourke bent the wizard's arm and drove the blade deep into his heart.

Vilnius stared at him, a faint look of victory flashing in his eyes before the life drained out of him.

Rourke stared at the fallen wizard, troubled by the gleam of triumph he had seen in the wizard's eyes.

With a muttered oath, Vega materialized beside Ana Luisa, one side of his face and neck blistered where the holy water had touched his skin. "Ana? Ana! Dammit, can you hear me?"

At the sound of his voice, her eyelids fluttered open. "It's a good thing . . . the blade wasn't silver," she murmured, and then her body went limp.

Vega looked up at Rourke. "Is she . . . she's not . . . ?"

"No. She will be all right. She is young and strong. Take her home. She will need rest, and fresh blood. You will be tempted to share yours with her. If you do, give her only a small taste. Call me if you need help."

Vega grunted softly. "What about him?" he asked, gesturing at the wizard's body.

Rourke shook his head. The body could lie there until it rotted for all he cared.

"Keep in touch," Vega said, then lifted Ana Luisa into his arms and left the house.

Rourke paid little attention to their departure. He looked at the painting and then glanced at the wizard's body. The enchantment Vilnius had cast on the painting should have been broken with the wizard's death, yet the painting remained intact, with Karinna still its prisoner.

Filled with a horrible premonition, Rourke moved closer to the painting.

"Karinna Adams," he called softly, "come to me."

A faint ripple of supernatural power stirred the air, then dissipated like smoke in a summer breeze.

"Karinna, come to me!"

Again, Rourke sensed a ripple of supernatural power, though it was weaker than the last.

He swore under his breath, quietly damning the wizard and his own impetuous act in killing the man. He knew now why Vilnius had looked so smug before death claimed him, why the spell had not been broken when the wizard breathed his last.

A choked cry of denial escaped Rourke's lips as the realization of what he had done knifed through him. In killing the wizard, he had forever trapped Karinna behind a wall of glass.

Filled with despair, Rourke lifted the painting from the wall. For the first time, he hoped Karinna wasn't aware of what was going on around her. He couldn't bear the thought of her knowing that he had tried to free her and failed, didn't want her to know that he had killed Vilnius and in so doing had killed all hope of freeing her from the wizard's enchantment.

A thought took Rourke to Karinna's house. Heavy-hearted, he hung the painting over the fireplace, where his own painting had hung not so long ago.

Would she eventually gain strength enough to move about in her painted world? Had she been able to hear him when he called her name? Did she know Vilnius was dead? Rourke swore softly. Even with his own preternatural powers, it had taken centuries before he had gained strength enough to move about within his prison. How much longer would it take a mortal woman? Was it even possible? If the wizard's daughter hadn't accomplished it in three hundred years, what hope did Karinna have?

"Karinna." He spoke her name aloud, wondering again if she could hear him, see him. Did she know where she was, or was she deaf and blind to her surroundings?

He clenched his fists as a fresh wave of remorse assailed him. As long as she was bound to that painting, so was he. He could never leave it, or her, not as long as there was a chance she would one day find the strength to communicate with him, as he had once communicated with her. It didn't matter if it took one year or a thousand; he would stay with her, wait for her.

He stood there for over an hour gazing at her face, wishing he had the power to free her, to speak to her, to offer her some measure of hope.

Because he didn't want to leave her in the dark, Rourke went through the house and turned on all the lights, and then, overcome with guilt and a growing sense of helplessness, he left the house to stalk the dark shadows of the night. A passing stranger provided him with the nourishment he craved, and then he moved on.

Hours later, he found himself knocking on Ramon Vega's front door.

After asking who it was, Vega opened the door. "Rourke."

"How is Ana?"

"Sleeping." Vega waved Rourke inside, then closed the door.

Rourke followed the other vampire into the living room.

Vega gestured at the sofa. "Sit down."

Rourke shook his head. "I need to talk to Ana."

Vega grunted softly. "What's wrong?"

"I cannot free Karinna from the painting."

Vega frowned. "Ana said her father's death would break the spell."

"I thought so, too, but when I called Karinna's name, nothing happened. I need to ask Ana if she knows what to do."

"I'll get her," Vega said, and left the room.

Rourke paced the floor restlessly. Ana was his only hope. He cursed himself for killing the wizard. He should have waited until Karinna was freed from the wizard's spell. He had known there was a possibility that Vilnius would employ a different incantation. He had known, and still he had acted rashly. And now Karinna would pay the price for his impatience.

He stopped pacing when Vega returned with Ana.

"Jason, I am so sorry," Ana said.

"You must help me."

"I do not know what I can do. My father has had years to perfect his magick."

"You can try, can you not?"

"Of course."

Moments later, the three of them stood in front of the hearth in Karinna's living room.

Moving closer to the painting, Ana closed her eyes, her senses reaching out, searching in the air for her father's signature. She felt it like a dark stain hovering over the canvas, knew her father had used Dark Magick to cast and bind the spell. Its power crawled over her skin like a loathsome spider.

With a gasp, she backed away.

"What is it?" Rourke asked sharply.

Ana wrapped her arms around her middle. "I can feel the spell, but I do not know how to counter it. I have never dabbled in the Dark Arts."

"What if we break the glass?" Vega asked. "Would that break the spell?"

"I do not know," Ana said. "It might."

"Or it might kill her," Rourke said, finishing her thought.

Vega glanced at Ana Luisa. "Is that right?"

Ana nodded. "Or she might already be dead."

"No!" The word was ripped from Rourke's throat.

"I am sorry," Ana Luisa said quietly, her eyes filling with sympathy, "but killing Vilnius may have killed Karinna as well. Perhaps that was why calling her name did not break the enchantment."

"No." Rourke shook his head, refusing to consider the possibility that Karinna could be lost to him forever.

"I wish I could help. Truly, I do." Ana Luisa laid her hand on Rourke's arm. "If I think of anything that might help, I will let you know."

Rourke nodded. A few minutes later, Ana Luisa and Vega left the house.

Rourke dropped to his knees on the floor in front of the hearth. Karinna couldn't be dead. He had no desire to exist in the world if she wasn't in it. He loved her more than his own life, could not go on existing if his thirst for revenge had cost the life of the only woman he had ever loved.

No, there had to be a way to break the enchantment. He swore softly. He would not give up, refused to believe that she was lost to him forever. He was a creature with remarkable abilities. He could change shape, compel others to do his bidding, influence the wind and the weather, move faster than the human eye could follow, and what good was any of it if he couldn't help Karinna?

Somehow, there had to be a way to break the spell that bound her, and he would find it if it took the rest of his existence.

In the last hour before dawn, he opened his senses, his mind seeking Karinna's, and finding only emptiness.

Fear iced its way through his veins. He had not fully considered how an ordinary mortal might react to being magicked into a painting, even if it was only for a short time. He remembered his own initial panic at finding himself trapped behind a wall of glass, remembered the endless nights when he had been helpless to move, and knew now that without his preternatural powers he surely would have gone insane. Was that already happening to Karinna? Was it the effect of the wizard's death that made her thoughts sluggish, or merely the effect of the enchantment? Or had her mind taken refuge in some stygian place deep within her soul where he would never be able to find her?

Refusing to consider that possibility, he tried again. After twenty minutes of concentrated effort, his mind touched hers.

"Karinna?"

"Rourke?"

"Hang on, sweeting," he implored. *"I know you are afraid. I know it is hard to hold on to your identity, but do not give up."*

"What . . . why . . . ?"

He knew what she was asking. Why hadn't he freed her? *"I do not know how to free you, but I will not give up trying, no matter how long it takes."*

He felt her fear, the tears she couldn't shed, felt the hot sting of tears in his own eyes when her voice whispered in his mind.

"I knew . . . you would . . . come for me."

Sitting on the sofa late the next night, Rourke stared at Karinna's painted image as he sought to connect with her mind once again. He smiled when he realized she was asleep. He had invaded her dreams before. If they could not be together in the flesh, perhaps he could again wander through her unconscious mind.

Closing his eyes, he followed the link between them into her subconscious.

"Rourke! How did you get here? Where are we?"

"Wherever you want us to be."

"I don't understand."

"You are asleep, sweeting."

He took her hand in his and led her down a narrow dirt path that led to a winding river bordered by lacy trees and tall ferns. Birds sang in the treetops, chipmunks ran back and forth. Overhead, an eagle soared against a clear blue sky.

"Is this place to your liking?" he asked. "If not, we can go somewhere else."

"I don't care where we are as long as you're with me."

Murmuring her name, he drew her down on a blanket that suddenly appeared beneath them.

"Rourke, what went wrong?"

"I do not know how to break the enchantment that Vilnius worked on the painting." He watched her face, saw the horror in her eyes when she realized what he was saying.

"Then . . ." Her voice broke. "I'm trapped in here? Forever?"

"No!"

"But if you can't free me . . ." Tears welled in her eyes and spilled down her cheeks.

"I will find a way to get you out," he said fervently. "And if I cannot . . . I will come in here and stay with you."

"No! How can you even think such a thing?"

"Would you rather be alone?"

"No, but . . . you already spent three hundred years imprisoned. I can't ask you to do it again."

"You did not ask."

"Rourke . . ."

He wiped the tears from her cheeks with his fingertips, then drew her into his arms and kissed her. Falling back on the blanket, he carried her with him, so that her body covered his. He kissed her again and yet again, his hands sliding restlessly up and down her sides, her back, skimming over her buttocks.

Kari reveled in his touch, in his nearness, and then drew back. "Are you sure this is a dream? It feels so real."

"I wish it were real," he said, his voice husky with yearning.

He lifted the hem of her gown, his hand sliding up to caress the inside of her thigh.

"Oh," she murmured. "That feels wonderful."

"I can make it feel even better."

Her breath escaped her lips in a long, shuddering sigh. "Rourke . . ."

"Relax, love." He rained kisses along her neck, his tongue hot and slick as he laved the sensitive skin behind her ear.

With a sigh, Kari closed her eyes. It was only a dream, after all. She might as well do as he said and relax. But as his hands caressed her, arousing her, she found it impossible to believe that their bodies weren't really entwined, that everything that was happening was only happening in her mind.

* * *

Rourke stayed linked with Karinna until he felt
the sharp sting of the rising sun. Promising that he
would return as soon as the sun went down, he
broke the connection between them and retreated
to his lair in the shed.

Drifting on the brink of the Dark Sleep, he smiled
as he thought of the hours he had spent with
Karinna, even if it had only been in her dream. But,
dream or not, he had enjoyed every minute of the
time they had shared.

Still, he wanted more than dreams, more than
just memories.

Tomorrow night, he would explore another means
of spending time with her. It was more risky than linking his mind with hers, but it might give him some
idea of how to break the spell that bound her.

Rourke inhaled deeply. If his plan failed, Vilnius
would have the last laugh after all.

Chapter 32

Rourke woke with the setting of the sun. After leaving the shed, he went into Karinna's house. His nostrils filled with her scent as soon as he stepped inside. For a moment, he simply stood there, drawing in the fragrance that was uniquely hers, remembering the nights they had spent together, the warmth of her smile, the merry sound of her laughter, the trusting touch of her hand in his, the sinfully sweet taste of her kisses.

Muttering an oath, he made his way up to the second-floor bathroom, where he took a shower, then changed into a pair of clean blue jeans and a dark blue T-shirt. He combed his hair and brushed his teeth, thinking that he very much liked the toothbrush and toothpaste Karinna had bought for him.

After pulling on a pair of socks and his boots, he went hunting. Being anxious to see Karinna didn't leave him time to be picky. He preyed upon the first single mortal he encountered, fed quickly and deeply, and sent the young woman on her way with no memory of what had happened.

Returning to the house, Rourke went into the living room and stood in front of the painting. If the plan he had come up with before he succumbed to the Dark Sleep the night before worked, he would be able to free Karinna. Of course, even if he could get into the painting, there was no guarantee that he would be able to get out again, but it was a risk he was willing to take. Linking his mind to hers was satisfying in many ways, but no matter how real what they shared seemed to be, it was little more than an illusion. If he had to spend the rest of his existence in a world of canvas and paint, so be it. Better that than to go on living without the woman he loved. Hopefully, he would be able to get into the painting and get them both out. If not, he was prepared to accept whatever Fate had in store for him as long as he could share it with Karinna.

Taking a deep breath, he focused on the canvas. He imagined he could feel the grass beneath his feet, smell the gentle breeze blowing off the lake, hear the birds singing in the trees. Ignoring the pale sun rising behind the trees, he willed himself into the painting.

He hadn't been sure it would work, but between one heartbeat and the next, Rourke found himself on the other side of the glass. He stood there a moment, every muscle taut, as he waited to see if the painted sun would ignite his flesh, but he felt no heat, no burning on his skin.

He breathed a sigh of relief when nothing

happened. For a moment, he wondered why the wizard's sun had no power over him when everything else seemed so real, and then he shrugged. What mattered was that he was inside the painting.

He took a minute to examine his surroundings. Vilnius had been a truly amazing wizard. Like the painting Rourke had inhabited for three hundred years, this one was more than mere paint and canvas. On this side of the glass, the grass was deep and fragrant, the water lapped gently against the shore. He noticed little things he hadn't noticed before, like the doe and her twin fawns resting in the shadows beyond the tree line, and the gopher peeking out of a hole. Birds chirped and twittered in the leafy green branches overhead, a bushy-tailed gray squirrel perched on a limb, scolding him as he passed by.

Hurrying to the water's edge, Rourke drank in the sight of the still figure of the woman he loved. He didn't know if Karinna was aware of his presence or not. She sat in the sailboat, unmoving, her gaze focused on the distant shore.

On a whim, Rourke sat down on the grass. After removing his shirt, boots, and socks, he dove into the water and swam out to the sailboat.

Hauling himself over the edge of the craft, he shook the water from his hair, then sat beside Karinna on the hard wooden seat.

She didn't move, didn't blink, but he could see the faint rise and fall of her chest.

"Karinna? Can you hear me?"

When she didn't respond, he spoke to her mind. *"Karinna, do you know that I am here, beside you?"*

"Yes. What are you doing here? How did you get in? What if you can't get out?"

"Let me worry about that. I have an idea, one I know you will not like."

"Will it get me out of this place?"

"I do not know," he replied honestly.

"At this point, I'm willing to try anything."

"I want to bring you across."

"No! Anything but that."

"I think it is the only way. Vilnius's death did not end the enchantment. Perhaps yours will."

"And if it doesn't?"

"Then I will stay in here, with you."

She didn't speak, but he could feel her inner turmoil, knew she was remembering what he had told her of his time inside the painting, how excruciating the pain had been because he couldn't satisfy his hunger. If bringing her across didn't break the enchantment, the two of them would spend centuries enduring that same kind of agony. Or maybe not. If he could enter and leave the painting at will, he could leave to feed, and she could feed from him, but he didn't tell her that. Best that she accept the worst than cling to some false hope.

"Karinna?"

"I don't know. There's no way to know if it will work. If it doesn't, I can't ask you to spend the rest of your life in this hell that's no life at all."

"My blood is powerful. Even if we remain trapped here, there is a good chance that my blood will enable you to move and speak, if not immediately, then in the near

future. There is a cottage in the woods, the surroundings are pleasant. It will be better than what you have now."

"Except that I'll be a vampire trapped inside a painting."

"It is not such a bad thing, being a vampire."

"Ana Luisa didn't seem to think so, either, but . . . if you make me a vampire, is there any way to undo it later?"

"No."

"So, I have two choices. I can either stay here, as I am, for who knows how long, or you can make me a vampire, which might break the enchantment. But whether it does or doesn't, I'll be a vampire for the rest of my life. Isn't there a third choice?"

"I am afraid not, sweeting. You need not decide now. Relax. Go to sleep."

"Will you make love to me in my dreams again?"

"If you wish."

"Don't you find it odd that I can sleep sitting up with my eyes open?"

"In this world, nothing is odd."

Which was true, Rourke thought wryly, even though he didn't fully understand why. He knew that if he left Karinna's side, he would be able to walk through her painted world. Even now, he could smell the water, the grass, the trees. He could hear the birds singing, the squirrels chattering at each other, the gentle lap of the water against the hull of the boat. He looked up at the painted sun, grateful that it had no power over him, yet it pleased him to look at it. He had thought when he was trapped in his own hellish existence that Vilnius had created a nighttime world because a painted sun would have destroyed him. He realized now that it had been nighttime in the painting simply because Vilnius wished to deprive Rourke of seeing the sun's light, even if it was only a pale imitation of the real thing.

He knew the moment Karinna fell asleep.

With a sigh, he kissed her cheek, then mentally carried her away from the boat and into the cottage nestled in the trees. He could have mesmerized her while she was awake, but it was easier this way.

Inside the stone hut, he took a moment to look around. It was a rather cozy place. It held a comfortable sofa and chair, a low table, a stone hearth, a box filled with firewood. A doorway to his left led to a bedroom and a bathroom; a doorway on his right led to a small kitchen.

He carried Karinna into the whitewashed bedroom, which was small and square, furnished with a wrought-iron bedstead and a wooden rocking chair. Dark green curtains hung at the single window, a colorful rag rug covered the raw plank floor beside the bed.

Rourke spared hardly a glance for the furnishings, though, in passing, it occurred to him that Vilnius must have expected Karinna to regain her mobility and come here at some point in time, else why bother to furnish the place? Rourke would have said that there was no kindness in the wizard's heart, yet the fact that Vilnius had furnished the cabin proved otherwise.

Grunting softly, Rourke laid Karinna gently on the mattress, then stretched out beside her, his mind melding with hers until they were no longer two, but one.

He kissed her and caressed her, his own desire rising with hers, not only the desire for her sweet flesh, but for the taste of her life's blood, her very essence.

She was fire and honey in his arms, a lover like none he had known before or would again. Her skin was warm and soft to his touch, her hair like silk in his hands, her mouth hungry for his kisses. A thought removed her clothing, leaving the beauty of her slender body open to his gaze as he caressed her from head to toe.

When she murmured, "That's not fair," he cast his trousers aside, then drew her into his arms once again, a sigh of pleasure emerging from his throat as her body pressed against his. He had heard people say they were made for each other and thought it wishful thinking, but no more, else how to explain the way Karinna fit into his embrace, the way her body molded so perfectly to his. If bestowing the Dark Trick upon her broke the wizard's accursed enchantment, he would take her for his wife and spend the rest of his existence trying to please her. If the curse remained unbroken, so be it. He had brought her to this end, and he would not abandon her.

He made slow, sweet love to her, reveling in the way she responded to his touch, in the throaty sounds of pleasure that whispered past her lips as his hands aroused her. He explored every inch of her body, a low groan of pleasure rising in his throat as her hands moved over him, each stroke firing his desire until he sheathed himself in her warmth. Afterward, he held her close in his arms while the sweat cooled on their flesh, and their breathing returned to normal.

They kissed and cuddled until he felt the night turning to day. Reluctantly, he broke his link with her mind, and then, as he had before, he left her world to seek shelter from the rising sun.

The next night, Rourke went to visit Vega and Ana Luisa. If Karinna agreed to accept the Dark Gift and it didn't break the wizard's enchantment, he would need someone to look after the painting and make sure that it wasn't destroyed.

Vega and Ana Luisa listened in silence as Rourke outlined his plan. When he finished, Ana Luisa shook her head.

"Are you sure you want to do this?" she asked dubiously. "If it doesn't work . . . what kind of life will that be, living inside a painting, leaving only to feed?"

"Not one I would have preferred," Rourke admitted, "but what other choice do I have? If not for me, none of this would have happened. I cannot leave her in that hellish prison alone. I cannot. I will not!"

"Don't worry," Vega said. "If the worst happens, we'll bring the painting here and lock it up in the back room. I'll paint the window black and board it up so you won't have to worry about the sun."

"And I'll put a spell around it," Ana Luisa said, "so no one will be able to break in."

Even as Rourke nodded his thanks, he hoped such measures would not be necessary.

"You must love Karinna very much," Ana Luisa

mused. Head cocked to one side, she looked up at Ramon. "Would you make such a sacrifice for me?"

Vega slipped his arm around Ana's waist and gave her a squeeze. "Don't you doubt it for a minute, chica."

Rourke's hands curled into fists as Vega and Ana exchanged heated glances. It wasn't fair! He had freed the wizard's daughter, and because of it, Karinna now shared Ana's fate. He had to convince Karinna to accept the Dark Gift. Deep in his heart, he knew it was the only way to free her.

"What about Karinna's house?" Vega asked. "Her car? Clothes? All that stuff?"

Rourke shrugged. "Do with it what you will."

"Well, legally, I suppose it will all go to the state," Vega remarked.

"I am not concerned about her house or anything else," Rourke said. "Only the painting."

Vega nodded. "Right. If we don't hear from you in a couple of days . . ."

"Then you will know I failed."

"Don't worry," Vega said. "We'll take care of everything."

A short time later, Rourke bid farewell to Vega, hugged Ana, and left their house, eager to return to Karinna. His plan had to work, he thought desperately. In spite of his brave words to Vega and Ana, in spite of the promise he had made to Karinna, he wasn't sure he could keep his vow to remain with her inside the painting. The very thought of returning to such a life filled him with dread. In spite of that, what he had told Ana Luisa was the truth. He couldn't turn his back on Karinna. She had freed him from a hellish existence, and no matter what the cost, if it was at all possible, he would return the favor.

And if he couldn't? How could he go back to living in a painted world, even one shared with the woman he loved?

How could he not?

Rourke shook such thoughts from his mind. He had to believe his plan would succeed.

A woman coming out of a drugstore saved him the trouble of hunting. He mesmerized her with a glance and took what he needed, giving little thought to the woman who stood pliant in his arms. He was after sustenance, not pleasure, and he fed quickly, then made his way back to Karinna's house, and into the painting.

As he had before, he paused on the lakeshore for a moment just to look at her, thinking that no artist, no earthly work of art, could capture the natural beauty of the woman herself.

A thought took him to her side.

"Karinna, I am here beside you."

"Rourke?" He heard the barely controlled panic in her voice. *"Rourke, help me! I'm afraid I'm losing myself. Today, I couldn't even remember my name."*

"Let me bring you across, sweeting. It is the only way."

"I don't want to be what you are."

Though he would have said it was impossible, a single tear slid down her cheek. When she spoke again, her voice was little more than a whisper. *"Rourke, I want you to destroy the painting."*

"No! Never! Do not ask such a thing of me."

He captured her tear on the tip of his finger and pressed it to his lips. They had been through much together. He loved her. He thought she loved him, though neither of them had ever spoken the words aloud. He swore under his breath. Being a part of his life had brought her nothing but trouble and pain. There was no guarantee that that would change in the near future. He would never really belong in this time and place. As long as she was mortal, there would always be a gulf between them that neither of them could bridge. Yet another reason to bring her across.

"I am asking," she said quietly. *"You said there was no third choice, but there is. I can't feel anything, so it shouldn't hurt. I'll just cease to exist."*

"No! No, no, no."

"If you love me . . ."

He heard the quiet desperation in her voice, the underlying note of fear and anguish.

If you love me . . .

He had heard that true love was unselfish, that one who loved deeply and sincerely put the needs and wants of his beloved before his own desires. But how could he destroy Karinna without destroying himself, he thought bleakly. And then he frowned. Perhaps that was the answer. He could ask Vega to burn the painting. In her current state, Karinna would not be aware of what was happening. As for himself, everyone knew vampires burned quickly. The pain, however excruciating it might be, would not last long.

He shook the thought from his mind. He would not destroy the painting. He would not destroy whatever chance of happiness they might have. He would not let Vilnius win.

"Rourke?"

"I cannot, sweeting." He shook his head. *"I cannot destroy you, not while there is a chance that we can break the curse and be together."*

"I know what you're thinking, and I'll hate you for it. You said I could choose."

He brushed a kiss across her lips. *"Hate me if you will. Hate me as much as you wish for as long as you wish, but let us hope you can do it on the other side of this accursed glass."*

She couldn't give voice to her unhappiness, but he knew she was weeping inside. Her anguish tore at his heart, but he couldn't let it weaken his decision, not now. It was their only hope. No matter how remote the chance of success, he had to try. Even if she never forgave him, even if he could never again hold her in his arms, he had to try.

He didn't put her to sleep this time. The moment he linked his mind to hers, she fought against him, but his will was too strong for her to resist.

Wanting to make the change as pleasant for her as possible, he mentally carried her into the cottage and lowered her onto the soft mattress, then covered her body with his own.

"No! No!" She struggled against him, but he held her down easily. And then he kissed her, ever so slowly and tenderly. Her nails raked his face, her fists pummeled his chest. He made no move to protect

himself as she bucked and twisted beneath him, but as his kisses deepened, her own body betrayed her.

His tongue laved her neck, and then, as gently as he could, he pierced the tender flesh below her left ear with his fangs, and drank. He closed his eyes as her life's essence flowed into him, thick and hot and sweet. He drank her life and her memories, drank until her heartbeat slowed, and she was at the point of death.

Pulling back, Rourke licked the wounds in her throat to seal them, then made a shallow gash in his left wrist and lifted it to her lips.

"Drink, love." It was a command, softly spoken, but a command nonetheless, one she was helpless to deny.

Caught up in his preternatural power, she did as bidden.

He threw back his head in ecstasy, reveling in the touch of her mouth against his flesh, in the hope that their mingled blood would have the power to restore her life and, hopefully, break the wizard's enchantment.

She tried to cling to his arm when he drew his wrist away, but she was no match for his greater strength. He ran his tongue over the wound in his wrist, then cradled her to his chest.

He held her close as long as he dared, then released his hold on her mind. Exhausted by what he had done to her, Karinna fell into a deep, death-like sleep.

As the sun's light chased the darkness from the sky, Rourke regretfully left the painting. It would have been pleasant to keep his mind linked to hers, to continue the charade that they were lying side by side on the bed in the cottage, but he couldn't remain.

Going into the linen closet in the hallway, Rourke grabbed a couple of thick blankets. After returning to the living room, he hung one of the blankets over the painting, then draped the other one over the curtains on the front window, lest the rising sun find Karinna and destroy her.

Her mortal body would die with the dawn. He only hoped the wizard's evil curse would die with her.

Rourke glanced at the sky as he hurried toward the shed in the backyard. He could feel the sun's rising like shards of glass pricking his skin.

Slamming the door shut behind him, he breathed a sigh of relief as blessed darkness engulfed him. Sinking down onto the bed, he closed his eyes, waiting for oblivion.

He would rise with the setting of the sun, and Karinna would rise with him, a newborn vampire, blood of his blood.

Chapter 33

Rourke woke with the setting of the sun. As always, his first conscious thought was for Karinna. Leaving the shed, he hurried into the house. For the first time in three hundred years, he was afraid of what the night might bring.

He came to an abrupt halt in front of the fireplace. He stood there a moment, filled with uncertainty, before he pulled the blanket off the frame.

The painting remained unchanged; Karinna sat in the boat, unmoving.

He swore softly. Had he failed? Was she now one of the Undead, trapped inside a painting with a vampire's needs, a vampire's hunger? Would it have been kinder to do as she had asked and destroy the painting?

He paced the floor in front of the hearth, torn by his need for the woman and his desire to end her pain.

Dammit! What had he done?

He was about to enter the painting when there

was a sharp crack. The glass shattered as the frame split in half. The canvas slid down the wall, over the mantel, and onto the floor, and Karinna stood before him, her face as pale as death, her eyes wide and unfocused. And empty.

"Karinna?" Fear like nothing he had ever known engulfed him. Merciful heavens, what had he done?

She stared at him unblinking, her eyes vacant, devoid of recognition.

"Karinna!" Grabbing her by the shoulders, he shook her. "Dammit, woman, answer me!"

She blinked once, twice, her expression turning to one of confusion. Color returned to her cheeks. She glanced past him, taking in her surroundings as if she had never seen them before. And then her gaze settled on his face. "Rourke?"

He nodded once, and waited. Would she sense the change immediately? Would she truly hate him for what he had done? Just then, he didn't care. Nothing mattered except that the curse had been broken and she was back in the real world, where she belonged.

Her eyes narrowed as she glanced around the room a second time. When she looked at him again, he knew that she remembered everything that had happened, and that she despised him for what he had done. Her hatred struck him like a physical blow.

"Why?" she demanded. She fisted her hands on her hips, her eyes blazing. "Why did you do it? I asked you to destroy the painting."

She stabbed a finger at his chest, driving Rourke backward.

Had she been mortal, her touch would have had no effect on him. But she was a vampire now, with a vampire's strength.

"I begged you to destroy me," she went on. "I told you I didn't want to be a vampire!"

Rourke shook his head, amused by her anger, delighted that she was free of the wizard's curse. She could hate him all she liked, but she was in the world again. With any luck, she might forgive him for what he had done in a hundred years or so. And if it took longer, well, he had all the time in the world to wait.

She glared at him, and then her expression turned thoughtful. "The wizard . . . is he dead?"

"Yes. He will never hurt anyone again."

"And his daughter? Where is she?"

"Ana Luisa is with Vega."

With a curt nod, Karinna brushed past him. She walked through the house as if seeing it for the first time, marveling at how big everything seemed. She ran her hands over her belongings, as if to reassure herself that they were real, that she was really there. She had spent only a few days trapped inside a world of canvas and paint, yet it had seemed ever so much longer. How had Rourke and Ana Luisa endured such torture without going insane?

She came to an abrupt halt in front of the mirror in her bedroom. She could see the wall behind her, the bed, the windows, but she cast no reflection in the glass. Feeling suddenly queasy, she ran her hands over her face and arms. She was flesh and bone, yet she didn't show up in the mirror. It made her feel as if she didn't exist.

Choking back the hot bitter bile that rose in her throat, she turned away from the mirror. She was a vampire. She ran her tongue over her teeth, but she didn't feel any fangs. Shouldn't she have fangs? Maybe they came later, she thought, and wondered how she would explain them to her dentist. Did vampires go to the dentist?

Shaking off her silly thoughts, she went into the bathroom and looked in the mirror over the sink. Her image wasn't there, either. How did female vampires put on their make-up and arrange their hair without being able to see their reflection?

She snorted softly. A minor inconvenience compared to everything else! How was she going to support herself when she couldn't go to work anymore? How was she going to explain this to her parents, to Tricia, and to the rest of her friends and acquaintances? This was all Jason Rourke's fault! She never should have bought that accursed painting, never should have brought it home with her, never should have helped him rescue Ana Luisa. . . .

She blew out a sigh of exasperation. There was no point in dwelling on the past. It couldn't be changed. So, she would find a new job, one where she could work nights, and when the time was right, she would tell her parents that she had come down with some sort of allergy to the sun, and . . .

She blinked rapidly as tears burned her eyes. She didn't want to make lemonade out of the lemon her life had become. She just wanted to be plain old boring Karinna Adams again. She wanted to be able to lie in the sun on a warm day and get a tan, and drink malts, and eat chocolate, and . . .

At the thought of food, her stomach knotted painfully. Of course, it was natural to be hungry; she hadn't eaten for days.

Leaving the bathroom, she went downstairs. She swept past Rourke without a glance as she made her way into the kitchen.

He hadn't followed her into the bathroom, but he followed her now, pausing inside the doorway while she opened the refrigerator and withdrew a bright red apple.

"Karinna . . ."

Ignoring the warning in his voice, she took a bite. The minute she swallowed it, she knew it had been a mistake. Pain speared through her stomach. Hurrying to the sink, she threw it up, then stood there gasping.

When Rourke took a step toward her, she put her hand out to stop him. "Just leave me alone."

"I only want to help you."

A harsh sound of derision rose in her throat. "You've done enough, thank you very much. Just go away."

"As you wish." Knowing there would be no talking to her until she had calmed down and accepted things the way they were, he left the house.

Kari stood in the kitchen, one hand pressed to her stomach as she listened to the front door open and close.

She was a vampire. No more dark chocolate ice

cream or candy. No more salty French fries. No more cheeseburgers smothered in onions. No more spaghetti and crusty garlic bread. No more suntans. No more iced tea on a hot day. No more hot days. . . . She blinked back her tears. No children. No grandchildren. No anything.

The room seemed to close in around her. Without a thought for where she was going, she left the house, turned left at the end of the driveway, and started walking down the street.

And walked into a whole new world. For a moment, she thought she was in the wrong place. Everything looked different and, yet, oddly the same. Though the sun was down and the world was dark, she could see everything around her. The colors of the houses and flowers and trees were as bright and clear as if the sun were high in the sky.

She heard bits of conversations as she hurried down the sidewalk, even though there was no one else in sight. It took her a moment to realize that what she was hearing were conversations taking place inside the houses that lined the road.

She took a breath and her nostrils filled with dozens of scents.

She slowed when she realized she was nearing Ramon Vega's house. How had she gotten here so fast? He lived on the other side of town.

With a shake of her head, she went up the walkway and knocked on the door.

It opened a moment later. "Karinna!" Ana Luisa exclaimed. "You are free. When . . . how did this happen?"

"Just tonight." Karinna couldn't help thinking that, clad in a pair of slinky red tights and a white T-shirt, Ana looked trim and happy.

Ana Luisa leaned to one side and glanced past Karinna. "Where is Jason?"

"I don't know. I don't care."

Ana Luisa frowned, then stood aside. "Come in."

Karinna followed her into the living room.

"Hey!" Vega said. "Nice dress."

"What?" Karinna looked down at herself, only then realizing she was still wearing the green gown she had been wearing inside the painting.

Ana Luisa gestured at the sofa. "Please, sit down," she invited, taking a place beside Ramon. "Tell us what happened."

"There's not much to tell." Kari sat down, her fingers pleating the material in her skirt. "Rourke came into the painting somehow. Last night, he made me a vampire. Tonight, the painting broke and"—she shrugged—"here I am."

Vega grunted softly. "So, the spell was broken when *you* died. Interesting."

Kari looked at Vega. "But I don't want to be a vampire."

"I take it he didn't give you a choice," Vega said.

"He knew I didn't want to be a vampire. I told him as much," Kari said bitterly. "For all the good it did me."

"Would you rather still be trapped inside that horrid painting?" Ana Luisa asked with a shudder.

"Of course not. I asked him to destroy it and me with it."

Ana Luisa's eyes widened. "You wanted him to kill you?"

"Yes. It would have been better than this."

"How can you say that?" Ana sprang to her feet, her hands planted on her hips as she stared down at Karinna. "You are here. You are alive. You are in love with Jason, and he loves you. Why would you rather be dead than spend the rest of your life with the man you love?"

Karinna blinked at the girl.

Vega tugged on Ana Luisa's shirt. "Calm down, chica."

With a huff, she resumed her place beside him.

"It's not all that bad, being a vampire," Vega remarked. "Sure, there are things you can't do, but hey, look at the bright side. You won't grow old. You'll never get sick. Your senses are all enhanced." He smiled at Ana as he slipped his arm around her shoulders. "And the lovin' only gets better."

Kari stared at the two of them thinking how perfectly matched they seemed to be and how well they complemented each other.

"I know you both seem to like being vampires, but . . ." Kari shook her head. "What about the blood?"

Vega shrugged. "You'll get used to it."

Kari glanced at Ana Luisa. "Isn't it disgusting?"

"No, it's quite sweet."

Kari stared at the girl. Blood, sweet? She frowned, surprised that the thought didn't make her sick, and a little disconcerted to find it even sounded . . . tempting.

"Have you fed since you were turned?" Vega asked.

"No," Kari replied, once again surprised that an idea she had once found completely repulsive now seemed almost . . . normal.

"You must be hungry," Ana Luisa said matter-of-factly.

Kari nodded, though she was reluctant to admit it.

"Vampires don't normally feed on vampires," Vega said, "but it won't hurt, this once."

"What do you mean?" Kari asked, although she was afraid she knew exactly what he meant.

"I mean if you're hungry, I'm offering."

She stared at him for several seconds, bewildered because the idea, which should have been repugnant, was suddenly vastly appealing. She glanced at Ana Luisa. "You don't mind?"

"As long as you do not make a habit of it," Ana Luisa replied with a grin.

"But . . ." Kari ran a hand through her hair. "I don't know how."

"It's easy," Vega said, patting the sofa cushion beside him. "Come here."

Sensing Karinna's reluctance to feed with someone else watching, Ana Luisa said, "Please excuse me," and left the room.

Kari hesitated a moment, then went to sit beside Vega. The talk of blood and hunger had awakened something deep inside her. She could feel it stirring, gaining strength. The tips of her fangs brushed against her tongue.

She stared at Vega's neck, and licked her lips. "Won't it hurt you?"

Vega laughed softly. "Not at all. Quite the contrary, actually."

Kari looked at him, uncertain as to what she should do. In the movies, vampires usually bit their prey on the neck. She licked her lips as the urge to feed grew stronger. Should she just grab him and go for it?

"Okay," Vega said. "Here's a quick course in How to Be a Vampire 101. You can take blood from the neck, the wrist, or anywhere else you like. Of course, some places, like the inside of the thigh, are more intimate than others."

Vega's thigh was out of the question. Kari glanced at his throat. She could easily imagine Ana Luisa drinking from there. Feeding from his wrist seemed more impersonal.

As though reading her mind, Vega held out his left arm, palm up. "Go on," he coaxed.

She was reaching for him when someone knocked at the door.

Vega looked up with a frown, then swore softly. "It's Rourke."

"What's he doing here?" Kari asked. "You don't think Ana Luisa called him, do you?"

Vega shook his head as he rose from the sofa. "I doubt it."

"Did you?"

"When would I have had time to do that?" he muttered over his shoulder, and then opened the door.

"Where is she?" Rourke demanded.

"In the other room," Vega said. "Come on in."

With a curt nod, Rourke swept past Vega and

stalked into the living room. He took one look at Karinna, at the hunger in her eyes, and knew why she had come here. Anger and jealousy rushed to the fore at the thought of her taking nourishment from another vampire.

"You will not feed off of him," he told Karinna brusquely.

"I don't know what you're talking about," Karinna said, knowing her extended fangs made a liar out of her.

"Don't you? You don't know how to feed on your own. You are too angry to ask for my help, so you came here, either to ask for his help or to ease your thirst." His eyes narrowed ominously. "If you need to feed, I will find prey for you, or you can drink from me. But not from him. Is that understood?"

"You're not the boss of me," Kari retorted, hating how childish her words sounded. "I don't have to do what you say."

"Okay," Vega said, stepping between them. "Just hold on a minute."

"You have nothing to do with this," Rourke said, his voice little more than a growl.

"Maybe not," Vega agreed. "But the two of you might want to cool off a little before you say anything you'll regret later."

Rourke glared at him. "Get out of my way. This is between me and my woman."

"*Your* woman?" Kari exclaimed as Vega distanced himself from the two of them. "Who said I was your woman?"

"Are you not?" Rourke asked, his voice suddenly

filled with tenderness. "Were you not mine the moment you first saw the painting in the gallery? Were you not mine, as I was yours?"

Kari looked up at him, all her anger melting away before the love she saw shining in his eyes. Why was she fighting him? From the moment she had first laid eyes on him, she had been helpless to resist him. She had spent hours, days, weeks thinking of him, dreaming of him, wanting only to be with him, and now he was here. He had made her what he was and, in so doing, had ensured that they could be together forever. He had taken the sun from her, but he had replaced it with the never-ending warmth of his love.

"Karinna?"

The sound of his voice moved through her, sweeter than honey.

She looked at Vega and smiled. "Thank you for your offer, but it's no longer necessary."

With a sigh, she slipped her arm around Rourke's waist. "Come on," she said. "Let's go home. We have a lot to talk about."

Chapter 34

"So, tell me what it's like to be a full-fledged, card-carrying vampire," Kari said as they settled on the sofa in front of the fireplace. "Tell me everything."

Rourke slid his knuckles down her cheek. "It can be a good life, sweeting, if you look on the positive aspects instead of the negative."

Once, she would have doubted there was anything positive about being a vampire. Now, she knew differently. She had been a vampire for only a short time, yet she was already changing. She could feel it happening inside her, feel the power growing within her. All her senses were magnified. She felt wonderful, stronger physically and mentally than she ever had in her whole life. She had always been a little afraid of growing old, of being alone. She wouldn't have to worry about that now.

"So, refresh my memory," she said with an impish grin. "What are the positives?"

He laughed softly. "After the time we have spent

together, I should think that you would know the good things better than most."

"Well, yeah, some of them, but I'm sure I still have a lot to learn, like how to turn into mist, and how to vanish into thin air, and all your other tricks."

He brushed a kiss over her lips. "And more than enough time to learn them all."

"You won't get tired of me, will you?" she asked, only half in jest.

"Perhaps," he mused, "in a thousand years or so."

"And what will we do for a thousand years?" Even as she asked the question, she couldn't imagine anyone living that long. What would the world be like in a thousand years? In five hundred? Would life as they now knew it even exist that far into the future?

His forefinger trailed down her cheek. "What would you like to do?"

"I'd like to travel," she said. "There's so much of the world I haven't seen. How about you? What would you like to do?"

"I would like to make love to you in every country and city in the world," he said with a roguish grin.

"Would you?" she asked, suddenly breathless as she pictured the two of them making love on the floor of a gondola in Venice, or wrapped in each other's arms at the top of the Eiffel Tower in Paris.

"Indeed." His smile grew wider. "It will be my pleasure to fulfill your every wish, your every dream and desire, no matter how large or how small. Starting here," he said, his voice suddenly low and husky with longing. "Starting now."

Impaled by the yearning in his eyes, Kari drew a

deep breath and expelled it in a long, shuddering sigh. "Sounds good to me," she murmured, then grinned inwardly as she imagined buying a map of the world and sticking pins in to mark every place where they made love.

She linked her hands behind his neck as he swung her into his arms and carried her up to bed. After undressing her, he quickly stripped off his own clothing, then stretched out beside her and drew her into his arms. He made love to her ever so slowly, adoring every inch of her body, from her sweet, sensual lips to the curved arch of her instep. And all the while, he whispered words of love and affection, needing her to know that he loved her as no other, that he would always love her.

Kari surrendered herself, heart and body and soul, to Rourke's touch even as she began an intimate exploration of her own. Rourke's body was a study in masculine perfection, a feast for feminine eyes, a magnet for loving hands and questing fingers. She had waited years to meet the man of her dreams, she thought, as she willingly yielded her innocence to him, and it had been worth every minute. They had made love in dreams and it had been wonderful, but the reality far surpassed the illusion.

He carried her above and beyond mortal limits, pleasuring her in ways no human male ever could, and when she teetered on the brink of discovery, her whole body yearning for something that beckoned just out of reach, he swept her over the top. The world as she knew it shattered, exploding into a million rainbow-colored lights that she could see and touch and taste.

She felt as if she were floating above the earth, and when she looked down, she saw that she really was floating, not above the earth, but above the mattress. She should have been scared, or at least surprised, but she wasn't. Instead, she closed her eyes and enjoyed every nuance of the strange but exhilarating sensation.

When, at last, the world righted itself, she knew she would never be the same again, and then she was drifting, down, down, through rainbow-colored clouds, sated, complete.

When her breathing returned to normal, she opened her eyes to find Rourke gazing down at her. Was it her imagination, or did he look just a trifle smug?

Well, he had a right to, she thought. He had promised to fulfill her every desire, and he had delivered. Oh, my, had he delivered!

Propping herself up on one elbow, Kari leaned forward and licked his cheek, then raked her nails down over his chest and his hard, flat belly to that part of him that should have been exhausted but wasn't.

"You know," she murmured, "I'm not sure a thousand years will be long enough."

Dear Reader:

I hope you enjoyed Rourke and Karinna's story. It was fun to write, and I enjoyed visiting Transylvania, if only via the Web. Vampires fascinate me, and with the popularity of *Moonlight*, *Blood Ties*, and *Twilight*, I know I'm not alone.

My next book, *Everlasting Kiss*, is one of my favorites. Of course, I think I say that about all of them! But I just can't help loving my dark and dangerous heroes. My thanks to those who write and/or e-mail to say you love them, too.

Amanda
www.amandaashley.net
DarkWritr@aol.com

And don't miss Amanda Ashley's newest book,
EVERLASTING KISS,
coming in February from Zebra!

Erik sipped his drink. It satisfied his physical thirst, but he found no pleasure in it. It was like hungering for milk and being given water, though in reality, he had no taste for either.

He had just ordered a second glass when a woman entered the club. A pretty woman in her mid-twenties, with lightly tanned skin and heavily lashed green eyes. Her hair, a deep reddish-brown, fell halfway down her back. She wore flat-heeled white boots, blue jeans, and a long white leather jacket over a white shirt. His nostrils flared as she passed by him on her way to a vacant stool not far from his.

Erik frowned. She was human, but she smelled of vampire. No doubt she was one of the dozens of human females who frequented the club, getting their kicks from rubbing elbows with the soon-to-be famous and the infamous. Or maybe she got off on letting vampires feed off her. Drinking vampire blood was all the rage now, though only the very rich could afford it. The thought of her feeding off of him stirred his desire; the thought of him feeding off of her aroused his hunger. He ran his tongue over the tips of his fangs, imagined himself bending over her neck, licking her skin, tasting her life's essence.

As if sensing his thoughts, she whirled around to face him.

She was lovely, young, ripe. Erik put the glass in his hand aside, no longer interested in its watered-down contents. Not when there was a possibility he could score something better. Something hot and fresh, directly from the source.

Daisy stared at the man sitting at the bar, felt a rush of heat engulf her from head to foot when his gaze met hers with such intensity, it was almost physical. Dressed all in black, he was long-legged and broad-shouldered, with thick black hair and the kind of rugged countenance that made a girl look twice. But it was his eyes that captured her attention. Deep, dark eyes that seemed capable of penetrating her innermost thoughts, of probing the depths not only of her heart, but her very soul.

Shaking off her fanciful thoughts, she took a seat at the bar and ordered a strawberry daiquiri. Even though she was no longer looking at the dark-haired man, she could feel the weight of his gaze resting on her. Without moving her head, she slid a sideways glance in his direction, felt a jolt of desire sweep through her when her gaze again met his. Never, in all her life, had she felt such a strong attraction to a complete stranger.

Her stomach knotted as he rose smoothly to his feet and walked toward her, although walked didn't really describe the way he moved. More like a jungle cat stalking its prey. The thought made her mouth dry and her palms damp. Her gaze darted toward the exit, but it was too late to escape. He was already standing in front of her. He was tall, she thought, looking up. Very tall.

"I'm Erik."

His voice, as deep as ten feet down, raised goose bumps on her arms.

He gestured at her glass. "May I buy you another drink?"

"No, thank you." Was that pitiful whimper her voice?

"Are you sure?"

Daisy nodded. What was wrong with her? She was behaving like some teenager who had just met her favorite rock star.

His gaze moved over her face, warming every place it touched. When he smiled, her heartbeat kicked up a notch.

Pull yourself together, Daisy, she chided. *It's not like you've never talked to a handsome man before.* So why did this one have her tongue tied in knots?

"I suppose a dance is out of the question?"

She felt her cheeks grow hotter as she imagined being in his arms. She was about to decline when she heard herself say, "I'd like that."

He looked as surprised as she was.

And then there was no more time for thought. He held out one large, well-manicured hand. After a moment's hesitation, she placed her hand in his. A shiver of awareness coiled in the pit of her stomach as his fingers closed over hers, and then he was leading her toward the small dance floor, drawing her into his arms. Long arms. Strong arms that made her feel protected and endangered at the same time.

She had watched numerous scenes in movies where couples danced and everything else faded away—Kathleen Turner and Michael Douglas in *Romancing the Stone*, Michael J. Fox and Julie Warner in *Doc Hollywood*, Amy Adams and Patrick Dempsey in *Enchanted*. As much as she had loved those scenes, she had always found them hard to believe. Until now. She wasn't aware of the music or the other couples on the floor; she wasn't aware of anything but the man holding her close. Too close, she thought, but feeling his body brush against hers felt so good, she had no inclination to object. He was tall and dark and decidedly masculine. Being in his embrace made her achingly aware of her femininity, of the delightful differences between male and female, of the way their bodies had been created to fit together, complementing each other.

Her only regret was that the music ended too soon. Or maybe just in time, she thought, because as sure as she knew her name, she knew what was coming next. He was going to ask her to go to his place, and she didn't think she was strong enough to refuse. Just thinking about being alone with him made her ache in places no man had ever touched.

Murmuring, "thank you for the dance," she pulled her hand from his and all but ran out of the Crypt. She knew it was only her imagination, but she could have sworn she heard the sound of his amused laughter following her all the way home.